Twilight Rebel

Midnight Empire: New Dawn
Book 2

Annabel Chase

Red Palm Press LLC

Copyright © 2022 by Annabel Chase

All rights reserved.

No part of this book may be reproduced in any form or by any electronic or mechanical means, including information storage and retrieval systems, without written permission from the author, except for the use of brief quotations in a book review.

Cover Design by Trif

To join my VIP List and receive FREE bonus content, visit www.annabelchase.com.

❦ Created with Vellum

Chapter One

"Hurry up," I called over my shoulder. "You're like the tortoise and the turtle." Admittedly, patience was not one of my virtues.

The two werewolves trailing behind me exchanged glances. The flare of Tyson's nostrils signaled annoyance.

"Why can't we just be two turtles?" Bear asked, less annoyed.

Tyson didn't wait for me to answer. "If you'd let us shift, you'd be eating our dust right now."

"We've been over this. No shifting." As the lone witch among my werewolf companions, I found it easier to communicate with them in human form.

I heard the rustle of leaves behind me, and suddenly, I had a brawny escort on either side of me. Some girls had all the luck—if you considered living as an outlaw in the middle of nowhere lucky.

Bear ducked under a low branch. "The forest here seems healthier than where we live."

I observed the thriving cedar and spruce trees that

surrounded us. "That's because it's Locklear. They would've used more magic near a vampire enclave."

Built during the early years of the Eternal Night, Locklear served as a gated community restricted to vampires. If you lived in one of the ten sprawling houses, you were doing well for yourself.

We'd made it past the main entrance without issue—the security guards were too engrossed in a game of chess in their little shack to notice us. One of the few perks of vampire rule was their arrogance. They rarely expected anybody to challenge them, which left them vulnerable to petty crimes like the one we were about to commit.

I tugged the hood of my golden cloak over my head to keep the wind from blowing long strands of hair in my face. I should've worn a ponytail, but I'd been running behind schedule and decided my weapons were more important than my hairstyle. Go figure.

"Do you still need to wear that cloak?" Tyson asked. "Every vampire in The Wild knows who you are by now."

"It's her trademark style," Bear interjected. "I've been thinking about adopting my own signature color. Bonnie likes me in green. She says it makes my eyes pop."

Tyson cracked his knuckles. "I can make your eyes pop. No special color required."

I made a chopping motion, and we came to a stop. "This is it," I whispered.

A Japanese-influenced house loomed beyond the next gate. It boasted floor-length windows and sliding doors made of glass. With no sunshine to threaten them, some vampires went a little overboard with transparency.

"I bet that house is loaded with useless crap like gold-plated lotus flowers," Bear said in a low voice.

We had no interest in the treasures inside, though, only the cash that would soon make its way outside.

"Speaking of gold..." Tyson squinted ahead. "Do my eyes deceive me or is that gate made of it?"

Bear let loose a low whistle, and I clamped a hand over his mouth. We'd made it this far. I didn't want to get caught now.

"Maybe we should just steal part of the gate and call it a day," Tyson suggested. "Then we don't need to interact with anyone."

Bear shot him a curious look. "Since when are you averse to interacting with our targets?"

"The introvert in me wants to sit by myself in front of a crackling fire with a carving knife and a piece of wood."

Bear snorted. "Introvert, my furry ass. You'd talk all twelve ears off a scorpion if it didn't sting you first."

"They have twelve eyes, not ears," I corrected him.

"I babble when I'm anxious," Tyson said, "because I'm an introvert."

The gate creaked as it started to open, and I crouched lower. "Get ready."

"How much did you say he'd have on him?" Bear whispered.

"It's a minimum buy-in of two thousand," Tyson replied.

If there was one game vampires in The Wild loved to play, it was poker. Personally, I didn't get it. Losing money for fun seemed like a terrible waste of time and resources. Then again, it probably made sense to vampires, who had more time and money than any other species on the planet.

According to reports, this was the first time Jacy Nez had been invited to play in the monthly Klondike game. Nez had recently inherited a small fortune from his aunt, including this house, and had quickly risen up the ranks as a result. His inheritance had qualified him to mix with the local vampire elites—the ones with the most money to burn. We figured he'd be so excited to join the game that he'd forget about external threats like us.

See also—arrogance.

A silhouette stepped through the open gate, only he wasn't holding a bag of coins.

He was holding a crossbow.

"I know you're out there," he yelled. "And if you come any closer, you'll find a bolt where your nutsack should be."

Bear and Tyson glanced downward. "I guess that means you're up, Aster," Bear said. "You're the only one here who's nutsack free."

Sighing, I strung my bow. "Cowards," I hissed. I emerged from the shadows with an arrow aimed at our would-be attacker's crotch. "Two can play at that game," I said.

Now that I was closer, I realized he was only a man. "You're not Jacy Nez."

"No, my name is Alex Pierce. I'm in charge of house security for Mr. Nez."

Nez hired a human as his head of security? Interesting. I expected a vampire. I had no desire to threaten a human. Life was hard enough for them. Anyway, the whole point of stealing from vampires like Nez was to redistribute the wealth among the local villagers, which included Alex Pierce.

"Nice to meet you, Alex." I nodded at his crossbow. "I can tell you're new at this, so we'll make it quick and easy for you. Give us the money and we'll go on our merry way. Nobody gets hurt."

Alex aimed the crossbow at my head. "I don't think so, miss."

"Lesson number one, Alex. My weapon is much more effective than yours." At over seven feet long with a range of more than three hundred yards, my longbow is a force to be reckoned with—in my hands, at least. Six arrows a minute, deadly aim, and the ability to pierce chain mail or sheet armor. Sorry, crossbow. Not even close.

"Trust me," Bear said. "You don't want to test her. I've seen the damage she can do. You'll be pissing out of every pore in your body by the time she's done."

Scowling, Alex lowered his weapon. "You're that witch, aren't you?"

"She prefers the Hooded One," Bear told him with an air of authority.

I shot my companion a silencing look. "Aster is fine."

"You said you were here to rob me," Alex said, "but I'm afraid I don't have any money."

"Not you, sir." Bear grinned. "Just your vampire overlord."

"Mr. Nez isn't in residence at the moment, and if you step foot inside the house ... let's just say Mr. Nez's predecessor took precautions."

His response caught me off guard. "Nez already left?" Tyson's intel had Nez leaving within the next hour, along with enough money to participate in the poker game in Klondike.

"Mr. Nez received word that an old friend is in town and decided to see her before the game."

Bear gave a nod of approval. "Old flame, huh?"

"Mr. Nez's personal affairs are none of my concern."

I disguised my disappointment. This was meant to be

an easy job and now we'd have to return to the hideout empty-handed.

I lowered my weapon. "How did you end up working for Nez?"

"Because I'm human? You think I'm a traitor to my kind, is that it?"

"I'm thinking more about the fact that you're facing off against a witch and two werewolves. How do you like your odds?"

"Better than the odds of surviving as Nez's personal blood bank." Alex shrugged. "I had to choose. It was the only way to pay off the debt I owed him."

I didn't bother to hide my shock. "That's illegal."

He wore a vague smile. "Legalities have become fuzzy ever since the donation center was destroyed. Vampires seem to be bending their own rules to suit themselves."

"Nothing new there," Tyson remarked.

Bear joined me closer to the gate. "Does that mean there's another human in the house who feeds Nez?"

Alex shook his head. "Not yet. He's been interviewing, though."

Interviewing? I swallowed my disgust. Only the truly desperate would offer themselves up as a walking wine box to be punctured by our fanged oppressors.

"You could report him to the authorities," I said, knowing how lame that sounded but unable to stop myself.

Alex laughed. "Oh, sure. I have no doubt the other vampires will take my side in a dispute against their gambling buddy. And here I thought the Hooded One understood how our world works."

"Believe me, I do." I returned my arrow to the quiver. "We'll go now. Sorry for scaring you."

"If it's any consolation, the job isn't too bad," Alex said.

"I get to live in the house, which is much nicer than anywhere I've ever lived."

Instinctively, I glanced at the massive house behind him and tried to imagine sharing my personal space with a vampire. We all made compromises when it came to survival.

"You won't alert the main security guards?" Tyson asked.

"No harm, no foul." Alex waved the crossbow as he retreated. "Have a good day, folks. Stay safe."

The gate closed with a loud clink.

"We could try to track Nez," Tyson offered. "He might not be too far away."

Bear shook his head. "Then we'll have the vampire friend to contend with, too, and we don't have intel on her."

"Bear's right," I said. "Let's forget it and head home." I was supposed to be keeping a low profile anyway, after a recent brush with kidnapping and torture. I wasn't very good at biding my time, though, and Nez had seemed like an easy mark.

Halfway home, Bear sniffed the air with exaggerated force.

"Be careful or you might inhale the whole forest," I warned.

"Don't you smell that?"

I cut a glance at him. "The stench of a decaying forest? Been smelling it for years, my friend. You get used to it."

"No, wait. Now I smell it, too," Tyson said. "It's definitely the stench of decay, but it isn't the forest."

I heard the crunch of leaves to the left of us and pivoted toward the sound, notching an arrow in the process. It was unlikely somebody followed us from Locklear without one of the wolves picking up the scent.

Bear peered at the slow-moving figure. "What is that?"

"Looks like a woman to me," I said, although it was hard to tell.

"What kind of woman? A banshee?" He leaned forward as though the extra two inches might help his night vision.

"What's on her legs?" Tyson asked. "I think her pants might have disintegrated."

"Her shoulders seem abnormally large," Bear said. "Maybe she's a hunchback."

Her gait was slightly off, too, as though she favored an injured leg.

"Hey," I yelled. "Are you okay?"

The woman groaned, prompting Bear to spring into action. He rushed to her aid and immediately trotted backward to rejoin us.

"She's rotten," he whispered.

I looked at him. "How can you tell already? You only just met her."

Tyson scented the air. "No, he means she's actually rotting. She's the bad smell."

Eyes wide, Bear nodded. "Zombie."

The animated corpse ambled closer to us, carving a line straight through the bushes and anything else in her path. This was my first zombie encounter, and I wasn't entirely sure what the protocol entailed.

"Are zombies sentient?" I asked my companions.

"Depends," Bear said.

Very helpful. "What's your name?" I called.

"Tiffany Hazleton." Her voice sounded hoarse, as though it hadn't been used for a long time, which it probably hadn't.

Tyson tossed me a look. "Isn't Tiffany a kind of lamp?"

I frowned. "How would I know?"

"You didn't always live in a treehouse," Tyson replied.

"No, but the coven wasn't exactly awash in chandeliers. If you had multiple bulbs in one light fixture, you were rich."

Bear directed his gaze at Tyson. "How would *you* know about a Tiffany lamp?"

"I worked in an antique shop when I was younger." He paused. "Very briefly. The owner fired me, said he should've known better than to let a bull in a china shop, whatever that means."

Bear snorted.

"Are your shoulders swollen?" Tyson called to the zombie.

Bear shook his head. "What kind of question is that? Never point out a woman's abnormalities."

"If she has a disease, we might want to keep our distance," Tyson said.

"I think you've forgotten the zombie part," Bear told him. "We'll want to keep our distance regardless."

Tiffany twisted her neck ninety degrees for a better look. "Oh, those are shoulder pads."

"Why would anybody use material to make their shoulders look bigger?" Tyson asked.

"Didn't women used to do that to their chests?" Bear asked. "Maybe the extra padding migrated from her boobs to her shoulders."

I was less interested in her sartorial choices than her existence. Then again, her outfit was slightly distracting. She wore so many shades of pink, she looked like a rosy rainbow. Even her shoes were neon pink.

"What are you doing out here by yourself, Tiffany?" I asked, returning my arrow to the quiver.

"I woke up, and nobody was there."

Tyson waved a hand in front of his nose. "They probably evacuated the area as soon as the smell hit them."

I shushed him. No need to antagonize the zombie. "Where did you wake up?" I asked her.

"I... I don't know. It was so dark." She looked skyward. "Everything is so dark. Will it be sunrise soon?"

"Sunrise?" Bear echoed. "How old is she?"

Tiffany's bones cracked as she twisted her neck so that it was facing forward again. "Did you just call me old?"

Bear waved his hands. "No, no. You don't understand."

Tiffany clenched her hands into fists, causing each knuckle to make a popping sound. "And now you're calling me stupid?"

Bear raked a hand through his thick head of hair. "I'm starting to understand why Bonnie gets frustrated with me."

Tiffany charged. For an animated corpse, she was surprisingly agile.

"I think the shoulder pads might be enchanted," I panted, as I swung my quiver and knocked her on the side of the head. Despite the dent I left, she barely reacted.

"What the hell?" Tyson said, echoing my thoughts.

"She doesn't feel pain," Bear explained. "That's what happens when you don't have a working nervous system."

"Now you're insulting my nervous system?" Tiffany grabbed Bear by the throat and squeezed, losing a pinky finger in the process. Bear seemed more disturbed by the loss of a digit than the pressure on his windpipe. He brought his knee to her groin, and she let go.

"She's freakishly strong," Bear complained, rubbing his neck.

"Out of the way!" Tyson yelled, picking up a fallen tree branch.

Bear and I jumped aside as Tyson rammed the branch through Tiffany's torso.

"No internal organs either, apparently." Tyson gestured to the gaping hole he'd created in her abdomen.

Although I could now see straight through to the tree behind her, that didn't stop Tiffany. The zombie lunged at me. I resisted the use of magic, not wanting to draw more unwanted attention to us. For all we knew, there were rangers patrolling the woods in search of the zombie.

Tiffany tried to gouge my eyes with her disgustingly long nails. I jerked my head to the side and pulled her stringy locks, which only resulted in a handful of corpse hair. I'd trained for many types of attacks, but none that included the walking dead.

Tiffany's scream was unnatural, like everything else about her. She splayed her hand over the bald spot. "Look what you've done!"

"I have an idea." Bear snapped his fingers, and Tyson tossed over the branch. "Batter up."

I moved aside as he pulled back the thick branch with both hands and swung.

Tiffany's head cleared her exaggerated shoulders and flew across the woods. The body remained upright for another tense moment before crumpling to the ground. Her skin began to crack and peel as greenish-yellow pus oozed from her pores, releasing a noxious odor. Her nails were the first to fall off, followed by her fingers. The body disintegrated, until all that remained was a pile of pink atop a swirling pool of slime. Delightful.

"Beheading for the win," Tyson said, staring in awe at the zombie's remains.

I surveyed the forest. "Do you think the head survived?"

Bear blinked at me. "Why? Do you plan to mount it over the outhouse like a trophy?"

Tyson ran in the direction of the flying head. "It's gone," he yelled. "But there's a pretty headband with a lace bow if anybody wants it."

Bear eyed me. "Do you think Bonnie would wear it?"

I laughed. "If you're seriously entertaining that possibility, I think you need to reevaluate your relationship." Bonnie would likely behead Bear for merely asking the question.

"We need to figure out where Tiffany came from," I said, as we resumed our walk to the hideout. Between her name and her distinctive clothing, I figured it wouldn't be hard to find out more about her.

"I'd rather figure out *how*," Bear said. "If we're on the verge of a zombie apocalypse, I want to be prepared."

Tyson groaned. "Another apocalypse? We're still dealing with the aftermath of the last one."

The last one was known as the Great Eruption, when ten supervolcanoes blew their stacks at once, throwing enough debris into the atmosphere to block the sun. The earth's bowels spilled magma, ash, and monsters that had been previously allocated to the category of myths. Mother Nature wasn't the only one to suffer. As food became scarce and temperatures dropped, half the human population died. While the survivors attempted to regroup during the seemingly permanent eclipse, another species seized the opportunity of their eternal lifetimes. Vampires climbed out of the shadows and straight to the top of the food chain, forcing other supernaturals to make their presence known. In other, more civilized parts of the world, vampire Houses began to employ magic users to keep the world from falling into decay. They provided artificial light for plants, among other things. Elemental witches and wizards were, and still are, in the highest demand. They fuel wind power, geothermal energy, and hydropower. Electricity, like most other essentials, is at the mercy of vampires because they control the grids.

They control everything.

The Wild used to be more like other places, but not anymore.

Tyson was right—we were still trying to carve an existence out of the last apocalypse. Zombies would certainly add an unnecessary twist.

"How would you prepare for a zombie takeover?" Tyson asked.

"For starters, I'd gather the right kind of weapons," Bear replied.

"And what would those be?" I asked.

He sidestepped a cluster of thorny bushes. "Anything that can be used for beheading."

"Is beheading the only option?" I'd been too preoccupied with the threat of vampires, monsters, and demons to learn much about zombies.

Bear jumped over a tree stump and landed on the ground with the grace of a three-legged elephant. "I think you can blow them up, but I'd have to double-check."

We didn't have easy access to explosives anyway. Beheading was our best bet.

"Tiffany was one zombie," I said. "I'm not sure we need to strategize."

Tyson smiled wryly. "I'm sure that's what the humans said when the supervolcanoes exploded."

"No, that's what they would've said if only one supervolcano had erupted. There were ten," Bear pointed out.

We arrived at the hideout to find Scarlet pacing in front

of the campfire. "Where've you been?" the werewolf demanded. As my second-in-command, Scarlet was in charge of the hideout when I was away.

"We met a zombie in the woods near Locklear," Bear answered, unable to contain his enthusiasm, "but she died."

Scarlet didn't flinch at the mention of a zombie. "You promised to lay low, Aster. What were you doing so close to a vampire enclave?"

"You skipped right over the part about the zombie," I said.

Scarlet rolled her eyes. "Are we talking about a real zombie, or is this one of Bear's stories?"

Bear recoiled, indignant. "Hey!"

"Don't get distracted, Scarlet," Bonnie yelled from her treehouse. "Tell them!"

I tilted my head. "Tell us what?"

"Fire up the Beast," Bonnie said, as she climbed down the ladder from her treehouse. She leaned back awkwardly to avoid bumping her expanding stomach on the wooden slats.

"The Beast? Why?" We generally saved the 4x4 for longer journeys unless there was an emergency.

"We need to go to Clayton, like right now," Scarlet insisted. "There's a situation."

My pulse quickened.

"A zombie invasion?" Bear interrupted.

Scarlet's face darkened. "No, something much worse."

The knot in my stomach tightened. What could be worse than that?

Chapter Two

Clayton could no longer be described as a village. The few buildings left standing were missing necessary parts like a rooftop or a wall. Survivors in tattered clothing staggered amidst the wreckage. The cries ranged from wails to whimpers. Mothers clung to their children instead of the other way around. They'd be traumatized for life—I knew from experience.

The healer's office had been destroyed, so a makeshift healing station had been set up in the local school that had withstood the attack—mostly.

After a quick tour of the carnage, the crew and I gathered outside the school to discuss the situation.

"Someone took the scorched earth approach," Bear commented.

"Did you see anything that suggests a motive or even a specific target?" I asked.

Bear made a sweeping gesture with his arm. "Pretty sure the whole village was the target."

"What about the Ghost Pack?" Tyson suggested.

"Maybe they had a few too many pints at the pub and went berserk."

"And threw a thousand Molotov cocktails?" I shook my head. "No way."

"This isn't the work of werewolves," Scarlet agreed.

"Maybe not our kind of werewolves," Tyson countered. "What do we even know about their pack? The White Wolf is supposed to be some kind of insane badass, emphasis on insane."

My thoughts flitted to Max Kane, the self-proclaimed leader of the legendary pack. One look at him and it was hard to doubt his claim. He was built like an oak tree but moved with the stealth of a panther. He was also cocky as hell. Then again, why wouldn't you be when you commanded the most famous and feared pack in North America?

"What reason would they have for doing this?" I asked.

"Carving out new territory?" Tyson offered.

Bonnie blew a dismissive raspberry. "And they chose Clayton of all places? It's in the middle of nowhere."

I looked at her. "We live in The Wild, Bonnie. It's all the middle of nowhere." Known as Alaska before the Great Eruption, The Wild was sometimes referred to as the Forgotten Land because of its remote location. The meltdown of calderas had effectively cut us off from most civilization. Your best bet to travel to The Wild unscathed was via portal, but only if you were rich enough and fortunate enough to have access to one.

Despite my misgivings, I considered the Ghost Pack theory. "The pack has its pick of remote locations to rule. Why would they encroach on a village?"

"Maybe they've encountered issues we don't know

about," Tyson said. "It isn't like we can ask them. If they want to stay hidden, they will."

I wasn't so sure about that. Max had made it clear to me that he was interested in an alliance—more than an alliance, really, although I was pretty sure it was his arrogance driving that conversation. I got the distinct impression the White Wolf had little to no experience with rejection.

Bear lifted a charred wooden beam and flung it across the ground. "This isn't the work of wolves. No way. We're animals, but we're not *animals*."

Scarlet frowned. "That made no sense."

"Just because we're not capable of something like this doesn't mean the Ghost Pack isn't," Tyson pointed out. "You saw some of them when they showed up at the White Fortress. They were ferocious."

I winced at the mention of the White Fortress, the vampire stronghold in the mountains where I'd been taken by Lord Doran and tortured by a vampire named Vincent Dufresne, also known as the Master Inquisitor. He'd wanted to better understand my magic, and apparently, that meant relieving me of blood against my will. Nice guy.

"The pack wasn't ferocious enough," Bonnie grumbled.

"The whole pack wasn't there, remember?" Bear said. "I got the sense they were only there to see how things played out."

Bonnie shot him an aggrieved look. "Doran and Birney lived to torment us another day. That's how it played out."

"It isn't you they want to torment," Bear said pointedly.

Everyone looked at me, except Bonnie's look was more of a glare. "You should've killed them both when you had the chance," she said.

"Excuse me for focusing on my survival."

"She blinded Birney," Tyson argued. "Losing his

eyesight basically neutered him. I think that counts for something."

Bonnie folded her arms so that they rested on the slope of her belly. "He'll want revenge, which endangers the rest of us."

"We were already outlaws, Bon," Bear said, his tone gentler now. "We've been in danger for years."

We'd already relocated our hideout since the incident at the White Fortress on the off chance that Lord Doran's rangers might find us. The move was no simple task. As rudimentary as our treehouses were, we still had to scout a new spot that was close to water sources and in a dense part of the forest—preferably a part of the forest that wasn't close to death. In the spirit of recognizing my own strengths and weaknesses, I'd left the scouting to the wolves and only offered my stamp of approval.

"I think we should talk to more of the survivors," Scarlet said. "I'm sure at least one of them saw what happened."

I hesitated. The villagers had to be traumatized. The idea of grilling them for information when they were hurt and vulnerable felt wrong.

But also necessary.

"Scarlet and I will go inside the school," I told the crew. "Why don't the rest of you see if you can help with any manual labor?" My gaze flicked to Bonnie's round stomach. "Except you, Bonnie."

"I'm perfectly capable of manual labor," she snapped. "I'm a werewolf, not a human. You don't need to coddle me."

"Noted," I said, and turned to enter the building with Scarlet.

"You could've had Bonnie come with us," Scarlet said.

"We need to question these people as gently as possible.

Do you really think Bonnie can do that?" She was about as delicate as a sledgehammer.

"Point taken."

I scanned the huddled masses in the hopes of spotting a familiar face. A man nodded at me from across the room, and I recognized Dakota, the local leathersmith. Perfect.

"This way," I told Scarlet. As we cut through the throng of bodies, I tried to block out their suffering. My nightmare card had enough holes punched, thank you very much.

"Aster," Dakota greeted me with a soft handshake. His face was stained with black smudges, and his hair looked like it had been set on fire and then smothered with a blanket. Maybe it had.

"I'm so glad to see you. This is my friend, Scarlet."

Dakota only nodded at her. He didn't seem to have the energy for pleasantries with strangers.

"How are you?" I asked.

He offered a grim smile. "Alive, which is more than I can say for half the village."

"Can you tell me what happened?"

"I wish I could. I was working late when I heard what sounded like an explosion. I'd been wearing earmuffs, so it had to be incredibly loud. I ran outside and saw flames everywhere."

"You didn't see anything out of the ordinary? No rangers or wolves?"

I felt a tug on the hem of my shirt and looked down. A boy no older than six or seven stared up at me with a solemn expression.

"I saw a dragon," the little boy said.

His mother gave me an apologetic smile. "He thinks because there was fire that it had to be a dragon."

"No," the boy insisted. "I saw it. It had horns and giant wings." He spread his small arms as wide as they could go.

"Now, Albert, you know we don't have dragons in The Wild," his mother protested. She seemed mildly embarrassed by his proclamation.

"Did anyone else claim to see a dragon?" Scarlet asked.

"Even if they did, it could be hysteria talking," Dakota said. "Everybody's worked up right now. I wouldn't trust any so-called eyewitnesses."

The little boy glared at the leathersmith. "I saw a dragon." He pursed his lips, and I waited to see whether he'd stomp on Dakota's foot to emphasize his statement.

"All right, my darling. You saw a dragon. We believe you." His mother patted his shoulder and steered him away, mouthing an apology as she turned.

A woman called to Dakota. "I've got more bandages for you," she said.

Dakota excused himself, leaving us to speak with those in line behind him. We stayed at the school for another hour, assisting those we could. The burn victims were the toughest. They were in so much pain, yet there was nothing I could do for them. Healers had been summoned from neighboring villages, but even they were ill-equipped to handle the severity of the injuries.

Seeing so many inconsolable loved ones and hearing their constant cries brought forth memories I struggled to keep buried. After my grandmother staged her ill-fated rebellion against the vampire authorities, the entire coven was punished with an event known as the purge. I lost the last of my family that day, along with my home. I'd never forgotten the screams of agony that had accompanied the destruction.

And I'd never forgive those responsible for them.

Scarlet seemed to notice my state of mind because she guided me to the exit. "You seem like you need a break," she said.

"It's a lot," I admitted, once we were outside. Clayton and its people would never be the same after this. It would take time and money to rebuild—and it would take an eternity to feel safe again.

"I'll be honest," Scarlet said, "considering the damage, a dragon attack isn't out of the realm of possibility. It's certainly more plausible than werewolves."

"One dragon couldn't have caused all this destruction, though, could it?" Then again, I had as much experience with dragons as I had with zombies.

"I don't know. It seems unlikely."

And it seemed equally unlikely that no one would've spotted multiple dragons flying overhead during the attack. On the other hand, the sky was black and dragon silhouettes could've been camouflaged by smoke.

Scarlet regarded me. "I hate to suggest this, but what about vampires?"

"They attacked an entire village without draining anyone's blood? Doubtful."

"Maybe if the purpose was revenge." She tried to gauge my reaction.

"Revenge for what?" As far as I knew, nobody in Clayton had staged a rebellion. Hugo had been the most recent rabble-rouser, and he belonged to our crew. More importantly, he was dead.

"For Hugo's insolence," Scarlet said. "They can't find us, so they attack the people we try to protect." She shrugged. "I don't know. I'm just spitballing."

My gaze swept the ruined village. "I can't see Lord Doran doing this."

She grunted. "The same vampire responsible for the purge? That Lord Doran?"

I fell silent. The thegn of The Wild had aided my escape from the White Fortress once he realized what Lord Birney and the Master Inquisitor intended to do to me. A vampire who'd arguably developed a compassionate side couldn't be responsible for this kind of mass destruction, could he?

Maybe.

Scarlet wasn't wrong to suspect him. Doran had survived my grandmother's rebellion, and we'd all paid the price. Maybe Clayton was paying the price for his most recent survival. The question remained—why?

"I can see you're flagging. Let's find the others and go," Scarlet said.

Sometimes she knew me better than I knew myself. I would've pushed myself to exhaustion and become no good to anyone.

We found Bonnie with a group of people scouring the debris for usable items. To her credit, the werewolf seemed to have pitched in.

Bear and Tyson, on the other hand, appeared to have left the village. There was no sign of them anywhere, and they hadn't told Bonnie where they were going. I was about to head back to the Beast without them when we saw them emerge from the forest.

"Where were you?" I was too surprised by their disappearance to be angry. They didn't usually disobey orders, certainly not instructions to help people in need.

"We followed a trail," Tyson said cryptically. His body, typically all loose limbs and flexing muscles, was now rigid.

I examined him closely. "And?"

"You're going to want to see for yourself."

"Gee, that doesn't sound ominous," Bonnie said.

"We'll take the Beast in case we need to make a fast getaway," Bear said.

"And the plot thickens," Scarlet said. I could tell she was making an effort to keep the tone light after everything we'd just seen.

"Scarlet, you and Bonnie should head back to the hideout," Bear said. "We'll update you later."

Bonnie squared her shoulders. "If you're worried about me keeping up, I can manage."

Bear touched her arm. "It's not an insult. It's been a long day, and it's about to get even longer."

Fear flashed in Bonnie's eyes as she yanked her arm away. "Hell no. I'm going with you."

We'd left the hideout unattended for hours, which I tried to avoid. I looked at Scarlet. "If you could…"

She held up a hand. "I was already planning on it."

"We really should go now." Tyson started to turn but then seemed to think better of it. "Do you have any more weapons?"

"I have a dagger in my boot," Bonnie said. "Not that I can reach it anymore without sitting down first."

"And I have my arrows and my magic," I added. "Why?"

His face hardened. "Because we're going to need them all."

Chapter Three

The trail was littered with broken branches and charred remains. Thankfully I had a strong gag reflex because I'd seen enough today to trigger it ten times over. It helped that we'd driven the Beast and could observe the carnage from the safety of our stolen 4x4.

"Almost there," Bear said.

"Yes, but where is 'there,' exactly?" I asked.

Tyson sat beside me, his features arranged in a grim composite. "There's a canyon up ahead. We should stop here to keep a safe distance."

I had a feeling that whatever we were about to witness would throw 'safe' right out the proverbial window. And I thought I was already tense. Now I was as taut as a bowstring.

We parked the Beast alongside a row of naked trees and continued on foot. We'd only made it a few feet when Bear stopped to scent the air.

"What is it?" I asked.

He remained perfectly still. "Company behind us."

As I reached for an arrow, he stayed my hand.

"Rangers?" I mouthed.

He shook his head.

"Wait here," Tyson said under his breath.

"Like hell."

Sometimes their lupine instincts seemed to forget I was the most powerful one of us. I ripped an arrow from my quiver and whipped around to confront our stalker. About twenty feet behind us, a trio of silhouettes crested the hill. There was no mistaking the one in the middle. His form was like a mountain rising between two valleys. I didn't recognize the two women that flanked him. Members of his Ghost Pack, presumably.

"Max Kane," I said, without lowering my weapon. The tip of this arrow wasn't poisoned, which meant it would likely bounce right off the massive chest of the White Wolf. His body seemed more impenetrable than armor. If rangers had his physique, I wouldn't have been nearly as successful at robbing and dodging them all these years.

"Aster Goodfellow, as I live and breathe," the werewolf said.

Beside me, Bear and Tyson growled.

Max made a calming gesture with his hands. "Down, boys. Nobody's here for you, not that I couldn't take you with both hands tied behind my back."

I didn't doubt it.

Bonnie ambled between us. "Try it and you'll have me to deal with."

Max gave her the once-over. "I know better than to mess with a pregnant she-wolf." He cracked a smile. "Learned that one the hard way."

"I suspect that's the only way you learn anything," I snapped.

"Sidebar, Your Honor," Max said. He stepped out from

between his pack members and motioned for me to join him.

Together we walked toward the tree line, out of earshot of our companions.

"Why are you following me again?" I demanded.

He arched an eyebrow. "Somebody woke up on the cocky side of the bed. What makes you think it's you? Why can't I be tracking your wolves?"

I worked my jaw, but no words came out. I couldn't think of a response that didn't make me sound either delusional or as arrogant as he was. The longer the silence continued, the wider his grin stretched. Finally, he put me out of my misery.

"Two days ago, members of my pack disappeared. Their trail led me here."

"What were they doing?"

"Hunting. In case you haven't noticed, we're a large pack, and that means a lot of food."

I knew how much my crew consumed, and I could only imagine the amount of food the Ghost Pack required. "You didn't find any trace of them?"

"Oh, I found traces." His pleasant expression evaporated. "Suraj's boot. Annelise's hand."

My stomach turned. "Tyson and Bear picked up a trail from Clayton that brought us here."

"The destroyed village?"

"You heard?"

"Saw smoke and sent a couple scouts to check things out. They thought it might be some sort of vampire retaliation."

"That's one theory, but I think it's something else." I inclined my head toward the cliff. "And I have a feeling that something else is right over there."

"That's where we're headed. I guess we can explore it together. You don't mind the extra company, do you?"

"As long as you don't get in my way, I don't mind what you do."

He chuckled. "You sound mighty blasé for a witch that had to be rescued from Dracula's castle."

I balled my hands into fists. "I did *not* have to be rescued. I'd already escaped. You gave me a lift home, and that's the extent of your so-called rescue."

"You seem to have forgotten there was a battle."

"A battle that had nothing to do with me and everything to do with a misguided wizard named Hugo." I didn't come all this way to argue with an ego the size of Max's. That would take more power than even I possessed.

"You seem awfully defensive. Have I pressed your buttons?"

"As much as you'd like that, I'm more concerned with whatever is over that cliff."

His jaw set. "Whatever it is, it'll have to answer to me."

"I think you mean us." I motioned for my crew to join us, and Max did the same. Somehow the fact that they were both women didn't surprise me. The first werewolf was taller than I realized, but only because I'd first spotted her next to Max. Everyone looked small in comparison.

"This is Ina, my second," he said.

I could see why. Aside from the height advantage, her body seemed like a statue made purely of corded muscle. If she had a physical flaw, it wasn't obvious.

"Don't you mean your beta?" Tyson asked.

Ina stepped forward. "We don't use those antiquated terms. People don't know jack about wolves." She paused to look him over. "Present company included."

Okay, so maybe there was a personality flaw that offset the physical perfection.

Tyson's eyes glimmered with hostility. As long as nobody threw a punch, we'd be fine.

"Nice to meet you, Ina," I said, adopting a friendly tone. "I'm Aster. This is Tyson, Bear, and Bonnie."

"Is he your second?" Ina asked, her gaze fixed on Tyson.

"No, that honor belongs to Scarlet."

"Then why isn't she here?"

"We try not to travel together," I explained. "If I leave the hideout, she stays. Sort of a safety protocol."

Ina frowned at Max. "Why don't we do that?"

"Because we rarely stay in one place," Max replied. "If I left you behind, you'd still be in Russia."

"Good point."

Tyson snorted.

"I'm Lavonne," the second companion said. "I keep everybody sane." Although less muscular than Ina and shorter by an inch, her easygoing smile told me she wasn't exaggerating her role in the pack.

"How's that working out for you?" I asked.

Her gaze skated to Max. "Some days are more challenging than others."

"I bet."

Tyson nudged me. "Now that we're all good friends, can we get on with it?"

He wasn't usually rude. The presence of members of the Ghost Pack seemed to have unsettled him.

We advanced toward the canyon in a cluster. Max's long strides covered more ground in less time, and he was the first one to reach the cliff.

As we approached the edge, a strong gust of wind blew past us, forcing my eyes closed. When I opened them again, an enormous creature hovered in front of us with its jagged wings spread wide. Purple and gold markings glinted with each fraction of movement.

The little boy was right.

Max let out a low whistle. "Well, that explains a lot."

The dragon didn't seem to notice us. A relieved breath escaped me when it turned and flew in the opposite direction.

"Is this the culprit?" I asked, although the boy had mentioned horns, which could've been an embellishment.

Max beckoned me closer to the edge. "You might want to take a look."

I inched forward and peered over the edge. I wasn't the only one to gasp.

The floor of the canyon was flooded with dragons. Although it was difficult to see their colors from this distance, their varying shapes and sizes suggested they were different species. Some sported horns; others featured a head frill and spikes reminiscent of a triceratops. There were wings that appeared flexible and short like those of bats, whereas other, elliptical wings seemed designed for short bursts of flight. I counted at least four different types of dragons based on their wings alone. The mixture was surprising. Much like any other species, they usually fought each other for dominance and territory.

I was the first one to break the silence. "Biggest dragon horde in the world was not on my list of theories."

"What do you think they want?" Tyson asked.

Bear shrugged. "They're dragons. Do they want anything? I thought it was all chaos and destruction with these guys."

Tyson shot him a curious look. "And what? They flew

over Clayton and decided it seemed like a nice place to pillage?"

"They don't pillage," Max interjected. "They graze. And if you happen to get in the way of their grazing, they roll right over you."

I cast him a sidelong glance. "You sound like you have experience with them."

"You can't run a pack across undeclared territory without running into the occasional nest, although I'm with you on this one. I've never seen a horde quite like this one."

"How could no one have seen them?" I asked. No one except one little boy.

"They were too busy running for their lives," Tyson replied.

"It's probably a coping mechanism," Max said. "Like before the Great Eruption, when people would see things that defied belief, they developed alternate theories that made sense to them."

As we spoke, a dragon occasionally rose into the air and hovered, but none came as close to us as the first one.

"I feel like they're waiting for someone to call the meeting to order," Bear quipped.

"I feel like they're waiting until they're hungry again," Tyson countered.

"They wouldn't eat us." I paused to look at Max, recalling the remains of his missing pack members. "Would they?"

"Most of them wouldn't on purpose," he replied, "but I see at least one species down there that's carnivorous. They don't care what they're eating, as long as there's meat on the bones."

Lavonne gulped audibly.

"What do we do about them?" Bear asked. "We can't exactly send them an eviction notice."

"Don't think they'd comply if you did," Max said, his eyes twinkling with mischief.

I watched the dragons as they moved through the canyon. "I wonder if Lord Doran knows about them."

"If not, somebody should tell him," Tyson said. "Maybe the vampires will actually prove useful for a change."

"It stands to reason they'd take action," Max agreed. "If the dragons wipe out whole villages, that won't leave many donors for their food supply."

Bear's face hardened. "They didn't seem to care too much when people were dropping dead from sickness." He was still bitter about the Green Death, mainly because it nearly took the life of Bonnie and their unborn child. I'd bargained with a demon to save them. It had been a risky move, but I was glad it had paid off.

"They cared about the Green Death," I insisted. At least I knew Doran did. Then again, it was hard to know how much of what the vampire had said to me was truthful or merely an act to lull me into a false sense of security. He'd been trying to determine whether I was, in fact, the Hooded One. I'd convinced him I wasn't, only to show my hand—literally—upon my escape from the White Fortress. Before that, I thought we might've reached an understanding when he'd helped free me from the clutches of the ruthless Lord Birney and the Master Inquisitor. Now I had no idea where we stood, and I wasn't sure I wanted to find out.

"It could be a couple bad apples ruining the bushel," Bonnie offered. "The rest of the dragons might not realize what happened to Clayton."

"Why have they chosen to gather in a canyon?" Ina asked. "It's not typical for them."

"It's large enough to accommodate them and keeps them hidden from view," Max replied. "If you ask me, it's pretty smart. They must have a good leader."

As though on cue, one of the larger dragons separated from the horde and rose to the top of the canyon. The two horns on its head glimmered silver. Long and narrow wings suggested speed and accuracy, and if it was a fire breather, we were well within range.

Nobody moved. The dragon assessed us, continuing to hover as though debating its next move. Dread coiled in my stomach. If a single one of us so much as scratched an itch, we'd identify ourselves as prey. Thankfully, I was surrounded by werewolves, and they weren't likely to—

"Shit," Bear's voice rang out in the canyon like a bell in a church tower.

I quickly realized the reason for his response. Another dragon had appeared behind us. Given its immense size, I was surprised how easily it had snuck up on us. That was probably its main predatory attribute. If you were as large as this dragon and could maneuver unnoticed until the last second, the odds of a successful attack were in your favor.

This one didn't seem eager to attack, however. It seemed to be working in coordination with the silver horned one.

Sharp chills racked my body. It was one thing for a mixed group to blow through a village. Two different species working together on a microlevel like this was something else entirely.

"Any ideas?" Bear whispered.

"Your leader has two magical hands," Max said quietly. "Now might be a good time to use them."

"Absolutely not." If I lit up the sky in order to defend us against two dragons, we'd have fifty more chasing us before we made it to the Beast. In this situation, my powers were suicide.

"Guess it's up to me then," Max said. "Do us all a favor and don't scream."

Scream? Why would anybody—

Max leaped from the cliff's edge.

"What the hell?" Bear yelled.

Lavonne rolled her eyes.

The horned dragon reacted by straightening its wings in preparation for flight. Max's hand shot out and gripped the dragon's leg as he fell.

Bear gaped at the spectacle. "What's he doing?"

There was no time to find out. The second dragon interpreted Max's leap as a threat and unleashed a mighty roar.

Bear sniffed. "Minty fresh. Didn't expect that."

I was too preoccupied watching Max and the horned dragon to answer.

"You want a piece of me?" Tyson turned toward the second dragon and thumped his chest.

I edged forward and kept my attention on the werewolf, who'd managed to climb onto the dragon's back. His arms were wrapped around the thinnest part of the neck, and he was in the process of squeezing. What was his goal? Kill the dragon and enrage the horde? And here I thought my magic was suicide.

The dragon flapped it wings in a frenzy as it twisted and turned in an effort to dislodge the uninvited rider. I was forced away from the cliff's edge as they moved closer to us. Max's face grew various shades of purple as he continued to hold the dragon's neck in a tight grip, and I wondered whether he was somehow depriving himself of oxygen too.

I glanced over my shoulder to see that the rest of the group had surrounded the second dragon. They seemed to have reached a stalemate. I turned back to Max in time to see the dragon slump to the ground in a heap.

"If your plan is to stand there and look attractive, you're mastering it with finesse," Max said as he dismounted.

I stared at the mass of scales in front of me. "Did you kill it?"

"Nope. Pressure points. Just giving him a few pleasant dreams, although he'll be plenty mad when he wakes up."

Hopefully, we wouldn't be around to witness that part.

Behind us, the second dragon roared again, and Max bolted toward the rest of the group. I ran after him, trying to think of a way to contribute. If we wanted to avoid drawing the attention of more dragons, we had to handle this one just as quietly. I doubted anyone else in the group possessed Max's strength and skills, not that it mattered. This dragon wasn't letting us get close enough to apply pressure to whatever points there were.

Then I remembered my stash of arrows. There were a few tipped with a potion that would render the target unconscious. One arrow was usually sufficient for a full-grown vampire, so I figured three might be enough to knock the dragon out long enough for us to flee to safety. Dragons weren't great trackers like wolves. They wouldn't be able to follow our scents back to the hideout and wherever the pack was holing up these days.

I notched the first arrow and aimed. "Max, out of the way."

The werewolf turned to look at me as an arrow skimmed his earlobe. His hand clamped the side of his head. "A little more warning next time!"

"Sorry," I said, as I watched the arrow land in the soft, fleshy part of the dragon's body between the scales.

I launched a second arrow and sent it sailing into another of the dragon's vulnerable spots. Max wasn't the only one with knowledge of anatomy. I started to wonder what else he knew and how it might benefit me later.

I shook off the salacious thoughts as I strung a third arrow and let it fly. This one hit the sweet spot—the underbelly. The dragon flopped forward, prompting the werewolves to scramble.

"Time to go, kids," Max ordered. "Playtime's over."

"There's room in the Beast," I offered, sprinting in the direction of the 4x4.

"We're faster in fur," Max retorted. He shot a quick glance at my companions. "So are they."

Bear rushed forward to run beside me. "We stick with Aster."

Max seemed to realize if he expected to win my favor, then leaving me in the dust probably wasn't the way to my heart. Not that I felt abandoned. The Beast was fast enough to get us out of here. Besides, I'd been taking care of myself in The Wild long before the White Wolf ever showed up.

With Bonnie on Bear's lap and Tyson behind the wheel, all seven of us crammed inside the Beast. I would've marveled at the ingenuity of our positions if I weren't in fear for my life. I checked over my shoulder every minute or so to see whether we'd picked up a dragon tail, but only darkness stretched behind us.

"Those dragons are deadly. Why didn't you kill them?" Bonnie asked.

Max stared straight ahead. "Because Aster didn't want me to."

Bonnie frowned. "I didn't hear her say that."

"She didn't have to."

"I'm with the mama wolf," Ina said. "They killed members of our pack. They deserve to die."

"We don't know which dragons were responsible for the deaths of your friends or the people of Clayton," I said.

Ina glowered at me. "What do you propose—that we hold a trial first?"

"I think we need more information before we act," I told her.

Ina snorted. "Sure. Get a few more of us killed, then act. Sounds like a good plan."

"Ina," Max said in a warning tone.

We drove for another thirty minutes before Tyson brought the Beast to a stop and turned to the back seat.

"We're heading to our hideout from here," he said.

Max hopped out of the vehicle. "Thanks for the lift." He looked at me. "Now that you've met the two most important women in my life, I'd like to introduce you to the rest of the Ghost Pack. You can find us in the Aleutian Valley. Any particular day convenient for you?"

I recoiled slightly. "Why would you want to do that?"

"Because you're an important figure in this region. The pack should learn to recognize you on sight."

"Or by scent," Ina added.

"Maybe we can work together to solve this dragon problem," I said.

Max raked a hand through his hair. "Agreed. I think it would be wise to join forces."

"That means don't do anything rash," I said.

"Like jump off a cliff?" He grinned. "You have yourself a deal."

The trio shifted into wolves and ran until they were swallowed by the night.

"You know when he says, 'join forces,' he means get in your pants," Tyson said as we continued on foot to the hideout.

"He wants more than what's in your pants," Bear chimed in. "I hear wedding bells."

I elbowed his ribs. "Nobody's getting married, and nobody's getting into anybody's pants. Consider my zipper firmly shut."

"You're missing out." Bear's words were followed by a quick frown. "Not that I would know anything about Max's skills. I just mean..." He started to stumble over his words.

I gave his arm a gentle pat. "I know what you mean."

"He's devilishly handsome," Tyson said. "And at least he's on our side, unlike the other one."

I knew he meant Doran, but I wasn't in the mood to talk about the stoic vampire. We had a destroyed village and no idea when the dragons might decide to take another joyride. This situation had to take precedence over vampires.

"You have experience leading a bunch of wolves," Bear said. "Max couldn't do much better if he wanted to choose someone outside his pack."

"No more Max talk unless it pertains to the dragon horde," I snapped. Since when did my crew view me as a woman willing to get married to the first guy who showed interest? Why did they think I'd want to get married to anyone at all?

"Seriously," Bonnie interjected. "What's with you guys?"

"I'll make my own choices when it comes to my personal life, thank you very much," I told them. "Right now, all I care about is protecting The Wild from another rampage."

"You and me both," Bear said, snaking an arm around Bonnie's expanding waistline.

"What do we do next then?" Tyson asked.

"Give my feet a rest, that's what." Bonnie winced. "I spent too much time on them today."

Bear scooped her off the ground like she weighed no more than a doll. The advantages of werewolf strength.

I smiled up at Tyson. "First we're going to cook food in front of a warm fire because I'm starving, then we're getting much-needed sleep. Tomorrow, I'm taking a team to Oglethorpe to hit the books."

The taller werewolf blinked. "Books?"

An image of Max subduing the horned dragon flashed in my mind.

"Knowledge is power, Tyson. If you want to defeat the dragons, you need to learn how."

Chapter Four

My dreams consisted of fireballs raining from the sky and burning trees. Okay, technically those qualified as nightmares and not very imaginative ones at that.

"It's research day," I said, yawning and stretching as I strode toward the campfire in time for breakfast. Although I'd eaten plenty before bedtime, I still woke up ravenous. To be fair, I felt like I was in a perpetual state of hunger.

Bear grimaced. "Yippee?"

My shoulders sagged. "Come on. Who's with me?"

Scarlet's hand shot up.

"Shouldn't you stay here if Aster is going?" Tyson asked.

Bear glanced up from the kebab he was roasting. "I'll hold down the fort. Scarlet's better at research anyway."

"Why is research the next stage?" Tyson asked. "I feel like we should be taking action."

"Now you sound like Ina," I told him.

"Research will help us take the *right* action," Scarlet said.

"Know thy enemy," Bonnie chimed in. She tore into a kebab like she'd just chased it through the woods.

"Enemy seems a bit strong," I said. "We don't know what we're dealing with yet. Maybe they're lost and confused."

Bonnie licked the meat juice from her fingers. "We have dead people, a destroyed village, and a zombie. I think it's safe to say we're not dealing with a friend."

Scarlet's ears pricked. "Do you think they're all related?"

I chewed slowly. "I don't know what dragons would have to do with a zombie. I've never heard of a type of dragon that could raise the dead."

"I'd still like to find out more about our corpse, Tiffany Hazleton," Bear said.

"I can follow that lead," Bonnie volunteered.

"The priority is shoulder pads," Bear told her, biting into the meat on his kebab. "I'd like to know their history." He paused. "Really, I want to know the reason for their existence."

"What about the lace gloves she was wearing?" Tyson said. "They were fingerless. What's the point of them?"

"Maybe the material was worn away over time," Scarlet proposed.

I sort of liked the idea of fingerless gloves. They'd keep my magic hands from acting on impulse without getting in the way of stringing my bow.

Bonnie saluted him. "On it, boss."

Bear leaned against her. "Would it be horrible if I asked you to stay here with me?"

"Because I'm pregnant?"

"You complained all night about your sore feet," he said. "You even complained in your sleep."

"I had muscle cramps in my calves. Am I supposed to ignore them so you can sleep?"

Bear's brow furrowed. "Yes?"

Bonnie smacked his arm.

"I think staying put today might be best," Bear said.

Bonnie kissed his forehead. "Fine. Anything for you."

"I'm going to hunt," Tyson announced. "Our supplies are getting low."

"That would be easier with two of us." Scarlet tugged a piece of meat off the stick with her teeth.

I stood upright. "I can manage on my own. It's only research."

"Are you sure?" Scarlet asked, sounding less than certain herself.

"Absolutely." I also needed to restock the sleeping potion for the arrows. Hugo had made the previous supply. Now that he was dead, I had to find another source.

"Scarlet's too busy anyway," Bear said. "She's been working on that list again."

Scarlet scowled. "You mock the list, but mark my words, one day you'll be happy I wrote it."

"Is this the charter?" I asked.

"Naturally," Bear said.

I looked at Scarlet. "What number are you up to now?"

"Sixty."

Sixty changes she wanted to see implemented by House Nilsson in The Wild. She referred to it as The Wild Charter. It was a pipe dream, of course, but we indulged her. We all needed a version of hope to cling to.

I guzzled a second cup of water before leaving the hideout. Dehydration was best avoided in The Wild. It left you weaker in a fight and vulnerable to infection, two things that could kill you—and I had no interest in dying, not while there was work to do anyway.

I arrived at Oglethorpe with an uncomfortably full bladder, the downside of staying hydrated, and waltzed straight into Olive Branch, a used bookstore and cafe. It helped that I knew the location of the restroom and, even better, I knew the owner, Olive McMurtry. Olive was human and had moved from Juneau to The Wild as a teenager. She fell in love with the area and decided to put down roots.

When I emerged from the restroom, Hattie pounced. "I thought that blur was you. What are you doing here?"

Eighteen-year-old Hattie had been a werewolf in my crew until Olive made her an offer she couldn't refuse. As much as it pained me to lose another member of our merry band, I knew the move was best for young Hattie.

"I'm hoping you can help me find books about dragons," I said.

"Why do you want to learn about dragons?"

"Can't I be curious?"

"I know you, Aster. You don't pursue knowledge for the sake of it. No offense." Her face paled. "Wait. Does this have something to do with what happened in Clayton?"

"It might."

"Should I be concerned?"

"No more than usual."

The young werewolf smiled. "Gee, that's comforting. There be dragons this way."

"Thanks."

She crossed the room to a row of books. There was a spring in her step that hadn't been there when she lived at the hideout with us. She'd been too busy crushing on Bear and scowling at Bonnie to enjoy herself. As I suspected, village life seemed to suit her better.

"Do you know which species?" she asked as she studied the titles on the spines.

"Not sure." I described the ones I had seen. Hattie's eyebrows seemed to inch higher and higher with each new detail.

"Is this all one dragon?" Hattie asked.

"No."

Her brow creased. "I can't decide whether to be relieved or terrified."

I joined her at the shelf to read the titles. "I should probably start with the broadest book you have to help me narrow down the variety of species."

"You might want to speak to Jacob Farmer," Olive interrupted, appearing behind the counter.

"Where did you come from?" I asked. I hadn't noticed her in the room.

"I'm working on the floor back here," she replied, a little too quickly. "Untidy files in constant need of organization."

"Who's Jacob Farmer?" Hattie asked.

"An old man who likes books about world wars," Olive explained. "But he's also knowledgeable about dragons. You can usually find him at the Dancing Dragon, in fact."

I smiled. "Why am I not surprised?"

"He and Rita like to discuss history, or so he tells me," Olive said. "I think he enjoys the company of clever ladies."

"As long as Glenn doesn't mind," I said.

My comment sparked a laugh from Olive. "Glenn has nothing to fear. Jacob is about a hundred years old and looks every inch of it. He's an absolute gem, though. Every time he comes in here, I feel as though I've earned a degree."

Hattie lit up. "Will you introduce me the next time he comes in? I'd love to meet him."

Olive's head bobbed. "Oh, I fully intend to. You two are destined to become the best of friends, I just know it."

Hattie appeared delighted by Olive's prediction. She pivoted to face me. "Maybe I could come with you to the Dancing Dragon."

"If Olive can spare you, I'd love the company."

Hattie shot her boss a pleading look.

"Only if you promise to bring back one of Rita's pies for supper. I'm a decent cook, but I'm not too proud to admit that Rita is the true master."

Hattie danced a little jig. "This day keeps getting better and better."

Olive smiled at me. "It doesn't take much to please her."

I wanted to say that's what happens when you grow up in the woods without access to food and indoor plumbing, but I bit my tongue. Nobody had it easy in The Wild unless you had fangs and a thirst for human blood.

"You're welcome to take any of those books as long as you bring them back when you're finished," Olive told me.

I perked up. "Really? You don't mind?"

"Sounds like your research is for the greater good. If this is how I can help the cause, then I'm happy to lend them."

Hattie tugged three books from the shelf and handed them to me. "If you want to go broad, these are your best bets."

"Thank you." I'd have to divide reading duties when I got back to the hideout. Bonnie wouldn't be thrilled, given her disinterest in books, but I knew she'd pull her weight. Now that her pregnancy was more advanced, she realized she was eating and sleeping more than usual, and I could tell it bothered her. Bonnie liked to be active. A research task might help her feel useful.

"Do you need a backpack?" Hattie asked. "I've got spares."

"No, I drove the Beast. I can leave them in there while I'm in the pub."

Olive glanced at the cuckoo clock on the wall. "I only ask that you be back in two hours so I can close on time."

"No problem. Thank you." Hattie practically skipped out the door ahead of me.

The Dancing Dragon was located in the neighboring village of Berthold. Its Bavarian charm was apparent the moment you crossed the border. The buildings were mainly painted black, white, and brown, but even the dull color scheme failed to detract from the grand and dynamic style of the architecture. Their primary vegetation consisted of beets and potatoes, which seemed in direct contrast to the village's Bavarian flair.

As far as I was concerned, the Dancing Dragon was the heart of Berthold, and its owners were, unsurprisingly, beloved by the villagers, as well as my crew. Glenn and Rita Arbor served beer and pies, along with wise counsel to those in need, and they'd been helpful to me more times than I could count. Their teenage twins, Meredith and Marcus, worked at the pub too. I had no doubt they'd one day continue to run the place every bit as successfully as their parents.

Marcus was behind the bar when Hattie and I entered. His hand shot up in greeting, but he quickly lowered it again. It took me a moment to recognize the problem. Six burly vampires in uniform sat at a table by the fireplace.

Rangers.

I maintained a casual demeanor as I steered Hattie to a stool at the bar. The werewolf started to jitter, and I tightened my grip on her arm until I felt her relax.

I kept my back to their table and was relieved I'd worn a plain black cloak instead of my golden one. Vampires didn't tend to patronize the pub, especially rangers. It was considered too banal and rustic for the top of the food chain.

Marcus handed me a menu. "There's a chill in the air today."

"Yes, there certainly is," I agreed and pretended to study the menu.

Marcus leaned over and whispered, "I expect them to leave soon. Meredith dropped off their bill about fifteen minutes ago, and their glasses are empty."

I nodded. "How are the mixed greens?"

"The beets are fresh."

Hattie stiffened when one of the vampires called for the owner. Marcus and I exchanged glances.

"He's on a supply run," Marcus told them. "Is there something I can do for you?"

The vampire ambled over to the bar and positioned himself directly next to my stool. I kept my head down and studied the menu.

"We didn't like the potato pie," the vampire said. "We want it stricken from the bill."

I had a feeling this was typical ranger behavior in a human-owned establishment.

"No worries. I can take care of that for you." Marcus swallowed hard as he took the bill and corrected the amount.

The vampire pivoted toward me. "You don't want the potato pie. Trust me. Tastes like cardboard."

"Thanks for the tip," I said without looking at him.

Relief washed over me when he tossed money on the counter and sauntered away. Only when the rangers left the pub did I release the breath I'd been holding.

"Do they do that often?" Hattie asked.

"All the time," Marcus replied. "They love the potato pie. Order it every time they come in."

Hattie shook her head. "You should complain to the authorities."

Marcus snickered. "They *are* the authorities."

"Is your father really on a supply run?" I asked.

His head bobbed. "He should be back soon. Left hours ago."

"Is your mother here? There's something I need to ask her."

"I'll fetch her." Marcus disappeared into the kitchen and returned a moment later with Rita right behind him. She broke into a smile at the sight of us.

"Aster and Hattie, two of my favorite ladies."

"I've got two more names I'm hoping you recognize."

Rita leaned across the counter. "Shoot."

"Does the name Tiffany Hazleton ring any bells?"

Rita tapped her nails on the wooden countertop. "Doesn't sound familiar, and with a name like Tiffany, I'd remember."

"You could check the blood bank records," Marcus suggested. "They keep a database of every registered human in The Wild."

"Aster's an outlaw," Rita interjected. "She can't go waltzing over to Klondike and demanding confidential information."

"Did the database survive the fire?" I asked. In addition to the recent rebellion, Hugo had also been responsible for the destruction of the donation center.

"You'd have to ask Lord Doran's office about that," Rita replied.

Well, there was no chance of that happening. The

thegn of The Wild might skewer me where I stood if he saw me again. I couldn't take the chance.

"I could try," Marcus offered. "I can tell them she's a relative I've been trying to find."

I regarded him. "Are you sure?"

The teenager nodded. "What's the harm? They'll tell me yes, no, or get the hell out and don't come back." He shrugged. "I can handle any of those outcomes."

Rita seemed less confident. "I don't know, Marcus. You don't want to put yourself on their radar unnecessarily."

Glenn emerged from the kitchen and set a cardboard box on the end of the counter. "Aster's done plenty for this family. If Marcus wants to contribute in this way, we should let him."

"I'd appreciate that. Thank you."

"What's the other name?" Rita asked. "Is there someone else you need him to find on the registry?"

"No. I'd like to speak to Jacob Farmer. Any idea when he might be in?"

"No, but it'd be easy enough to send for him," Glenn said.

"He's old, isn't he? Seems cruel to make him come to me."

Glenn wore a vague smile. "He won't complain about being summoned to the pub, trust me. Marcus can give him a ride on his bicycle. He's got the sidecar attached." He leaned over. "Comes in handy when you've got a customer unable to walk a straight line."

He gave Marcus directions to the old man's house. Marcus cast me a speculative look as he exited the pub.

"You've done a good job with the twins," I said.

He kissed his wife's cheek. "Oh, it's all down to Rita. I'm just ornamental."

I knew that wasn't true, but I went along with the joke. Hattie ordered a pie to take back to Olive Branch, and I ordered fish pie to split with Jacob, his favorite according to Rita.

The minutes ticked by, and Hattie started to shift on the stool. At this rate she'd be needed back at Olive Branch before I finished with Jacob.

"Maybe I can drive you to Oglethorpe and get back here before Jacob arrives," I offered.

"No, that's silly. I can shift and run back."

"With a pie?"

She frowned. "Good point."

"I can take her," Meredith volunteered, wiping her hands on an apron as she left the kitchen. "I'm finished my shift now."

"Do you have a sidecar, too?" Hattie asked.

"No, but I have a tandem with a basket for the pie." She tilted her head. "You can ride, can't you?"

"No, but I have two working feet. I'll figure it out." Hattie's smile faded. "But then you'll be coming back here on your own. I don't want to put you in that position when there are rangers around."

Meredith tugged on a chain around her neck and produced a whistle. "It makes a sound that's painful to all supernaturals. It won't hurt anybody, but it will buy me time to get away."

I marveled at the small device. "Where did you get that?"

"Dad bartered for it. A customer got a pitcher of beer and a meat pie, and we got a defensive weapon."

I nodded my approval. "Good deal."

I thanked Hattie for her help and watched them depart as I dug into my pie. I was hungrier than I realized. By the time I finished, Marcus had returned with an elderly man. His shock of white hair looked like it hadn't been combed in a decade, and his stooped shoulders suggested too much time spent hunched over a table.

"Mr. Farmer," I greeted him with a handshake. "I'm Aster Goodfellow."

He squinted at me. "Maya's daughter?"

"Granddaughter."

He removed a pair of glasses from his shirt pocket and slipped them onto the bridge of his nose. "You're the spitting image. It's like stepping into a time machine."

"I didn't realize you knew her."

"Who didn't know Maya Goodfellow? She's something of a legend in these parts."

Glenn snorted. "Unlike the Hooded One."

I kept my focus on the old man. "I understand you're something of a history buff."

Jacob's eyes sparked with interest. "Which subject are you interested in? World War III? I hate to call it a personal favorite because mass casualties aren't to be enjoyed, but the strategies involved in ending the war..." He offered a chef's kiss.

"I'd actually like to talk about dragons."

"Oh." His expression crumbled. "I mean, dragons are cool and all, but have you ever wondered how three thousand soldiers ended up at the bottom of the Grand Canyon in one fell swoop?"

Glenn chuckled and set a full pint glass in front of the old man. "Here. This might encourage you."

Jacob wrapped his hands around the glass. "I'll talk about dragons all day as long as you keep the beer coming."

"I've got a fish pie, too."

Jacob snapped to attention. "You just got better looking."

"I need information about certain types of dragons. If I draw them for you, do you think you could identify them?"

"Depends on how good of an artist you are." He seemed to savor the beer, closing his eyes as he drank and smacking his lips at the end.

Glenn hurried over with a sheet of paper and a pen. I started with the two dragons we'd encountered up close and turned the picture, so it was right side up for Jacob.

He bent over the picture and pushed his glasses back to the bridge of his nose. "That horned one is a Corniger."

"You're sure?"

He tapped his temple. "I've got a photographic memory. It's both a blessing and a curse, let me tell you."

"Have you ever seen one in person?" I dug into the pie while it was still warm.

"Not that kind, but I've seen others. I did a lot of hunting trips in my youth." He stuffed a forkful of fish into his mouth and released a soft moan of pleasure.

"Whereabouts?"

"Yukon, mostly. One time we ventured as far as Inuvik, but a storm forced us to turn back."

"You covered a lot of ground."

He shrugged. "Desperate times."

"More desperate than now, without the help of a coven?"

"That year we lost crops to a beetle infestation. No matter what magic the coven threw at them, they refused to quit. Finally, we couldn't wait anymore, so we gathered a party and hit the road." The light faded from his eyes. "We lost four villagers on that journey."

"To dragons?"

He shook his head. "An unfortunate encounter with nasty creatures called the Pey."

"Never heard of them," I said.

"Consider yourself lucky." Jacob shuddered. "I still have nightmares about that day." He poured more beer into his mouth as though rinsing away the memory.

"What was your experience with the dragons you met?"

"They were only territorial if we got too close to a nest. As you can imagine, those were easy to spot, being dragon sized and all."

"What about this dragon?" I tapped the other picture.

"That's a Ustrina. Lots of fire power. Saw a group of those in the Yukon about twenty years ago. None of them was fully grown. We figured they were orphans. To be honest, we weren't sure if they'd survive without adults."

"I did."

He gave me an appraising look. "I'd expect nothing less of Maya's granddaughter."

Rita strode toward the table, maintaining a friendly smile. She placed a hand on my shoulder. "Got a report of more rangers headed back this way. I'd recommend a quick exit."

I looked up at her. "Are they searching for something?"

"Not sure and would rather you not be here when I find out."

It was possible the rangers in here earlier had discovered my presence, although it was unlikely anyone in the village had ratted me out. Still, better safe than sorry.

I rose to my feet and slung the quiver strap over my shoulder. "Thank you." I pivoted to Jacob. "And thank you for sharing your knowledge."

Jacob's gaze slid to the door. "Go on. Don't be wasting

precious time with pleasantries. I fully intend to continue our conversation another time."

"I'd like that." And next time I'd make sure Hattie joined us. Olive was right—those two would get along swimmingly.

"Through the kitchen door and out the back," Rita suggested. "You can bypass the town center."

Nodding, I hurried toward the kitchen. It wouldn't be the first time rangers had interrupted a pleasant meal—and, sadly, it wouldn't be the last.

Chapter Five

The sound of thundering hoofbeats forced me in the opposite direction of where I'd hidden the Beast. I'd have to circle back to it once the rangers had gone and hope they didn't discover it in the meantime. We'd stolen the vehicle from rangers; no doubt they'd be more than happy to reclaim the 4x4. The vehicles were designed for rough terrain, which was mainly what The Wild had to offer.

With my longbow poised and ready for a quick response, I headed deeper into the woods. This wasn't my usual escape route. The paper birch were thin and leafless here, although they were so numerous that they stood clustered together like rows of soldiers pale from fear. A sweet aroma drew my attention to the right where I spotted a decent-sized clearing. Instinctively, I turned in that direction to find the source of the delicious smell. It was possible there was a rogue maple tree amidst the birch. It was moments like this that a werewolf's keen sense of smell came in handy.

I entered the clearing and walked straight into a hard

surface—except there was absolutely nothing in front of me. Not a tree. Not a bush. Not even a stump. Frowning, I stepped forward again and was met with resistance. No, not simply resistance.

A wall.

Hands up and palms out, I felt my way along the invisible barrier until my fingers curled around what felt like a knob. I turned it and heard the soft click of a door opening.

Bingo.

As I crossed the threshold, the world around me shimmered and popped. The pale birch trees disappeared, and I now stood inside a rustic cabin. The furniture was basic and sparse, and the decor was lacking, none of which was unusual in The Wild. The cabin's invisibility, however, was another matter.

A woman with wiry gray hair stood behind the kitchen counter with narrowed eyes, brandishing a wooden spoon like a weapon. "Stay right where you are, or you'll find this spoon lodged in a place with even less light than the great outdoors."

"I believe the expression is 'where the sun don't shine.'"

"It's the Eternal Night. The sun don't shine anywhere, Red."

"It's auburn."

She maintained her threatening position. "How did you get in here?"

I gestured behind me. "You didn't lock the door."

Her face relaxed. "Don't normally need to lock a thing no one can see."

"Who are you?"

"Patricia Aldridge." She lowered the spoon and resumed mixing the contents of the bowl on the counter.

"Aster."

There was a moment of awkward silence.

"Cookies?" I asked.

She shrugged. "I have a sweet tooth."

I returned my arrow to the quiver and my gaze landed on a glass jar filled with eyes of newts. "You're a witch." And an old-school one at that. I was still a child the last time I saw any part of newt anatomy.

Patricia offered a dismissive grunt. "Congratulations. You possess deductive reasoning skills. Let me find my stash of gold medals."

I looked around the cabin. "What kind of spell are you using to hide this place?" It would take powerful magic to make an entire house disappear, even one as small as this.

Patricia set down the wooden spoon with a reluctant sigh. "I'll show you, but if my cookies come out flat, I'm blaming you."

She dipped her hand into her pocket and produced a bluish stone, handing it to me on her way to the door. I joined her on the welcome mat that hadn't been there when I discovered the doorknob, or at least it hadn't been visible to me. Written on the mat in stark white letters were the words 'go away.' Well, if nothing else, she was blunt.

Patricia swiveled to face the cabin. "Look and learn."

The entire front of the house was covered in black markings. Although I couldn't identify them, I recognized them as runes.

I whistled. "And I thought I lived off the grid." I hefted the stone in my palm. "This breaks the spell?"

"No." She swiped the stone from my hand and returned inside, closing the door behind us. "It's a reveal stone. Helps me find my way home without showing the cabin to anyone else. Once you cross the threshold, you don't need it."

I took a closer look at the cabin's interior. The kitchen

appeared to be the most used portion of the cabin. There was an old-fashioned cauldron tucked in the fireplace, as well as cast iron pots and pans hanging from hooks on the ceiling.

"You weren't part of my coven." I would've remembered a witch with magic like this. Runes weren't commonly used in my circles.

"I moved here last year from Anchorage."

"What brought you to The Wild?"

Her face remained flat. "What brings anyone to a remote place like this?"

"Couldn't tell you. I was born here."

She angled her head and examined me. "In some ways, I think that's better."

"Were you ostracized?" I'd heard of witches and wizards who'd been shunned by their covens for a variety of reasons. It wouldn't surprise me to learn that thieves and other rule breakers retreated to The Wild.

Patricia's left eye twitched. "It was a mutual agreement."

"Did you steal?" I paused. "I won't judge you for it. I've built an entire reputation around thievery."

"I'm aware."

I raised an eyebrow. "You know who I am?"

She zigzagged a finger in front of me. "Didn't know your name was Aster until now, but you carry a longbow like it's your third arm. You can't swing a dead newt in The Wild without hearing a tale or two about the Hooded One." Her brow creased. "Thought your cloak was supposed to be yellow."

"Gold, and it depends on the day's tasks."

"Gold is for thieving, is it? I suppose I can rest easy then, seeing you in black." Her smile resembled an uncomfortable pucker. "In case you didn't know, the people here adore you."

"The vampires not so much."

Her pucker morphed into a scowl. "They love none but their own kind."

I observed the cabin. "You escaped to a remote location, yet you still feel the need to hide."

She spooned dollops of cookie dough on a baking tray. "A feeling you would understand, no?"

I didn't respond. I was too distracted by the delicious smell of the dough. Cookies were a luxury item unless you owned a bakery or a restaurant. "How did you manage to source all those ingredients?"

"You don't survive as long as I have without knowing how to barter." She slid the tray in the oven and closed the door.

"You run a pretty big risk using so much magic to hide the cabin. If the vampires get wind of it, they'll kill you without hesitation."

She set the timer on the oven and turned to face me. "I'd rather die than not use magic. It's as much a part of me as my lungs or my heart." She waved a hand at the counter. "Don't keep standing there. It feels intimidating. Sit down, and I'll get you a drink. That way I get to tell folks I had tea with the Hooded One. I'll be the envy of all the other ladies in the knitting circle."

"You're in a knitting circle?" It seemed to me someone desperate to stay hidden would do just that.

Her sigh was regretful. "No, but I used to be, once upon a time."

I approached the counter and sat on the lone stool. It seemed Patricia wasn't equipped for company, which shouldn't come as a surprise given the cabin's secrecy.

"I hope you like lavender tea."

"Water is fine, thank you." Lavender could disguise another substance, and I wasn't entirely certain I trusted the witch. If anything happened to me inside the cabin, I might never be found. I hated to be suspicious of strangers, but such was the world we lived in.

Patricia lifted a pitcher and poured a cup of water. "You don't mind if I have tea, do you?" She slid the cup across the counter to me.

"Knock yourself out."

Patricia opened a jar of loose tea leaves, and the scent of lavender mingled with the sweet smell of fresh cookies. Memories stirred.

"You heard about Clayton, I assume," I said. If I was going to think about tragedies, it might as well be one in the present that I might be able to do something about.

Patricia scooped tea leaves into a small sachet and secured it. "Smelled the stench of death from here. Part of me wanted to see what was happening, but my survival instincts told me to stay home, so I did."

Smart witch.

"It isn't the image you want burned into your retinas. I'll have nightmares about it, that's for sure." And already had, in fact.

Patricia poured boiled water over the sachet of tea leaves. "I assumed it was vampires, but now I hear dragons are to blame." She shook her head. "Never thought I'd see a dragon in my lifetime. They never came to Anchorage."

"Why do you think that is?"

"Dragons are clever. They must've decided there were too many sea monsters big enough and spry enough to jump right out of the water at them."

An image of the Uktena flashed in my mind. I'd wrestled a dog from the jaws of the serpentine creature. The element of surprise had given me an advantage, but I could understand dragons wanting to avoid an encounter with the ancient monsters.

Patricia slurped her tea. It was evident that she'd lived alone for a long time. Bonnie would cut you in your sleep if she had to listen to that sound on a daily basis. Actually, she'd cut you midslurp and then finish your tea.

"Would you like insight into the dragon problem?"

I straightened on the stool. "What kind of insight?"

She nodded to a small pouch on the edge of the counter. "We can read the runes. See what they have to tell us."

"I don't have anything to offer you in return."

"Oh, but you do." She eyed me over the rim of her teacup. "Your silence."

I finished the water and slid the cup away from me. "You have a deal." I had no desire to reveal the witch's whereabouts to the authorities anyway.

Patricia gave the pouch a gentle shake and passed it to me. "Close your eyes and count out seven tiles."

I followed her instructions, dumping a pile on the counter and separating seven tiles from the group. When I opened my eyes, Patricia had placed the tiles in a horizontal line with the runes facing me. I didn't recognize any of the markings, not that I expected to.

"Does the order matter?" I asked.

"Does the order of letters matter in a sentence?" She leaned over the counter and studied the tiles. "The position of each tile answers a specific question." She tapped the second tile. "For example, this rune tells us what forces might be working against your solution to the dragon problem." She shifted her finger to the third tile. "This one tells us what might be helpful."

"I'd definitely like to know the answer to that."

Her eyes grew sharp. "I see a falcon."

"Archers and falcons are like bread and butter."

She cocked an eyebrow. "You have one then?"

"No. Birds aren't as common here as they once were." Not since the forests started to decay.

"I noticed." She squinted at the rune. "I don't think this one has anything to do with dragons. In fact, I think this entire reading is meant for you alone."

"Okay, then what does a falcon have to do with me?"

She shrugged. "Could be the connection to archers, as you say."

I observed the lines across her forehead. "But you don't think so."

"No, I don't. That's simply a connection that already exists. It doesn't tell us anything new."

"I wouldn't know how else to interpret it, other than a falcon might help us deal with the dragons in some way."

"It could be suggesting you send a message for help to someone via falcon." She slurped her tea again. "I admit, I'm baffled, which doesn't happen very often."

"You wouldn't be the first witch I've stumped. I also don't have an aura. Maybe I can't be read by runes either, so they're giving you facts instead."

Patricia lifted her gaze from the tile to me. "No aura? I've never heard of that."

"I bet you've never known anyone with light magic either, yet here we are."

Her attention shifted to my hands that rested on the counter. "Would you show me?"

I pulled my hands to my lap. "I don't think that's a good idea." I didn't take my power lightly. "What does this rune mean?" I pointed to the one that resembled a bowtie.

She contemplated the tile for a long moment. "That tile tells us the outcome."

"Of the dragon situation?"

"Not if this reading is meant for you specifically."

"What does the rune signify?"

"It's Dagaz," she said simply.

I looked at her. "And?"

"Dagaz implies both a beginning and an end. There will be completion, but that end will usher in the start of something new."

"That's pretty vague."

She smiled. "Welcome to runes. Despite the algebraic symbols, it doesn't share the certainty of mathematics."

The timer dinged, and Patricia slipped on an oven mitt to retrieve the baking tray. The cookies were puffy and perfect.

"You're lucky," she said, setting the tray on a rack to cool. "If they'd come out flat, I might've been tempted to turn you into a frog."

"Can you do that?"

Patricia flicked a tile. "Runes can be surprisingly powerful if you know how to use them."

She nudged aside the jar of newt eyes to make room for a spatula and two plates. It was then that I glimpsed another jar filled with a thick, golden substance.

"What's in that other jar?"

"Nothing," she said quickly, and moved the jar of newt eyes back into its original position.

"Is it mead?" I'd read about the nectar of the gods. Whatever that substance was in the jar, it was exactly how I pictured mead.

She guffawed. "That's a good one. Do I look like Athena to you?"

Whatever it was, she clearly wanted to keep it to herself. "I've seen a lot of ingredients in a witch's kitchen, but I don't recognize that one."

"Because it's too hard to come by."

"Is it dangerous?"

She cackled. "Only if you bathe in it and wander the forest looking for bears."

"Good luck finding a bear here." Although there was no official reporting agency, I suspected bears in The Wild were now extinct.

"Wonderful creatures. A pity to lose them."

I was still transfixed by the golden substance. "You said you've heard of me." I raised a hand and wiggled my fingers. "Tell me what it is, and I won't hurt you." Patricia was a witch in hiding. What if the mysterious substance was connected to the dragons, or even the zombie? I needed to know more.

Patricia angled her head to observe my hands. "Can you really shoot lightning from your fingers like Zeus?" She frowned. "Maybe I shouldn't have made that Athena joke."

"Trust me. You don't want to find out."

Her tongue swiped her upper lip as she debated her response. "It's honey."

"Magical?"

She shook her head. "As natural as it comes."

"Where did you get it?" There were no bees in The Wild to my knowledge, and given the amount of time I spent in nature, I should know.

"Anchorage." Her eye twitched again. Somebody had a tell, it seemed. I'd have to advise her to avoid poker games with the vampire elite.

I leaned forward and lowered my voice. "Tell me where you really got it."

"I bartered for it."

"What did you barter?"

"I'm not sure that's any of your business."

I splayed my hands on the counter. "Perhaps you can ask Lord Birney what happens when you get on my bad side."

Her jaw tightened, and she dared to meet my gaze again. "I offered a service in exchange for a jar."

I pinned her with a hard stare. "And what was the service?"

She bit her lip.

"Patricia, if you think for one second I'm willing to walk out of here without this information, you're delusional. Why not make it easier on both of us and tell me before I'm forced to resort to unpleasant means?"

"The people speak so highly of you. Do they know what a bully you are?"

"They know I protect them." I thought of Clayton, and guilt squeezed my heart. "Whenever I can," I added, and cleared the emotions from my throat.

Patricia squeezed her eyes closed and exhaled. "Fine. I'll tell you, but not because you threatened me."

"Then why?"

"Because now that I've met you, I've had a change of heart."

"A change of heart about what?"

"A vampire asked me to develop a locator spell they can use."

"To find what?" Their missing zombie? Their horde of dragons?

Patricia played with the ends of her hair, back to avoiding eye contact. "Not what."

It took me a moment to catch on. "Me? They hired you to find me?"

Her entire demeanor changed in an instant, and the demure countenance was replaced by desperation. "What would you have me do? This is *honey*. Do you know how valuable this is? I came here with nothing. My coven tossed me out on my backside without letting me collect a single belonging. I've been trying to claw my way back to a normal life ever since."

Her client had to be a vampire with deep pockets and access to rare goods, which ruled out many of them. Although vampires were better off than the general population, that only meant they weren't struggling on a daily basis and that the laws favored them. Only an affluent and powerful vampire could acquire a substance as coveted as honey.

"Who hired you?" It could've been Doran; the vampire had sent his rangers after me for years without success—except when he finally got his hands on me, he'd let me escape.

"I'm afraid that detail is confidential."

"Was it Birney?" It wouldn't surprise me to learn the vampire was out for revenge. He certainly had the status to flaunt, even if he lacked the funds to procure the honey.

Patricia made a show of locking her lips and pretending to toss the key over her shoulder. As much as I hated to do it, I decided to let it go. There'd been witches in my coven whose entire livelihoods were built around discretion. One wrong word and they could've lost everything. Patricia had already been through that once, and I had no desire to put her through it again. Besides, vampires had searched in vain for me for years, and there was no guarantee her spell would be successful.

"Just out of curiosity, how could you craft a spell to locate me? I don't even know you."

She poked a cooling cookie, testing its firmness. "It's one of my talents."

"And this vampire knew about it? How?"

"We crossed paths in Anchorage, and then again here."

All signs pointed to Birney. Before I blinded him, he traveled regularly on behalf of House Nilsson.

"Did they tell you why they want to find me? I'd be more than happy to attend a party if someone's extending an invitation."

Patricia didn't smile. "They didn't offer the information and I didn't ask. That's how my business works."

"I understand. We had a locator witch in our coven." Kylie had died during the purge. Even if she hadn't, she was the kind of witch who would've sacrificed herself later in order to keep my identity and whereabouts safe. No doubt vampires would've tried to exploit her magic in order to find me.

"Had," she repeated. "You lost many from what I've heard."

"Arguably, we lost everyone." Half of us may have survived, but the coven itself didn't. We were forced to scatter like mice. Many of them made a point of staying away from the others so as not to arouse suspicion and draw the attention of rangers. Nobody wanted to be accused of collusion. Of course, that was the point of the purge. Divide and conquer. A coven was far more dangerous than an individual witch or wizard.

Unless that witch was me.

"For what it's worth, I don't know how accurate my spell will be. Maybe they've already tried and it failed."

I thought of the rangers and wondered whether the

spell had brought them back to the Dancing Dragon. "Then what happens to you?"

"Nothing. No guarantees. It's in my contract."

"I hope you did business with the kind of vampire who honors their agreements."

"There are procedures and safeguards for that sort of thing."

I laughed. "This is The Wild, Patricia. We have our own way of doing things here."

Her mouth formed a straight line. "So I'm learning." She picked up a spatula and slid a cookie onto a plate. "They're cool enough now. Would you like one?"

I contemplated the cookie. "You first."

She cackled again. "You don't trust me."

"Can you blame me? You just admitted you gave me up for a jar of honey."

Patricia made a show of biting the cookie. Her eyes closed as she savored the taste. Finally she smiled. "See? Still standing."

Leaning across the counter, I swiped a cookie from the tray. "I'll take this one for the road."

Patricia thrust another cookie. "Take two. After all you've done for the people, you deserve them."

"Thank you," I said, not without hesitation. "If anyone else asks you to find me, do me a favor and decline." I had enough to deal with right now and didn't need the extra worry.

She offered a mischievous wink. "They'd have to find me first."

Chapter Six

The Aleutian Valley was named in honor of the Aleutian Islands off the coast of Alaska that were lost during the Great Eruption. Far enough from civilization to be left alone by rangers but close enough to pop in and out of the villages undetected, the location was a wise choice for the large pack of wolves.

"Do you think he'll be surprised to see you?" Tyson asked.

I snorted. "Have you met Max? He probably has a bottle of sparkling wine on ice in anticipation."

Now that I had a vampire offering expensive jars of honey in exchange for my location, I decided it might be prudent to accept Max's offer of meeting the rest of the Ghost Pack. I needed alliances and, arrogant or not, Max was a good one to have. Tyson and I drove the Beast north, stopping briefly to refuel. Patricia wasn't the only one who knew how to barter.

As usual, we kept to the lesser traveled roads to avoid a run-in with rangers or anyone else who might recognize two outlaws in a stolen 4x4. It wasn't hard to do given our destination.

We parked the vehicle between two boulders about a mile from the valley. Trees were sparse in this region, which left few options for camouflage.

Tyson climbed out of the passenger seat and scented the air. "This place reeks of wolf."

"Good, that means we're in the right place."

He looked at me askance. "You brushed your hair."

I curled an auburn strand around my finger. "You say that as though it's unusual."

"No, I mean you brushed it just now." He peered behind me into the 4x4. "Did you bring a brush with you?"

"It gets windy in the Beast," I said, a tad defensively.

"For someone who doesn't want to show interest, you're making quite the effort." He held up his hands. "Not that I'm judging."

"Good, because we're here to form an alliance." I started toward the valley.

"I wouldn't blame you for being interested. He's quite the catch."

"Stop."

Tyson stifled a laugh, and we continued the walk in silence. Three quarters of a mile later, he tapped my arm.

"The smell is overpowering here. We should let them come to us now, so they don't perceive us as a threat."

"We were invited."

"You and I know that, but whoever's on patrol might not know that. I'm a wolf that doesn't belong to their pack. They won't know how to interpret my presence."

I nodded. "How long do you think it will take?"

"If their patrol is any good, I'd say..."

A low growl caught us off guard. I spun to the right to see two wolves crouched in a ready position.

I held my hands in the air, and Tyson followed suit. "I'm Aster. This is Tyson. We're here to see Max."

The growling ceased as the wolves sniffed the ground around us as though the scent would somehow confirm my statement.

The wolves turned away and began to trot in the direction of the valley.

Tyson and I exchanged glances. "I can't swear to it, but I think we're in," he said.

We trailed behind the wolves, careful not to close the gap in a way that might seem aggressive. The slope was so gradual that I barely noticed we were headed downhill until I spotted the outline of tents in the distance.

"Wow, the Ghost Pack," Tyson said under his breath.

The note of awe didn't escape me, and I felt a momentary pang of envy that there was no witchy equivalent to the legendary Ghost Pack. Their setup reminded me of temporary army camps I'd read about in history books.

Lavonne was the first familiar face to greet us. "Hello again, Aster. Max has been expecting you."

I resisted the urge to make a snide remark. "You remember Tyson."

"Of course." Her gaze lingered on Tyson a beat longer than necessary. "Right this way. Max will be happy to see you."

We maneuvered our way through tents that seemed haphazardly placed. If there was a rhyme or reason to their location, I didn't see it. Finally, she stopped outside the largest tent in the valley, because of course it was.

"Go ahead in," Lavonne said. "He knows you're here."

As Tyson stepped forward, Lavonne placed a hand on his broad chest. "Just Aster. Not to worry, though, you and I can spend time getting to know each other while they do the same."

I held my tongue, excited to reference this moment the next time Tyson gave me a hard time about Max. My crew and I were nothing if not mature.

I ducked inside the tent and immediately cut to the chase. "I'd like to take you up on your offer."

My gaze traveled up Max's six-foot-six frame. He was naked from the waist up, revealing a body wrapped in corded muscle. The ends of his white-blond hair stuck up like it was freshly washed. Two blue diamonds glinted in the low lighting of the tent.

"Unable to resist me, huh?"

I rolled my eyes. "Your offer to work together."

"Right." He held out his hand. "I look forward to our partnership."

I stared at his hand. "That's it?"

Max kept his hand in place. "Were you expecting a parade?"

Reluctantly, I shook his hand. "You said you wanted me to meet the rest of the pack." A parade wasn't out of the realm of possibility, especially when Max was in charge.

He squeezed my hand but didn't let go. "Come on."

"Where?"

"Koda Rock. It's where I make all my important announcements."

Of course he had his own announcement rock. Why wouldn't he?

"Shouldn't you put on a shirt first?"

"And disappoint my pack? Never."

He guided me through the maze of tents, greeting pack members along the way, until we reached a large boulder.

"Need a boost?" he asked.

"I can manage."

"I don't mind. It's a pretty good view from the rear."

I glared at him before climbing to the top of the boulder. The sweeping vista captured the impressive number of tents, as well as a waterfall in the distance that likely provided a natural pool as their primary water source.

Max joined me atop the boulder and cleared his throat.

"What? No megaphone?" I asked.

"My commanding presence is enough."

"If you beat your chest, the partnership is off."

"You mean like this?" He thumped his bare chest and indulged in a primal yell.

"Good grief," I muttered, prompting a laugh from Max. He seemed to live to torment me.

Max summoned his pack with a howl that reverberated through the valley. I watched as members drifted from their tents and crowded around Koda Rock as they waited for their leader to address them. I spotted Tyson standing beside Lavonne and waved. Several hands waved back, which made me smile. At least the pack members thought I was friendly.

Once a sizable group had gathered, Max began his speech. "This is Aster Goodfellow, also known as the Hooded One. She's a witch with great power, and she's our best weapon against the vampires."

True or not, I didn't love being described as a weapon. I wasn't an object to be used for their benefit; I was a living, breathing witch with my own thoughts and feelings.

"Learn her scent," Max continued. "She is to be

protected, no matter what the threat. Dragons, vampires, monsters—your job is to make sure she survives."

If I was a weapon of great power, why did he think I needed protection?

The wolves howled their assent, their combined voices lifting into the air as one.

Max turned to me with a triumphant grin. "Now we can retreat to my tent and discuss our common dragon problem. Let them scent you along the way, but if anybody gets handsy, they'll have to answer to me."

His leap from the boulder formed a smooth arc, and he landed gently on the ground. My own departure was less graceful, but I doubted anybody noticed. Max was like the sun to his pack. Next to him, I was no more than a passing asteroid.

Ina fell in step with me on our return to the main tent. Max's second was far more serious than mine. Scarlet seemed like family to me, whereas Ina seemed more like a work colleague to him.

"Hello to you, too, Ina." I scanned the mob of werewolves. "Where's Tyson?"

Ina ignored my question. "He's got a thing for you."

"Not at all. Tyson and I are strictly professional."

"Not Tyson." She angled her head. "Max."

I laughed. "Max has a thing for Max. I must've accidentally stepped in front of his mirror."

Ina resisted a smile. "You'd have an ego, too, if you'd accomplished as much as he has in his lifetime. To be that young, too." She shook her head in amazement. "He's one-of-a-kind. If he were anybody else, I would've left the pack years ago."

"What's so great about him?" I was genuinely curious.

Ina grunted. "It's obvious to anyone with access to one

of the five senses. The fact that you even asked that question tells me you're interested, or at least considering it."

"I'm interested in a professional partnership. That's all."

Her lips curved in a slight smile. "Sure you are."

We arrived at the tent, and she motioned for me to go first. I was surprised to find a table laden with food and drinks. Little elves must've scampered inside while Max was making his announcement.

The White Wolf took his place at the head of the table. "Sit. We'll eat while we talk dragons."

Tyson entered the tent, along with Lavonne, and Max waved them over. Ina sat to the right of Max, and I sat to the left. Tyson sat beside me, across from Lavonne.

"Anyone else joining us?" I asked.

"Not today," Max said.

I surveyed the table. "This is a lot of food for five of us."

He grinned. "I have an insatiable appetite."

I stuffed a handful of berries in my mouth to keep from groaning.

Max told everyone to dig in and started the meeting.

"What do the dragons want?" Lavonne asked.

"Who cares? What matters is what we want," Max said, reaching for the meat platter.

I disagreed. If we understood why the dragons were invading our territory, we might be able to find a peaceful solution.

"Dragons don't attack for no reason," Lavonne said, "although I don't see how anyone in Clayton provoked them. The people there didn't even believe any dragons had been spotted in the area."

"The dragons aren't the only ones getting restless," Ina said. She'd already cleaned her plate and was in the process of serving herself seconds.

I glanced at her sideways. "Who else?"

She sucked the meat off a bone. "There's chatter among the elite vamps in The Wild. They're none too pleased about Lord Birney's benevolences."

Tyson snorted. "Benevolent? They've got the wrong vampire."

"No, she's talking about forced loans," I explained. I was concerned that I hadn't gotten wind of this already. We'd been falling down on the job in terms of intel ever since Hugo's attack on the White Fortress.

"Why would Birney need money from the elites?" Tyson asked.

Ina's gaze flicked to him. "That's a very good question and one we're determined to find out."

"Does Doran know?" I asked.

Ina compressed her lips. "Not sure. Would be interesting if he didn't."

It would.

"If the elites are unhappy about these benevolences, then why aren't we hearing more disgruntled noises?" I asked.

"Would you want to piss of Birney?" She laughed, apparently remembering my history. "Never mind."

"I don't think it's a very smart move to upset your base," Tyson pointed out. "If Birney pushes them too far, he might have a different kind of revolution on his hands."

"I'd really like to know what the money is for," I mused.

"Our intel suggests he's heavily in debt," Ina said. "No surprise for a vamp that likes to wine, dine, gamble, and live a generally lavish lifestyle without spending a dime of his own money."

Max downed a cup of water. "Think about it. Birney's stuck here now. Can't easily travel anymore and do the king's dirty work in the Outer Territories. Word of his affliction will spread. He'll be viewed as weak, yet he doesn't want to give up the power he has."

It didn't take me long to understand. "You think he wants to oust Doran."

Max shrugged. "Wouldn't that be your strategy? There's only one official seat in The Wild, and it's presently taken."

"Wouldn't the king object?" Tyson asked.

Max looked at him. "Is Stefan really going to care as long as someone has this place under control? The king wants whatever makes his life in Minneapolis easier. If that's Birney serving as thegn instead of Doran, then so be it."

His theory made sense.

"Is Birney a better option, though?" Lavonne asked.

Tyson snorted. "He's a vampire. There are no good options."

Max regarded me. "You've been up close and personal with both of them. Any thoughts?"

None that I could share. "I don't trust Birney. My guess is he's out of money and using those benevolences to fund his lavish lifestyle."

"But do you trust him more or less than Doran?" Max pressed. "If we can help tip the scales one way or another, which way do we go?"

I swallowed the seeds and nuts in my mouth and washed them down with water. "Whichever one is willing to help us with the dragons."

"That seems shortsighted," Ina said.

"Maybe it is," I agreed, "but we won't have much of a future if the dragons decide to go on another rampage."

"Annelise and Suraj would agree with that," Max said solemnly.

Lavonne and Ina traded glances. "You have more experience with the local vampires. We'll defer to you," Ina said, although she didn't sound happy about it.

As I finished my meal, I recalled my conversation with Poco, a fae fortuneteller I'd met at Aurora Hot Springs. She told me she'd seen a triangle in my future, but that it wasn't a love triangle. In fact, she specifically mentioned women, which ruled out Max and Doran. Sitting here now, I wondered whether she meant Ina and Lavonne. Maybe I had a role to play within the Ghost Pack that was greater than the object of Max Kane's affection. Only time would tell.

I steered the conversation back to dragons, sharing the information I'd received from Jacob Farmer.

"I do find the different species banding together to be an interesting development," Max said. "It's like our pack."

"It's like our crew," Tyson added.

I smiled. "I'm not sure four wolves and a witch are that diverse. And you're all the same type of wolf."

"Gray, right?" Max asked. He didn't wait for an answer. "They're the majority in our pack. You'd be right at home with us."

Tyson didn't respond.

"We should make a move sooner rather than later with regard to the vampires," Ina said, looking directly at me.

"I'll let you know when I decide."

"Which is the lesser of two evils?" Max asked. "Decide that and we have our answer."

I wasn't willing to throw Doran to the wolves just yet. At the very least, I felt like I owed him a conversation. After all, he'd helped me escape the clutches of the Master

Inquisitor. Of course, that was before he realized I was the Hooded One. I had no idea what to expect from him now, which meant I had to be prepared to defend myself.

I only wished defending myself wasn't so dangerous for my opponent. Just because I had the power to kill didn't mean I wanted to use it. My crew understood that. Now I needed to make sure the Ghost Pack understood that, too.

Chapter Seven

I hadn't seen Lord Doran since I'd hightailed it out of his secret stronghold during Hugo's misguided attack. It was only during my escape that the vampire discovered my real identity and learned what I could do. I couldn't imagine he was thrilled to realize I could kill him with the wave of a hand. How did I expect our conversation to go? *Hey, Doran. I sure am sorry about luring you into a false sense of security and then blinding your boss on my way out the door. Gee, I really love your wallpaper.*

I stuck to the shadows, wearing a black cloak and avoiding the lit paths. I couldn't raise the alarm and announce my presence at his home or office. Too risky. Instead, I ventured to the place where I knew he went every other Tuesday—one of the perks of tracking his schedule all these years. You would think he'd be more careful about a routine, but the top of the food chain rarely worried about their safety, which would work to my advantage today.

The Golden Heart Country Club was a vampires-only establishment west of Klondike that featured a golf course, restaurant, and indoor swimming pool. At ten o'clock, the schedule was cleared for Lord Doran's arrival. If you wanted to host a morning golf session for your organization, tough. You had to wait until eleven.

I expected to find Doran on the golf course, where he liked to whack golf balls into oblivion. A quick survey of the grounds, however, told me he was nowhere to be found. The raised flag confirmed he was in residence, so I crept along the perimeter in search of another option. A few yards later, I found it.

Peering through the tinted window, I noticed movement in the swimming pool. Powerful arms propelled his muscled body forward. His strokes were long and precise. For a brief moment, I found myself imagining that I was the water beneath him.

Nope. Not going there.

I snapped to attention and slipped through the entrance. No guards. No personnel. Gotta appreciate the arrogance of a vampire in charge.

I wandered over to the diving board and straddled it, my boots dangling above the water. It was a bold move, but I let my strange sense of confidence guide my actions. Probably misplaced.

Sensing a presence, Doran stopped when he reached the far end of the pool and turned to look at me. I wiggled my fingers.

"Fingerless gloves?" he asked. If he was surprised to see me, he didn't show it.

"I figured they would put you at ease." Tiffany had given me the idea, and it seemed like a good way to keep my powers from inadvertently blinding anybody else.

Doran dove beneath the water and streaked toward me. I maintained my position, my heart thumping as I waited to see his next move.

He climbed out of the pool, and I swallowed a gasp. I didn't know why I was surprised to find him so ripped. To prevent myself from gawking, I reached for the towel draped across the board behind me and tossed it to him. He wrapped it around his waist with a faint smirk.

"I didn't peg you as a prude, Miss Goodfellow."

"I'm not. I just wasn't expecting to see so much of you." Nobody told me that Doran swam in the nude.

"Should I bother to ask how you got past security?" He held up his hands. "Apologies. What a ridiculous question. You blinded them."

"I didn't blind anybody. The security here is nonexistent."

"I suppose I should remedy that." He tightened the knot on his towel. "Come to finish what you started?"

I swung my leg across the board and rose to my feet. "What *I* started? You can't be serious."

He grabbed a second towel from a nearby stack and rubbed it over his head. "If I were so inclined, I could launch myself at the diving board and sink my fangs into your skin before you had a chance to wiggle your finger again."

I raised my hand and wiggled my pinky.

His mouth twitched. "Smart ass."

"I'm not here to fight. I'm here to talk about dragons."

"I see."

"You know what happened in Clayton, I assume."

Nodding, he tossed the second towel over his shoulder. "I went yesterday to see for myself. It's devastating."

"What do you intend to do about it?"

"Still debating the options. I suppose you'd like to kill them."

"Well, I'd like to be able to defend innocent people, and

if that means slaying a few dragons in the process, then so be it." It wasn't entirely true, but I didn't want to appear soft to my mortal enemy.

"You should know that King Stefan has forbidden the slaying of any dragons in The Wild, so I'm afraid we'll need to get creative."

His statement took me by surprise. "Why? They're not all endangered. There's every species in existence in the horde."

"This isn't out of the goodness of his heart. He wants to use them."

I frowned. "Use them? As a method of transport?"

His face hardened. "As a weapon."

I burst into laughter. "He thinks he can tame them to act on his behalf? Is he mad?"

"He's ambitious."

"Why would he want to have dragons in his arsenal? Who's House Nilsson fighting?"

"There's a lot of unrest at the moment," Doran explained. "Some Houses are making changes the others don't agree with. It's having a ripple effect."

"What about the people of Clayton?"

He regarded me with mild interest. "What about them?"

"What are you doing for them now that their homes and businesses have been destroyed? Are you finding them shelter? Have you given them a break on tax payments?"

He stared at me for so long without speaking that I worried I'd pushed him too far. As long as he kept his fangs to himself, though, I'd mind my manners—and my magic.

"Why are you so concerned with the people of Clayton? According to my reports, you live elsewhere."

'Elsewhere' made me smile. It was too vague. I already

doubted he was the one who paid Patricia a jar of honey in exchange for my location, and his comment confirmed it. His rangers had tried to pinpoint my hideout for years without success. Given that we'd relocated after Hugo's rebellion, I knew there was little chance his vampires knew where to find me; they only knew I wasn't in Clayton.

"Do I need them to be my neighbors in order to care about them? I didn't realize proximity was a requirement."

His brow furrowed. "I don't understand. You have all this power. Why do you use it the way you do?"

I arched an eyebrow. "You'd rather I kill you where you stand?"

"Your grandmother would have."

The mention of her was unexpected and hit me directly in the gut. "She was braver than I'll ever be."

"I wouldn't be so sure about that."

"What's that supposed to mean?"

"Do you think you haven't killed me because you're not as brave as she was? Do you really think you blinded Birney and left him alive because you're weak and scared?"

"What happened to Birney was self-defense."

"Oh, I'm well aware, and I take no issue with it. Just don't confuse compassion with weakness, Miss Goodfellow. They are not the same."

A vampire—Lord Doran, no less—was lecturing me on compassion. Who would've thunk it?

"Birney isn't so compassionate, I'm afraid. He wants your head on a platter."

"No doubt."

"He rants and rages to anybody willing to listen."

"As long as that's all he does."

"He's threatened to send rangers after you."

"You've been doing that for years. Hasn't resulted in my capture."

Doran studied me. "You could've killed him. The fact that you stopped before that happened suggests you didn't intend to hurt him."

I regarded him coolly. "Does it matter?"

"It does to me."

"I only wanted to get away. I would've killed him if it was the only option, though."

He inched closer. "I don't understand. You had the perfect chance to take him out. To take us both out. Why didn't you?"

"Because the king would replace you."

"The devil you know. Is that it?"

I shrugged.

"Or maybe you can't control your powers? Is that it?"

"If you want to talk about magic, why don't we talk about making it legal so we can save The Wild?"

His thick eyebrows drew together. "Save The Wild?"

"You realize the forests here are dying, right? They've been slowly dying ever since the disbandment of the coven."

He shot me a quizzical look. "What makes you think that?"

Was he serious? Did vampires not pay attention to their environment? "The coven was tasked with using magic to keep the plants and trees alive. When you destroyed the coven, the members stopped infusing the surrounding forests with magic. I've been seeing evidence of decay for years."

He seemed genuinely stunned, which surprised me. What did he think would happen?

"How can we fix it?" he asked.

"You need to grant witches and wizards broader rights

to use magic so they can sustain plant life beyond their own borders."

"What about magicians?"

"We have far more witches and wizards in The Wild than magicians." Most magicians had vacated the area when my grandmother was young. She'd told me about their mass exodus into the Yukon and beyond.

He appeared thoughtful. "I don't think I can risk it."

"Risk what?"

"I have to weigh the pros and cons of allowing more magic. We've already stamped out two rebellions in recent memory."

"Hugo used magic without permission," I reminded him. "I think the people of The Wild would appreciate knowing you're invested in saving the environment. Without the forests, we'll die."

"People thought they'd die without the sun, too."

"And they would have, without magic," I fired back. Lord Doran seemed to forget how crucial magic was in keeping the world spinning on its axis. Vampires might rule in eternal darkness, but we'd all be dead by now without magic.

"Magic can be expensive."

"Birney is collecting benevolences," I said. "Maybe he intends to use the money to pay for it."

Doran froze. "Where did you hear that?"

Interesting. He didn't know.

"A reliable source."

He yanked the towel from his torso and used it to blot the remaining damp from his hair.

As tempting as it was to peek, I kept my gaze on his upper half. "Is this the part where I'm supposed to run away shrieking in terror?"

He flashed his fangs. "That can be arranged."

"Can we call a truce? I think it's important that we try to set aside our differences and work together, at least while we solve the dragon problem."

"And follow it up with a rousing rendition of *We Are the World*?"

"Never heard of it." I spread my arms wide. "Give it a go, though. The acoustics are pretty good in here."

"They're even better in the shower. Why don't I demonstrate?"

It seemed Lord Doran had been taking flirting lessons from Max Kane.

"Maybe another time."

To my relief, he returned the towel to rest on his hips. "As long as we're trading information, there's something you should know," he said. "Isobel Markham is here."

I offered a blank look. "Should I know that name?"

"She and Birney have a longstanding relationship. Let's just say they're a good match."

"And why do I need to know this?"

"Because she isn't happy about what happened to her precious Birney. She likes to be admired, and he can't do that in his current state. She's been making noises about vengeance."

"And did you remind her of your stance on vigilante justice?" As far as Lord Doran was concerned, he served as The Wild's judge, jury, and executioner.

"Like Birney, she believes herself above the law. That's what happens when you grow up in a royal household."

So now I had to watch out for Birney *and* his psycho paramour with a royal pedigree. Terrific.

"She's from House Nilsson?"

Doran shook his head. "We imported this one. Her

grandfather was a royal in House Troy. Made sure his granddaughters were married off to minor royals and those in positions of power to increase their bargaining power. Rumor has it there's a Troy in one form or another in every castle and compound in the world."

"She and Birney are married?"

"Oh, no. She was married to a lesser royal when she met Birney, who later died under mysterious circumstances."

I was beginning to get the picture.

"Where's your mail order bride then? Sounds like you missed out."

He snickered. "The Wild's never been deemed important by anyone. Why do you think the king appointed a thegn here instead of one of his own children? Wasn't worth it."

It was the location more than anything that made The Wild undesirable to most of the population. Even before the Eternal Night, the region was considered far from the mainland. Thanks to the Great Eruption, the area was almost cut off completely. If you managed to get here, it was due to luck or determination. Or both.

"Is this Isobel Markham powerful in her own right, or do I need to watch out for her hired help?" Best of luck to any assassin from the mainland that tried to capture me in The Wild.

"She's strong and wily. Sometimes she outsources, but I can see her wanting to handle this personally. If she asks me about you directly, I'll try to warn her off."

"No need to protect me, my lord. I'm more than capable of handling myself."

He smirked. "I wasn't planning to warn her for your benefit."

"As long as you're sharing information, any special talents I should be aware of?"

"I think discovery is half the fun." His gaze flicked over me, causing heat to spread from my core. It rippled all the way to my fingers and toes. Inwardly, I swore, annoyed that he managed to have such a powerful effect on me.

I quickly collected myself. "I meant Isobel."

"She's unassuming. That's probably her most worrisome trait. She'll sneak up on you when you least expect it."

"Then I'll simply expect it."

His mouth split in a grin. "Ah, yes. Problem solved."

"I appreciate the warning." And now I had a good guess as to who hired Patricia.

I left the country club, feeling mildly unsettled. Lord Doran seemed to have that effect on me. I nearly made it to the woods when a familiar figure on a bicycle caught up with me.

Marcus slowed to a stop beside me. "Aster, you're just the one I wanted to see. I have the information you wanted."

"The information?"

He nodded and paused to catch his breath. "Tiffany Hazleton."

I'd been so consumed by thoughts of Doran and dragons that I'd nearly forgotten about the zombie.

"There's no one by that name in the registry."

Hmm. "Any Hazletons at all?"

"One. Emily Brewer Hazleton. She lives at 17 Red Leaf Court in Poole."

Poole was a border town like Clayton, except northeast instead of northwest. The village was probably grateful for its coastal position in light of Clayton's misfortune.

"Thank you, Marcus. Great work."

The teenager beamed with pride. "Would you like me to accompany you there?"

"I appreciate the offer, but I think it's best if I take a member of my crew."

"You're going to need more members soon. You've lost Hugo and Hattie, and soon you'll lose Bonnie."

My smile faded. "What makes you say that?"

"Mom says there's no way Bonnie will want to keep living as an outlaw once the baby's born. That she and Bear will decide to settle somewhere more permanent." He seemed to realize he'd said too much. "Is that not what you think?"

I sighed. "I'm sure you're right, Marcus. I guess I've been avoiding the reality."

"You've got another few weeks to avoid it. According to Mom, Bonnie's carrying low. The baby will be here before you know it." He returned his feet to the pedals. "Let me know if you need any more information. I'm always happy to help."

"Thanks, Marcus. You're the best." I stared after him as he rode away, lost in thought. The crew was falling apart. The Wild was falling apart. I was attracted to the vampire who'd killed my grandmother and destroyed my coven.

It seemed my whole world was falling apart.

Chapter Eight

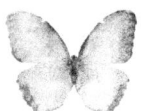

I returned to the hideout to collect Tyson and the Beast for the trip to Poole. I found the crew gathered around the embers of the campfire. Tyson stood on a small rock with his chest puffed out.

"And I, King of the Ghost Wolves, and my impressive pecs, officially declare my eternal devotion to Miss Aster Goodfellow," he announced.

The others broke into laughter, except Scarlet who spotted me before she could join in.

"Who wouldn't mind a little eternal devotion?" I asked.

Tyson's cheeks reddened, and he hopped to the ground.

Bonnie twisted to face me. "Tyson was filling us in on your meeting with the Ghost Pack."

"I figured."

"Any news?" Scarlet prompted.

"King Stefan has issued an order not to kill the dragons."

Tyson sucked in a breath. "Then how we are supposed to get rid of them before they get rid of us?"

"What about the calamity demon?" Bonnie suggested.

I snapped to attention. "What about it?"

The calamity demon had been accidentally released from an amulet where my grandmother had imprisoned it years ago. The demon couldn't be killed, only contained. It was fortunate that I'd been able to retrace my grandmother's spell and return the demon to its prison before it wreaked too much havoc.

"Why don't we use the demon to intimidate the dragons into leaving? That way we don't put our lives at risk." She rubbed her growing stomach. "Some of us have more to lose than others."

"We can't unleash a calamity demon in the hopes of controlling it. We could end up doing far more damage to the villages."

"If we let a demon loose on unsuspecting people, we're no better than King Stefan," Scarlet added.

Bonnie's lips formed a pout. "I say we fight fire with fire. Literally."

"No, we need to find a way to keep the dragons from encroaching on the villages," I countered. "There's no need for fire."

"I agree with King Stefan," Bear cut in. "They seem to be a ragtag group of outcast dragons looking for a home of their own, like us. Killing them all doesn't seem like the right answer."

Bonnie pinned him with a hard stare. "Do you think they'd extend the same courtesy to you? They're far more destructive than we are."

"We can talk more about this later," I interrupted. "I'd like to head over to Poole. Ready, Tyson?"

"Depends. Do we need to talk about my reenactment of yesterday's meeting?"

I gave him a coy look. "What reenactment?"

He grinned. "I'll fire up the Beast."

"You're too easy on him," Scarlet said in a low voice. "If you want to be the leader, you need to command respect."

I thought of the cordial relationship between Max and Ina. "I don't know. Maybe I'd rather have a family."

Scarlet's face softened. "We are family, Aster, but every family has its matriarch, and, however unconventional, you're ours."

Next to Clayton, the village of Poole looked like a luxury resort. It was obvious from the bustling crowds in the marketplace that some displaced villagers had taken refuge here.

"I've never seen it like this," Tyson said.

The extra residents were straining the already limited resources of the outer village. An argument broke out in the line for the bakery as we passed by.

Tyson cast a sidelong glance at me. "How about I meet you at the address?"

I nodded. "See if you can soothe any flaring tempers." The people seemed ready to turn on each other, which would only make a bad situation worse.

I left Tyson to play diplomat and walked around the bend to a cul-de-sac. The interior lights of the houses provided the only illumination here. The infrastructure of places like Poole was even worse than in the villages closer to Klondike. I didn't want to use magic, so I retrieved a small penlight from the recesses of my cloak to check for number 17 on the mailboxes.

"Found you, Emily."

The house was a simple rectangular structure with nothing to recommend it. Some villagers placed plastic flowers in pots in order to liven up their properties, but Emily's yard looked abandoned. If it weren't for the light blazing inside, I would've thought the house was empty.

I knocked on the metal storm door. Scuffed and slightly askew, it had seen better days. The door opened slowly, as though the person behind it knew that one wrong move could tear the door from its hinges. An older woman stood in the doorway. Her ash blonde hair was streaked with age, and her pale blue eyes were hard and beautiful like two aquamarine stones.

"Can I help you?" The woman averted her gaze, and I realized I was still holding the penlight upright. I turned it off and slipped it into my pocket.

"I'm looking for Emily Hazleton."

"You found her." She scrutinized me. "Are you who I think you are?"

"My name is Aster Goodfellow."

Emily folded her arms. "Well, roll me in a ditch and call me a rock. What on earth are you doing out here?"

"May I come in?"

"Yes, of course. Sorry, I'm so flabbergasted to have the Hooded One on my doorstep. You might as well be one of those killer dragons I keep hearing about." She stepped aside and waved me in. "I don't have much to offer in the way of hospitality. I've got a half-eaten pumpkin loaf."

"I'm fine, thank you." A quick survey of the house told me Emily held the interior of her house in the same regard as the exterior. It was a place to eat and sleep and not much else. As someone who lived in a treehouse, I understood.

"Sit down." She darted forward and swept a stack of papers off the loveseat onto the floor. "Don't mind my artwork."

I glanced at the top sheet that featured a charcoal drawing of a dog. "You draw?"

"It's how I pass the time."

I perched on the edge of the loveseat. "I need to know if you have a relative called Tiffany."

She stared at me blankly for a moment, as though still awaiting the real question. "Tiffany?"

"Yes."

"I don't know off the top of my head, but I know how we can find out."

Emily dropped to the floor in front of me and reached between my feet. I lifted my legs and swung them to the other side of her. She slid a box out from under the furniture and dusted off the top.

"This is where I keep official records." She opened the lid and rooted through the documents stashed inside. "Here we go. I drew it years ago for an assignment at school."

She handed me a long sheet of paper on which she'd drawn a family tree. I scanned the names for Tiffany. I found her, just not where I expected.

Emily peered over my shoulder. "There she is. What's this about?"

I gaped at the picture. Tiffany died in 1985, long before the Great Eruption.

"Can you tell me anything about your family?" I asked.

"Other than it's been filled with disappointment, not really."

"Do you know anything about your family's burial customs before the Eternal Night? Would they have been cremated?"

"No, she died way before the cremation rule. Tiffany would've been buried in the family plot."

I stiffened. "Where can I find it?"

"There's a small cemetery about five miles from here. It's not in use anymore, obviously. The Hazleton family has their own section."

"Can you draw me a map?"

"Sure can." She fetched a pen and paper and drew a crude map from her house to the cemetery. "It's pretty remote. No need to worry about rangers there."

Good to know. I took the map and thanked her.

Emily returned the family tree to the box and closed the lid. "I knew your grandmother, you know. She used to come to Poole and teach the younger ones how to use a bow."

I smiled at that. "Sounds like her."

"Even now, the little ones clamor to learn. They want to be you when they grow up. Hell, they want to be you now. It's all 'I can't wash the dishes now. I need to practice my archery first.' 'Course we don't have a big arrow supply, so they end up practicing with sticks." She chuckled. "Not quite the same results, let me tell you."

"I wish they didn't have to feel the need to arm themselves."

She slid the box under the loveseat and resumed an upright position, joints cracking with each movement. "You were a child who learned to defend herself. So was I."

"Yes, but wouldn't it be nice if we could make sure future generations didn't have to endure what we did?"

Emily blew out a breath. "From your lips to the gods' ears. Sadly I don't see anything changing in my lifetime. A real shame, too. I used to have hope when I was younger, but that fades with each passing year of more of the same."

A question gnawed at me. "What do you remember about Hecate's Revolt?"

She sniffed. "Not much. I remember the purge better. Horrible affair. Had the desired effect, too. Put you all in your place. I remember that bastard Lord Birney marching through the village with his rangers like it was a victory parade." She scowled. "Despicable vampire."

"Birney but not Doran?"

"No, Birney was the one who liked to remind us what would happen if we stepped a toe out of line. Used any and every example at his disposal. He's all about instilling fear as a means of control."

I didn't remember much about the time immediate after the purge. I'd been too young and too traumatized.

"Face it, Aster. You're an inspiration. You should be proud of what you've done for The Wild. For all of us."

I didn't know how to respond, so I simply said, "Thank you."

"Is there anything I need to know about Tiffany? Was she a secret vampire or something?"

"No, nothing like that." I didn't have the heart to tell her the truth.

"I hope those dragons don't decide to make a meal of us in Poole. I don't think I'll be to their taste." She laughed awkwardly, but I could tell she was genuinely nervous about the threat of dragons.

"We're working on the situation. Everybody's concerned."

"As they should be. We've got half of Clayton trying to squeeze in here while their village is being rebuilt, and we all know that'll take years with vampire bureaucracy."

"I'll see what I can do about that."

She smiled. "So much like your grandmother. Wonder if I'm anything like Tiffany."

I noted the blonde hair and blue eyes. "I bet there are a few similarities."

I left the house to find Tyson lingering outside. "How'd things go on your end?" I asked.

"There's a good pub half a mile from here. I took a few people there for a round of drinks, and they calmed down."

I smirked. "An excellent use of time."

"Where to next?"

"A cemetery." I gestured ahead of us. "Right this way, according to the official map." I showed him Emily's handiwork.

He whistled. "An actual cemetery. Not something we see every day. The others are missing out."

"Let's see what we're dealing with first before you make a statement like that."

We returned to the Beast and drove the five miles to the rural cemetery.

"How would a corpse survive intact all these years?" I asked. "Her hair. Her clothing."

"I know. She ought to have been nothing more than a skeleton at this point."

I stopped outside the gates. "Here we are."

The cemetery was exactly as described, and we found the Hazleton section without any trouble.

"Here's Tiffany's headstone," I said.

Tiffany Noelle Hazleton. Born in 1967 and died in 1985. Loving daughter and sister. Unfortunately, there was a rectangular hole in the ground that suggested Tiffany might've grown weary of her burial spot.

We leaned over and peered at an empty casket.

"Well, I guess we have confirmation that this is where she came from," Tyson remarked.

"She died young."

"You say that like it's unusual."

"I thought it was back then." We both knew what 'back then' meant. Before the Great Eruption. Before the Eternal Night. Before the world collapsed in on itself like a dying star.

"People died young for all sorts of reasons then. Cancer, accidents, diseases." Tyson motioned to the grave. "Humans have been dying early since the dawn of time."

"Don't think humans existed at the dawn of time, but I take your point."

As I turned back to the vacant grave, I noticed deviations in the shades of earth and crouched to examine the area. I ran my fingers through the dirt and raised a handful to my face to smell it.

"Tiffany didn't climb out of here on her own," I said.

"You think they buried two people in one grave?"

"No." I held up my hand for inspection. "I mean she had a little help."

He sniffed the collection of dirt. "Yew. What's the other smell?"

"Mullein."

Tyson blew out a breath. "Necromancer?"

"Seems likely."

"I didn't think we had any in The Wild."

"Maybe they're new or maybe they've been honing their skills in secret."

"What's the goal?"

"Might not have one. Might be a case of seeing whether they could for the hell of it." Emily Hazleton drew pictures of dogs to pass the time. This person raised the dead.

Tyson stared at the empty grave. "Well, they proved themselves capable. Now what?"

I tucked the handful of evidence in my cloak pocket. "We need to find them and make sure they don't do it again.

We have enough problems without a rogue necromancer on the loose."

"I wonder if they got scared of their own Frankenstein and ran off. That might be why we ran into her."

"Frankenstein was the doctor," I said. "Technically, Tiffany would be the monster."

"Those shoulder pads support that statement."

I laughed. "You've seen pictures of how people dressed in the olden days. You're lucky she wasn't sporting a bouffant and wearing a hoop skirt."

Tyson scratched the back of his head. "Um, Aster."

"What?"

"I don't think Tiffany is our only zombie."

I followed his gaze to the back row of headstones. Each one was underscored by a hole. Terrific.

"If there are other Tiffanys roaming The Wild, I think we would've heard about them by now," I said.

"Unless rangers found them first and took care of them."

Too bad I'd already used and abused my one private audience with Doran. I'd have to get the information another way.

Tyson glanced behind us. "We should get this place warded so our necromancer can't strike again before we find them."

"Illegal magic? Is that a good idea?"

"Who's going to know all the way out here?"

"The witch we ask to ward it," I said pointedly. "She'll know." And that would make her a liability.

"We're already outlaws. You blinded the Earl of the Outer Territories, for crying out loud. I think we're well past coloring within the lines."

He made a good point. "Fine. We'll talk to someone."

Tyson flashed a grin. "How about that pretty someone who lives in Oglethorpe?"

"Margot?"

"Big brown eyes and a very squeezable body?"

"I can confirm the eyes. Can't speak to how squeezable her body is."

"I can. Let's go now."

I was hungry, but the village was on the way back to the hideout, and we could stop in to see Hattie.

"As long as you promise to behave yourself. If I need to use the phrase 'down, boy,' or anything within that category, you'll be on latrine duty for the next two weeks."

Tyson's brow inched up. "If you use the phrase 'down, boy,' we're going to have bigger problems than my libido."

Margot Royce had been a member of my coven. Younger by a year, she'd followed me around like a pesky little sister. I'd searched for her after the purge and had been relieved to find her alive. She'd suffered multiple injuries and lost her mother. Her father also survived, although he died a few years ago during a routine journey to Fairbanks.

Margot still lived in the same cottage where she and her father had settled after the purge. Our interactions were few and far between, mainly because of my outlaw status. Given our history, I trusted her not to reveal any magic she performed for us, but I tended to avoid asking for her help so as not to endanger her. I knew she'd do anything I asked, and that was a powerful position to be in. I didn't take the responsibility lightly.

We approached the front door. As I knocked, Tyson smoothed back his hair. "How do I look?"

"Like a werewolf who's been hanging out in a cemetery."

He glowered at me. "That bad?"

I smiled. "You look fine, but this isn't a social call, remember? Besides, I thought maybe you and Lavonne sparked a connection."

He gave me a lopsided grin. "You noticed that, too? I thought maybe I imagined it."

The door swung open, and I burst into laughter at the sight of Margot's swollen belly. Better luck next time, Tyson.

Margot broke into a broad smile at the sight of me. "Aster!"

"Hi, Margot. I guess congratulations are in order."

"Isn't it wonderful?" She embraced me, although I bumped awkwardly against her bump.

"Is there something in the water?" Tyson complained.

"You remember Tyson," I said.

Margot gave him a demure smile. "Of course."

"Mind if we come in?"

"I would love the company." She nudged the door open further and stepped aside. "Jason is on a hunting trip, so I've been on my own the last few days."

"Do I know Jason?" I asked.

She gestured to the table and chairs. "I don't think so. He moved here two years ago from Anchorage."

"Wizard?" I asked.

"Human." She beamed. "He loves that I'm a witch. Thinks it's the most amazing talent in the world."

"When are you due?" I asked.

"Two months to go." She puttered to the stovetop. "Can I interest either of you in a cup of tea? I've been drinking it like crazy. Jason thinks I've become a mint tea addict." Her laughter tinkled in the air. She seemed genuinely happy.

"You and Bonnie are going to have kids around the same time," I said. "Too bad you don't live closer."

"And too bad Bonnie lives in a hideout," Tyson added.

I wasn't sure that she would once the bean was born. I had a feeling that Marcus was right, that she and Bear would seek a safer environment for their child, not that anywhere in The Wild could be deemed safe. The world was perpetually on fire, and the main objective was to dodge the flames.

"I'll take a cup of tea," I said.

"Nothing for me." Tyson seemed disgruntled by Margot's current situation. As much as I wanted to laugh, I didn't want to endure his grumbling all the way home.

Margot busied herself with the tea. "I'm so pleased to see you, Aster. I've missed you."

"I've missed you, too. How did you meet Jason?"

"I needed help fixing up the cottage after my father died. He'd just moved to the village and needed work." She smiled dreamily. "I'd bring him food and drink, and he'd stop working to join me at the table. After a couple weeks, I already felt like we were an old, married couple. It was nice."

"When did you get married?" Tyson asked.

"We didn't." She shrugged. "We both agreed we didn't want to register or give them any official records."

We all knew to whom 'them' referred.

"Any names picked out?" I asked.

"Jason thinks it's bad luck to choose a name before the birth." She delivered two cups of tea to the table and placed one in front of me. "But I have a couple in mind. Arthur for my father and Darla for my mother."

"That'll be a nice tribute," I said.

"How about you?" Margot's gaze flitted between us. "Are you two involved?"

Tyson made a dismissive noise at the back of his throat. "Aster's like family, and not the kind you get horizontal with. Besides, she's got two interested parties, and I wouldn't want to get on the wrong side of either one of them."

Margot paused midsip. "Two suitors? Lucky lady. Tell me more."

If looks could kill, Tyson would be on the floor and his body riddled with arrows. "There are no suitors. Tyson exaggerates." I drank my tea, careful not to slurp which was apparently one of the manners I failed to master in my youth. "We're here to ask a favor."

Margot's eyes widened. "What kind of favor?"

"I don't think we can ask her now," Tyson said.

I looked at him askance. "Because of the pregnancy?"

"Does it involve manual labor?" Margot asked.

"No." I lowered my voice. "Magic."

"We can't put her at risk," Tyson insisted. "If she gets caught..." He shook his head.

"We need a ward placed around a cemetery north of Poole. It's remote, and someone's been busy digging up graves."

Margot flinched. "Vampires?"

"Necromancer," I replied. "We want to block them from access."

Margot sipped her tea. "Easy. I can do that."

"I know you *can*," Tyson said, "but I don't think you should."

She met his gaze. "I don't think it's up to you, though, is it?"

Tyson swore under his breath. "You sound as stubborn as Aster."

Margot smiled. "It's the witch in me. She can't resist a challenge."

"Can you get the materials you need without drawing attention?" I asked.

She nodded. "I have a supplier."

"Don't tell them what it's for," Tyson said. "We need to keep this quiet."

"They never ask, and I never tell," Margot assured him.

"There seems to be a lot of that going around," I murmured, thinking of Patricia.

"How quickly do you think you can do it?" Tyson asked.

"By the end of the week. Does that work?"

"Take an escort," Tyson told her. "Don't travel there alone in case the necromancer comes back. We don't know what their end game is."

"We'll be searching for them in the meantime," I said. "Hopefully, you won't encounter any trouble."

Tyson licked his lips. "If Jason won't be back in time, I'll go with you and keep watch."

Margot's face softened. "That's sweet, Tyson. Thank you."

"Promise me you'll take him up on his offer," I said. "I'd never forgive myself if anything happened to you."

"I promise," Margot said. "I've endured far too much discomfort to let anything bad happen at this point."

If only we could choose the timing of our misfortunes. Unfortunately, nobody was that lucky, not even a witch.

. . .

By the time we arrived at Olive Branch, Tyson claimed to be "weak from hunger."

"Good thing Olive sells food then."

"Yes, but she doesn't sell real food. It's all sandwiches and snacks."

I looked at him sideways. "It's food, Tyson. Does it really matter that it isn't a slab of raw meat on a stick?"

"Not to you," he grumbled.

We entered the building and greeted Hattie, who was busy wiping down tables in the cafe area.

"Twice in a week?" Hattie exclaimed. "How'd I get so lucky?"

"We were in the neighborhood," I told her. "I figured we'd stop in and do a little more research."

She tossed the cloth into a bucket. "What is it this time?"

"We need to figure out how to get rid of the dragons without killing them. King's orders."

Tyson raised a finger. "Any chance we could eat and talk?"

I rolled my eyes. "He's wasting away. His stomach rumbled so many times, I was sure someone had let loose the calamity demon."

Hattie chewed her lip, thinking. "What about using the demon to scare off the dragons? Maybe it could cause a landslide and force them to fly away."

"Bonnie suggested the same thing, but I think we can come up with a better option."

Hattie brightened. "I have an idea!"

"Already?"

She raced across the room to the bookshelves. "I was reading about this special stone earlier. Maybe it can help us."

Tyson remained rooted in place. "Could I have a sandwich?"

"Help yourself," Hattie said, distracted by the book in her hands. She flipped to a page in the middle. "There's a crystal called the Ulunsuti stone."

I joined her across the room. "And?"

"And the way this book describes it, it's the most powerful object in the world. It can even control light and dark."

"Sounds good for beating back vampires, but how will it help with our dragon problem?"

"Maybe you can use the crystal to control the dragons. Command them to leave the populated areas."

I glanced at the open page. "I'm listening."

"The crystal is also said to offer a window into the past and future."

"Sounds nifty but that's not really relevant to our issue."

"I guess not, but it's a cool skill to have."

My breath caught in my throat when I read the rest of the paragraph. "Wait a minute. You're talking about the crystal on the Uktena's forehead?"

"Yeah. The Uktena is some sort of horned sea monster."

"Oh, I know." I'd fought one in Fairbanks when I foolishly agreed to rescue a lady's dog from the monster. The dog survived. If I'd realized what I'd be fighting, though, I wasn't certain I'd make the same decision again.

"They use rivers, lakes, and springs to travel between here and the underworld," Hattie continued.

"Yes, I met one in a river. You don't remember my story about the Uktena I met in Fairbanks?"

"I don't think you told me. You probably thought I was too young to hear it. My delicate ears couldn't handle the violence."

I flipped to the next page. "Where did you find this book?" It had so much more information than what Poco had told me.

"It was in the stockroom," Hattie said. "Olive has more books than she can display, so she keeps the rest in a separate room, and I bring them out when there's space on the shelves."

"This is a great find, Hattie."

"Do you think the information is helpful?" I heard the hopeful note in her voice.

"Absolutely." I wasn't appeasing her. The Ulunsuti stone was our best chance yet of dealing with the dragon situation without starting a war with House Nilsson.

"It says you must carry the crystal in a buckskin pouch."

"I'll be sure to purchase one before I even attempt to acquire the crystal. What happens if I don't store it in buckskin?"

Hattie glanced at the page. "It doesn't say."

The answer was probably nothing, but I'd get the pouch anyway. This wasn't the time to discover that ten supervolcanoes exploded because somebody forgot to use a buckskin pouch.

"You can only kill it by wounding its heart. It says anyone who captures the crystal will become..." She paused. "I think the translation means a miracle worker."

"That probably goes without saying if you manage to extract the stone from the giant horned serpent monster."

Hattie tapped the page. "Shouldn't you have an alternate plan in case you can't get the crystal?"

"I'm a big fan of having a Plan B. If you have any ideas, feel free to share them."

She blinked at me. "Know any rounders?"

I smiled. "Not around here." Rounders were basically

cowboys for dragons. They'd cropped up in other places to corral dragons and keep them from invading magically enhanced farmland. I'd never heard of rounders in The Wild, though.

"Not anybody can use the crystal," Hattie said. "If it falls into the wrong hands, it won't work."

"In other words, don't let Bonnie hold it."

She laughed. "I'm glad you're the one who said it."

"I have no intention of letting Bonnie take control of an object as powerful as this one. If we manage to get one, and that's a big 'if,' we're going to use it for the sole purpose of protecting ourselves from a dragon invasion without pissing off vampires in the process."

"But what if Bonnie wants to know more about her pending offspring? The stone can show her the future."

I snorted. "She'll have to wait until the big reveal like the rest of us."

Exhaling, Hattie pushed away the book. "It's such a roll of the dice."

"Whether we can get the crystal?"

She looked at me. "That, too, but I was talking about having children. You have no idea what you're bringing into the world, whether they'll be able to handle it or whether they'll grow up to be a monster like Lord ... Birney."

I had no doubt she nearly said 'Doran' and changed it at the last second for my benefit.

"If you ask me, every day is a gamble regardless of your parental status. Each decision we make has the potential to result in catastrophe."

Hattie's shoulders slumped. "Gee, no pressure then."

I laughed. "Sorry, that came out more dismal than I intended."

Hattie's face softened. "Do you think you'd ever have a child?"

I chose my words carefully, not wanting to sound too negative. "I'm an outlaw. I'd be doing a child a disservice if I tried to raise them in the current climate. The child would become as much of a target as I am."

"Don't you think little Bonnie Bear will face the same problem?"

Nodding, I chewed my lip. "Which is why I think Bonnie and Bear will be leaving me soon."

Her eyebrows shot up. "Have they said that?"

"Not in so many words, but I know it's coming. I don't blame them. They have to do what's best for their family."

"You won't have much of a crew left without them."

I shrugged. "I'll cross that bridge when I come to it. Right now I have more immediate issues to address."

Hattie cocked her head. "Do you worry your child's magic might be even more powerful than yours?"

"In what way?" It was hard to imagine anything more powerful than simulating sunlight.

"I don't know. A type of magic that's even harder to hide or control. Like, what if they glow as a baby and that makes them too hard to hide?"

I grunted. "Well, I hadn't given it much thought before, but now that you mention it... Thanks, Hattie. Something new to consider."

"Don't go borrowing trouble," Olive said, entering the room with a stack of books. "Unless there's any chance of you becoming pregnant, don't give it a second thought."

"No chance," I said. "I'm not scratching any itches. I have too many other plates to spin."

Olive smiled. "Got another idiom you'd like to squeeze into that response?"

I tapped the book. "This has been a big help, Hattie."

The young werewolf beamed. "You know I love to read." Her smile morphed into a pucker. "Ooh! There's something else I found you might want to read when you get a chance."

"A book?"

"Even better. A journal."

I wasn't sure why a journal would be better until she handed it to me and I recognized the neat, crisp handwriting.

The journal belonged to my mother.

"You found this here?"

She nodded. "Olive said a lot of items ended up here after the purge. She never had time to go through all of them, so I volunteered."

I stared at my mother's handwriting, so familiar and yet so foreign to me now. "Did you read it?"

"I skimmed. When I realized whose it was, I set it aside for you. I'm sorry I forgot. I've been so busy lately."

"I understand. Thank you. This means a lot to me."

Curious when my mother stopped writing in the journal, I opened to the last entry.

Maya is as obsessed with killing vampires as they are with depriving us of our blood. I fear this obsession will be her undoing. My only hope is that she doesn't take us all with her when it happens, especially my Aster. She is our very own bright flame, the ray of sunshine that sustains me.

I slammed the journal closed and wished I hadn't read it. Not right now anyway. There was no time to revisit the past when the present was in dire need of attention.

"Let's go, Tyson," I called.

The werewolf looked up at me with a hangdog expression. He swallowed whatever was in his mouth. "Already? I only ate one sandwich."

"You can eat at the hideout." An idea was forming in my mind, and I was anxious to hash it out with the rest of the crew. It wouldn't be without its risks, of course. As with so many of our adventures in The Wild, the plan could either result in the end of our dragon problem—or the end of us.

Chapter Nine

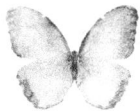

I waited for everyone to gather around the campfire for dinner before launching into my plan. I suspected Scarlet would reject it as untenable, and she didn't disappoint.

"Are you crazy?" she blurted. "You were lucky to survive the first encounter with an Uktena. Now you're proposing to hunt one down on purpose?"

"The crystal is the answer to our problems. We get that stone, and there won't be any bloodshed."

"Except the blood you shed trying to get the crystal," Scarlet shot back.

"I won't go alone. This is where our alliance with the Ghost Pack comes in handy."

Bear stared at his charred kebab. "Where do you plan to look? Fairbanks?"

Bonnie rubbed her side. "I can't manage the bumpy ride all the way to Fairbanks."

Bear squeezed her shoulder. "We wouldn't ask you to."

"I'll talk to Max tomorrow and decide on the party size," I said.

"Are you sure this is the best option?" Bonnie asked. "It seems pretty risky. What if you don't get the stone? Then we're back to square one."

"Then we'll be no worse off."

"Unless you're dead," she replied. "That's officially worse off."

After dinner, I dragged myself to the treehouse for much-needed rest. As much as I worried about nightmares, that didn't stop me from falling straight to sleep. It seemed my mind was just as exhausted as my body.

I awoke a few hours later, feeling refreshed and ready to initiate my plan. I gathered my fully packed quiver and bow and drove the Beast to the Aleutian Valley to see Max. The White Wolf was asleep when I arrived, and Ina seemed to delight in waking him to announce my presence.

Max shot to a seated position, hair sticking up at the ends. I was beginning to suspect this was his usual hairstyle.

He motioned for me to sit on the edge of the bedroll. "Ina, make sure no one interrupts us."

She offered a crisp nod and vacated the tent.

"I've pictured you in bed with me many times, but not quite like this." Even groggy, Max operated at full libido.

"I have a plan and thought it best not to wait." I told him about the crystal and the Uktena.

"I know what the Uktena is. Tell me more about the crystal. All this time I thought it was nothing more than a distinctive feature like horns on a rhino."

"Legends suggest it acts as a window to the past and future."

"Not really helpful."

I smacked a hand on the bedroll. "That's what I said, but the crystal has power that we might be able to harness to get the dragons to obey us."

"There's been a sighting of an Uktena in Unalakleet," Ina called from outside the tent.

Max frowned. "You're not supposed to be eavesdropping."

Ina ducked her head inside. "You told me to keep others out. You didn't say anything about not listening."

He sighed. "Where did you get this intel?"

"Kerry and Luke scouted the area a couple days ago, looking for more dragons. They didn't find any."

"But they found the Uktena?" I asked.

"Reports from local fishermen," Ina said.

Well, Unalakleet wasn't close, but it was closer than Fairbanks.

Max ran a hand through his hair in an effort to tame the unruly strands. "How soon can you leave?"

I'd told the crew that we'd formulate a plan, not execute it, but that was before word of an actual sighting. We had to strike while the iron was hot.

"Now works for me," I replied.

His gaze slid to Ina. "You're in charge."

Ina lifted her chin a fraction. "With all due respect, I should go with you."

Max stood. Suddenly, his body seemed to fill the entire tent. "You'll stay here and act in my stead."

Ina's gaze flicked to me, and her nostrils flared in annoyance. "As you wish."

"I wish. Have Lavonne pack us supplies." He swiveled to face me. "Give me five minutes."

He took ten, but I didn't hold it against him, mostly because he brought snacks.

We traveled eastward toward the coast. Max seemed mildly uncomfortable cooped up in the Beast, but there was no way on the gods' scorched earth that I was riding on his lupine back all the way to Unalakleet.

When we reached within three miles of our destination, I found a place to hide the Beast until our return.

"We'll travel the rest of the way on foot," I told him as I vacated the vehicle.

"I would've traveled the whole way on foot, but nooo. Somebody didn't want to wrap her legs around me for hours." He gave me a pointed look. "And somebody's missing out."

I ignored him and started toward the village. There was a place where the river met the sea that seemed like the ideal place to start our search.

I felt the vibrations beneath my feet before I spotted them. A sea of white horses surrounded us, squeezing us into a tight circle. The riders were all male and each member of the group held a silver spear. There was no obvious leader.

"What's with the coordination?" I asked. "Are they requirements to join your boy band?"

One of the horses trotted forward. "Show us your teeth," the rider said. There was nothing to indicate his authority. He seemed no taller or stronger than the others, and his coat was the same brown sheepskin.

I didn't see the harm in complying. I opened my mouth. "I'm a witch," I said with my jaw still open wide. It sounded more like *I'm rich*, which I hoped they didn't take as a sign to rob me.

Using the tip of his spear, he motioned to the others in my group to do the same. For a fleeting moment I thought Max might make an issue of it, but when he opened his mouth, silence followed.

"Wolves and a witch," the rider said. "What brings you to Unalakleet?"

"There've been sightings of a sea serpent in your waters," I told him. "We'd like to find it."

He observed me coolly. "You seek the Uktena. Why?"

Max stepped between us. "How about we discuss this at eye level?"

The rider smiled, showing his own set of crooked teeth. "In other words, come down off my high horse?" He dismounted, still gripping the silver spear. "Gladly."

The rest of the riders followed suit.

He closed his spearless hand and held a fist to his chest. "I am Farid."

"Aster."

"Max."

Farid looked between us. "You work together. Why?"

"Common goal," Max answered before I had a chance to respond.

"What common goal involves the Uktena?" Farid asked.

"We've been besieged by dragons," I explained.

"We have as well," Farid said. "We lost two of our men to them last week."

Maybe that tragic fact would make him more inclined to help us. "Our research indicates that the Uktena can help us without bloodshed."

His thick eyebrows drew together. "Yours or the dragons'?"

"Both," I said.

He nodded slightly. "You think the crystal is capable of that kind of magic?"

Okay, so he knew about the crystal. It shouldn't come as a complete surprise if the Uktena frequented these waters.

"It's worth a try," Max said. "If not, we move on to our alternate plan."

Farid regarded him. "Which is?"

Max shrugged. "We'll let you know when we figure it out."

Farid laughed. "Perhaps we can assist you in your quest. We were on our way to eat when our scout alerted us to your presence. Join us."

I glanced at the other sheepskin coats and pictured the scrawny bodies beneath them. Nobody was eating three square meals a day in this group. "You have food you can spare?"

Farid's smile evaporated. "No, but we have food we can share."

"We have our own rations," I said, "but we'd be happy to join you and find out everything you know about the Uktena before we start our search."

Farid addressed his riders and divided us among them. Max seemed reluctant to ride a horse.

"I can keep up," he insisted.

"It's a friendly gesture," I said through clenched teeth. "We should accept it."

Max imitated my forced smile. "But what if I don't want to?"

I compressed my lips in frustration. "Get on a horse, Max," I ordered.

Max contemplated its broad back. "I'm too big. I'll break its spine."

"And I'll break your spine on the ride home if you don't accept their kind offer," I ground out.

Reluctantly, he mounted the horse. I knew it was a werewolf thing, but I didn't care. I admit I also took mischievous pleasure in watching him struggle on horseback.

Farid guided us to a cave not far from the water's edge. His companions set to work; each one seemed to know his task and carried it out on autopilot.

"How do we know they're not leading us to a werewolf-sized roasting spit?" Max whispered.

"They're people," I replied. "They don't eat werewolves."

"They're cannibals for all we know," he hissed. "They live in the middle of nowhere with their matching ... everything."

"We live in the middle of nowhere, and we're not cannibals," I pointed out.

Farid twisted to look at us. "Our diet mainly consists of seafood, but I would be lying if I said Kamran's thigh didn't look tasty every now and again."

The rider beside him straightened. "Hey!"

Farid laughed.

"Why aren't your horses afraid of wolves?" I asked.

"We've trained them to be fearless," Farid said. "Our mounts are all we have. We can't afford to lose them during one werewolf encounter."

Smart. "How do they react to vampires?"

Farid stroked the mane of his horse. "We've trained them to alert us to their presence without a show of fear."

"We don't see many vampires along the coast," Kamran added.

"Fewer people," Farid explained. "Means less blood for them."

"You're not worried about sea monsters rising up from the deep?" I asked. That was the primary reason people stopped living along the coast years ago. After one attack too many, they decided the proximity to a food source wasn't worth it and opted to try for survival elsewhere.

Farid twirled his spear. "We're always prepared."

The fish were wrapped in paper and promptly distributed. This group clearly had a system that worked for them. I was a bit envious.

"You seem to be coping well with your environment," I said, after sitting on the cave floor to enjoy my fish and bread roll.

"We appeal to Mithra, and he provides for us," Farid said.

Max's brow furrowed. "Didn't he fight Godzilla?"

"That was Mothra," I said.

He looked at me askance. "How do you know that?"

"Right back at you." I imagined Max in the wilderness from birth. No exposure to movies or anything else from the pre-Eternal Night world.

"Mithra is the god of the rising sun," Farid explained. "He battles the forces of darkness and restores order."

Max snorted. "Well, he's fallen down on the job. You might want to let him know."

"The gods are long gone," I chimed in. "Trust me, your prayers are wasted on that guy."

Farid pointed the end of his fish at me. "It is exactly that attitude that keeps Mithra away. Were he with us today, you would be more enlightened."

"You said appeal and not worship," I said. The word choice seemed deliberate.

Farid gave me a small smile. "You noticed."

"What's the difference?" I prompted.

"It's hard to worship one that isn't present," Farid said. "Instead, we appeal to him to return."

"And bring the sun with him?" Max asked.

"That's the idea."

I chewed my roll. "What does appealing to Mithra involve?"

Max blew out a breath. "Mark my words. This is the part where he tells us we're the next sacrifice."

Laughing, Farid shook his head. "No sacrifices to Mithra. That isn't the path to enlightenment."

"Celibacy is," Kamran interjected.

Max started to choke on his mouthful of food. "No sex of any kind? Nobody in this group is getting it on with each other?"

"No sex of any kind," Farid confirmed.

"And you think that will appeal to Mithra?" Max asked, regaining his composure. "I would think that would keep him away longer."

"Mithra won't have any followers left if none of them can reproduce," I pointed out.

Farid looked at me. "We're aware of the downsides."

"But you believe Mithra will return before that's a real issue," I said, as more of a statement than a question.

"That is our belief, yes." Farid tipped his head back to regard the dark blanket stretched across our heads. "In the meantime, we do what we can to persuade him to return order to this world."

"Vampires might argue the new world order is doing fine without Mithra," I said.

Farid smiled. "I'm happy to let Mithra deal with the vampires and their opinions."

"What else besides celibacy?" Max asked. He now seemed fully invested in this conversation.

"We treat each other with honor and respect," Farid said. "We try to live a life that Mithra would approve of."

"We ride white horses as he would have," Kamran interrupted. "And carry silver spears, too."

"We can't manage the gold bow and arrows," Farid said regretfully. "We do, however, honor Mithra by ending each day with a haoma tonic."

"What's that?" I asked.

"Haoma is an ancient plant associated with Mithra," Farid told us.

"I've never heard of it," I said.

"Its identity today is unclear, so we've created what we believe is haoma's equivalent."

Max's mouth curved in amusement. "It's the thought that counts, right?"

"We'd like to end our meal with a special tribute to Mithra." Farid poured a greenish-brown liquid into a cup and passed it to Max. "Join our appeal by drinking with us."

Max sniffed the contents. "It smells better than it looks."

"Tastes better, too," Kamran said.

I pursed my lips. "I'm not sure about this. What are the effects?"

"What makes you think there are any effects?" Kamran asked.

I gave him a pointed look. "You drink this every day to honor a god. There has to be a payoff."

"The payoff would be the return of Mithra," Kamran replied.

"Bullshit," I shot back. "You also do it because you enjoy it."

Kamran tapped his cup against Farid's. "I suppose there is a grain of truth in that."

Max held the cup out to me. "Maybe you should drink it, and I'll keep watch."

I pushed the cup back toward him. "If Mithra is spying on us from outer space with some pervy Eye of Sauron, then he'll want to know the White Wolf is appealing to him. Mithra doesn't give a rat's ass whether Aster the Random Witch drinks his special plant."

Max's gaze flicked to me. "Fine. I'll drink if you do."

"Deal." As much as I hated to admit it, I was willing to do a lot more than drink a gross tonic if it increased our chances of restoring the sun.

I swilled the thick liquid. I was right. They must drink it every day because they enjoy it. The only negative attribute was the way it looked. It smelled delightful and tasted good, too. It was only after I downed the entire cup that I noticed the frenzied behavior of the ones who'd drank theirs before me.

"Somebody needs to teach them new moves," Max said.

Farid's men were dancing like no one was watching. They tossed their hair and kicked out their legs as though every twitch was a direct message to Mithras.

Max observed the fevered dancing with a critical eye. "How are they drinking this every day and not having sex with each other?"

"Maybe they are and they don't remember," I whispered. I stared at the bottom of my empty cup. "Promise me you won't tell me tomorrow if I do anything stupid."

He bit back a smile. "Where's the fun in that?"

"Keep an eye on me," I said. "Actually, wait." I tugged a pair of fingerless gloves from my cloak pockets and put them on.

"You don't want to be cold?" he asked.

"I don't want to kill anyone." I had no idea how the tonic would affect me. It seemed that I'd simply dance around and make a fool of myself. Better that than burn someone to a crisp.

Max grabbed me by the gloved hands and pulled me to my feet. "Time to show them how it's done!"

"Uh-oh," I said quietly. "I don't know if I like where this is going."

Despite my misgivings, I ran hand in hand with Max toward the others. I felt energized. My body wanted to move; it didn't matter how.

Max twirled me around and dipped me. We were a couple dancing our way around a ballroom floor. A prince and princess performing for our subjects. I'd never felt so light on my feet.

I threw my hands in the air and shrieked at the sky, "Mithra, come back! We need you!"

Max grabbed me around the waist and twirled me around until we both fell backward on the ground. My arm knocked into a rock, and I felt a jolting pain.

Max's laughter warmed my ear. "Oops. That's going to bruise."

"I heal quickly."

"Good to know." He rolled us both across the ground so that he was now on top of me. "I wouldn't say I like it rough, but sometimes it just escalates."

"Sounds like a personal problem."

We stared at each other for a prolonged moment.

"No sex," I reminded him. "That's part of the appeal."

His hand slipped beneath my cloak and skimmed my waist. "Doesn't sound very appealing to me. I highly doubt Mithra would be on board."

"Celibacy is the key."

"To unlocking the chastity belt."

We laughed. At some point during the haoma-induced nonsense, I dozed off. When I opened my eyes again, Farid's face loomed over mine.

"Good, you're awake," he said. "I have an idea."

I shifted to a seated position. "You could try knocking."

"On the ground? Besides, I find a hard stare much more effective."

I blinked the sleep from my eyes and noticed the slight man standing beside him. "Is your friend here to stare at me, too?"

"This is Benjamin. He can help you."

Benjamin waved.

"Is Benjamin here with a cup of coffee and a painkiller? Otherwise, I'm not sure how he can help me."

"Your journey requires you to be underwater for an extended period of time. As I understand it, you don't possess water magic, which means you'll drown before you reach your destination."

"Thank you for that inspiring message."

Benjamin crouched beside me. I scooted backward because he was a little too close for comfort.

"I have something that can protect you from drowning."

Well, that was promising.

"A scuba suit?"

"Magic."

I peered at him, still not fully awake. "Care to elaborate?"

"When I was a boy, I discovered I had the power to adopt the skill of another species for a short timeframe."

"And how does one discover this exactly?"

"It started with a bird. One day I was working on a potion when a feather drifted into the bowl. I reached in to remove the feather, and when my hand touched the liquid, my bones turned hollow, and I discovered that I could fly."

"Must've been quite a shock," I said.

"The first time was terrifying. Flying was fun, but I

didn't know whether I'd be stuck with hollow bones forever." He made a noise at the back of his throat. "I was called Bird Boy for years afterward."

I could imagine. "But the effect wore off eventually."

He nodded. "I began to experiment with other animals. I was able to inject venom like a snake. It was a natural progression to fish."

I frowned. "Will I actually grow gills?"

Benjamin cracked a smile. "Don't worry. They're not permanent." He thrust a cup at me. "Drink this."

I'd had more than enough of their elixirs for one visit. "What is it?"

"Tastes like peppermint," Max chimed in.

I leaned to the side to see Max raising a cup in the air in salute. "You dove right in there, didn't you?"

"Leap of faith, babe. You should try jumping more often. Might bring more joy to your life."

"My life is plenty joyful," I grumbled.

"The peppermint disguises the fishy smell." Smiling, Benjamin held the cup toward me. I accepted it with a grunt of resignation. Max was right; a pleasant burn filled my mouth as the liquid passed to my throat.

"How long will it last?" I asked, once I'd swallowed completely.

"I've relied on it for up to twelve hours," Benjamin said. "It might go longer, but I haven't tested it. Haven't needed to."

There was no telling how long our task would take.

"Ready when you are, mermaid," Max said.

I climbed to my feet and checked for any sign of fins or gills. All my limbs were still intact.

"My name is Max Kane, and I'll be your server this

evening." He bowed with a flourish. "Catch of the day will be Uktena with a crystal garnish."

Benjamin licked his lips. "I think you've still got haoma in your system, son."

I laughed. "He's got Max in his system." And I was starting to think he'd infiltrated mine, too.

Chapter Ten

It was entirely possible that formulating a plan while under the influence of an ancient, unknown substance wasn't the best idea. This thought occurred to me, along with several others, including my moment of weakness with the tempting werewolf, as Max and I prepared to enter the river.

It was a scenic spot. The narrow body of water gently curved around the land like an undulating snake until it kissed the ocean. If there wasn't so much at stake, I might have allowed myself to enjoy the view, as well as the company. The more time I spent with Max, the more he surprised me. I was on a dangerous mission, yet I was—dare I say it—having fun.

Max shook his arms and legs, warming up his muscles. "Is the crystal always on its forehead or is there a chance it might be embedded in its toenail or something?"

"As far as I know, it's always the forehead."

"How inconvenient. The opposite end from its teeth would be better."

I smiled. "I'm sure that's by design."

Max positioned himself at the edge of the bank. "Count of three?"

I frowned at him. "Are you sure you want to go? I could go alone, and you could wait for me here."

Max looked at me blankly. "Why wouldn't I go with you? I thought we were a team."

"Because you're a werewolf."

"Since when does that matter? You spend most of your time with wolves."

I gestured to the river. "You'll have to swim."

"So? I love the water."

"Not my crew," I said. "They avoid it unless absolutely necessary. I even have to add incentives for them to bathe."

He chuckled. "If we couldn't swim, we would never have been able to travel as far as we have. Some areas could only be crossed by water."

They'd adapted to their environment for survival. We had that much in common.

"Ladies first or together?" Max asked.

I responded by executing a shallow dive into the frigid water. I was suddenly grateful for the effect Max had on me. I would've turned and headed straight back to shore if my blood weren't pumping so hard.

We started here because it was an easy access point for us, but it was unlikely a sea monster the size of an Uktena would opt to squeeze into the narrow space. We'd have to explore further out.

Max swam ahead like he was competing for a trophy. Then again, guys like Max always seemed to be competing for something. It was one reason I didn't tend to find his type attractive. Their prize was inevitably an object, and if they had their eye on you, then they viewed you as an object, too. They were often courageous, but not because they were striving for an ideal or a better world. It was simply to win. To be 'the best,' whatever that meant. Sure, he was easy on the eyes and immensely likable when he wasn't being a smug bastard, but those qualities weren't enough to sustain a relationship, even if I was interested in one.

Which I most definitely wasn't.

I kicked my feet and propelled myself forward until I reached Max. He seemed to take my presence as a challenge and increased his speed. It wasn't hard for him. His long, muscular arms moved like two motors. I wasn't foolish enough to think I could compete with his strength or his speed. I had my own talents, though, as we both knew.

I focused on the murky depths and looked for any sign of the sea monster. I already knew the creature liked dogs. Maybe the wolf would be an acceptable substitute. I held back a fit of laughter, not wanting to test the parameters of Benjamin's magic.

The water seemed darker and thicker here than the Chena River that ran through Fairbanks. Here I felt like I was pushing my way through oil, likely because of the absence of city lights. Everything was darker.

I veered away from Max and ventured through an underwater passageway. Every so often I released a small burst of light to allow me to see far enough to choose a path. Benjamin's tonic seemed to be doing its part, for which I was grateful.

I pushed my way through tangled seaweed and emerged in a deeper section of the river. I suspected we were getting close to the ocean now. I peeled a silky string of seaweed off my forehead and flung it to my right.

And there it was.

The crystal gave the creature's position away. Without

the shining light of the jewel, the Uktena would've blended in with the murk.

I swam with minimal movements and tried to reach the monster before it noticed me.

No such luck.

The sea creature turned abruptly and started to swim in the opposite direction, toward the ocean. I swam faster, scissor kicking my legs as fast as possible in an effort to grip the tail. I started to resent not having access to an indoor swimming pool in Klondike.

I felt movement in the water behind me and watched Max rocket past me with a smug smile. Instinctively, I gripped Max's ankle as he passed and found myself brought along for the ride.

He grabbed the monster's tail and managed to scramble up the creature's backside, just as I had when I'd encountered the Uktena in Fairbanks. I lost my hold on him in the process, but I traded his ankle for the monster's tail.

The Uktena wasn't thrilled with the unexpected passengers. The monster bucked and twisted in an effort to get rid of us. Although we held on, we were unable to make any further progress. The Uktena somersaulted, and I lost all sense of direction. There was no way to tell which way was up and which was down. If the tonic failed and I needed to reach the surface for air... I pushed the thought aside.

I could do this. I had to.

The Uktena abandoned its plan to shake us off and instead swam faster and deeper. Max made a bit of headway using his claws to gain purchase and climbed higher along the monster's back.

The monster raised its tail and swept me to the side. I lost my grip but quickly regained my bearings and swam after it. Max had also been ejected from the monster's back because he appeared beside me, swimming past me with powerful strokes.

It was only when the darkness receded that I realized our surroundings had changed. A rocky beach was straight ahead, yet we hadn't broken the surface.

The monster crawled onto land. I could see its colorful markings more clearly now, and they were similar to the first Uktena I'd met, although not identical.

Max charged onto the beach after it. The monster was sorely mistaken if it thought it could outrun the White Wolf on land.

By the time I waded to shore, Max had the creature in a headlock and was about to snap its neck.

"No! Don't kill it."

Max froze with his giant arms still wrapped around the monster's neck. "How else do you expect to get the crystal? This guy's not going to let me wrench it out of his head with my bare hands."

"I don't expect you to do anything." I marched toward the monster and stood in front of it. "Close your eyes."

Max obeyed, for once. Unfortunately I wasn't talking to him.

"Not you, the Uktena." I made eye contact with the creature. "I don't want to hurt you."

The monster seemed to understand and closed its eyes. I held out my hand. My arm tickled as the magic slid toward my open palm. A beam of light broke free and streaked toward the crystal. I focused on the Ulunsuti stone, controlling the scope of the light so that it only hit the stone and nothing else. If Doran could see me now, he wouldn't question my control over my powers.

The stone vibrated with energy, and for a moment, I

worried I'd crack it. I expanded my focus to the crystal's outline so that I loosened it rather than broke it. Finally the crystal dislodged and slid away. Max snatched it before it could hit the ground.

Relieved that it worked, I closed my hand and sank us once more into darkness. The monster released a pathetic cry before slinking away.

Max examined the crystal. "It's one of the most beautiful things I've ever seen."

I gazed at the pale yellow stone, feeling the energy emanating from it. I was in no doubt of its power. I only hoped it was the kind that could help us.

"I think we might have wounded the poor guy," Max said.

"Only its pride." Hattie's research told me that the monster didn't need the crystal to survive. "Besides, you were ready to kill it. Now you feel sorry for it?"

I pulled the buckskin pouch from my pocket and held it open, prompting Max to drop the stone inside. I tugged the mouth closed and returned it to my pocket.

Max dragged a hand through his hair. "Why are we not wet?"

I'd been so preoccupied by our achievement, I hadn't noticed. "I think we might've passed into another realm. We're on a beach, but we never surfaced."

Max contemplated the water. "Do we try to swim back?"

I wasn't sure that we could. The Uktena had taken the lead, and I hadn't exactly left breadcrumbs behind us.

A moan echoed from the direction the Uktena had gone. Max gave me a look.

"What?" I asked.

"You want to check on it, don't you?"

I paused. "Maybe."

"Me, too." Max cupped the back of my head. "I think you might be rubbing off on me." He broke into a grin. "I like how dirty that sounds."

"Very mature." I shook off his hand and started after the Uktena. If I had injured it, maybe we could treat the wound.

Max hurried after me. "I guess we'll also try to find another way out of here."

"Sounds like a plan."

We vacated the beach and walked until we reached a wall so high that it seemed to stretch into eternity. We followed it until we arrived at the base of a winding set of wide, rocky steps. There was nowhere else to go.

"It can't be that injured if it managed to climb," Max observed.

"It might have turned left at the wall where we turned right." I hadn't heard any sounds of distress since that first moan.

"Good point." Max surveyed the options. "What do you think?"

"Maybe the steps will take us to the surface."

He climbed the steps two at a time. I followed behind him, thinking about the passage from our world to the next.

"This is the underworld," I said, as we continued to climb.

"How can you be sure?"

"The Uktena uses waterways to travel between the two realms. It tried to escape us by swimming to the underworld, thinking it would lose us."

"Well, it didn't lose us, but we're definitely lost."

The rocky steps didn't deliver us to the surface either. Instead, they opened into an enormous cavern. It looked like the hollow center of a volcano, and we were on its ridge. A bridge floated above an abyss.

I inched forward and peered into the seemingly bottomless cavern. "What do you think is down there?"

"Don't know. Don't want to know." Max remained focused on the bridge. "It's suspended in midair. How do we cross it?"

I cast him a sidelong glance. "How's your long jump?"

"It's yours I'm worried about."

Fair point.

"I don't suppose you have any magic that involves super long stilts or flying?" he asked.

"I'm not a circus witch."

"Too bad. Might be fun." He regarded the opposite side of the chasm. "What if it's the wrong way? Maybe the bridge is a deliberate attempt at misdirection."

"A structural siren?" I asked, only half joking.

"For all we know, there's a giant lying in wait on the other side. He'll end up using our bones as toothpicks."

"Do I detect a note of fear?" I found it hard to believe that Max Kane, the leader of the Ghost Pack and White Wolf himself, would be intimidated by the unknown.

He gave me a long look. "Again, it's not me I'm worried about."

Got it. "Well, let me put both of our minds at ease."

"How do you propose to do that?"

I steeled myself for my next statement. "I can do a thing."

"Congratulations."

"A thing that will help us know what's on the other side."

"That's a bit better. Anything I can do to help?"

I looked at him. "Protect me."

"That's a given."

"Protect my body. It's going to be empty for a few minutes."

His eyebrows inched up. "Curiouser and curiouser."

I moved closer to the rocky wall and slid my bottom to the hard surface. "I may not be able to fly, but I can switch to the astral plane, which is the next best thing."

"Your soul leaves your body?"

"I don't know that it's my soul, but it's part of me. My consciousness, maybe? While I'm gone, my body is vulnerable. If there's an attack, I won't be able to defend myself."

His expression turned stony. "I'll defend you."

"I know you will." It was the only reason I felt comfortable enough to do this. If I trusted Max with my life, it seemed ridiculous not to trust him with my secret as well. On the other hand, I trusted my merry band of wolves and hadn't told them. And Hugo's betrayal only confirmed it was the right decision.

There was something different about Max, though. Forget his arrogance and his relentless flirtation. When he said he'd defend and protect me, the belief settled in my very core.

I crossed my legs and closed my eyes, blocking out all thoughts of Max and my crew. All thoughts of the perilous journey we'd undertaken. I concentrated on separating from my physical form. Peeling away a layer of myself and joining the astral plane.

I felt a snapping sensation, and my eyes jerked open to see my astral form hovering above the abyss. I observed Max standing guard over my body. My eyes were closed and my head was slumped to the side. I thought I spied a trail of drool along my cheek. Very attractive. If Max still hit on me after this, his interest was genuine.

I floated to the bridge to see whether there was a way to access it that wasn't obvious from our vantage point. There were indentations in the rocky wall that could be used as steps. They wouldn't get us all the way to the floating bridge, but they'd get us closer than the floor level.

I drifted across the bridge. The pieces were intact. No sign of loose boards or traps that would dump us into the abyss. It was a strange design, and I wondered for whom it was meant. If you could fly, you'd simply fly across the chasm and skip the bridge. Lazy fliers then— they reached the bridge and needed a rest until the next leg.

I continued to the other side and glanced over my shoulder to check on my body. Max was crouched beside me with an object in his hand. Maybe he'd spotted the drool and was sparing me the indignity by wiping it away.

I turned back to the task at hand and slipped between the gap in the boulders. It was wide enough for us if we entered sideways, which begged the question—what would I find at the end of this trail? Certainly not a giant.

I floated through the darkness like a will-o'-the-wisp against a black canvas. I sensed *something* ahead.

Silver lines glinted ahead of me. There seemed to be some sort of metal suspended in midair, like the bridge.

Once I drew near enough, I realized the objects weren't suspended but attached to a far wall. Even better, the objects weren't useless pieces of metal.

They were weapons. An entire cache of them.

A staff. An axe. A sword. Every one of them was made of a dark silver substance I'd never seen before. Whatever it was, it was clear these were no ordinary weapons. They glowed with a faint light, suggesting they'd been blessed by the gods. Incredible.

I returned to my body to see that he'd written on my

face in blue marker. *I love Max.* Well, 'love' was a heart, which he'd also completely colored in.

Very mature.

I rejoined my body and opened my eyes, causing Max to jump backward. "Boo," I said. "How did you manage to carry a blue marker in your pocket all this time?"

"I keep it for emergencies."

"What kind of emergency is resolved with a blue marker?"

"You'd be surprised."

I wiped my hand across my forehead.

"It won't come off that easily," he admitted.

"You'd better hope the water washes it off during our swim back."

He nodded toward the bridge. "Will there be a swim back?"

"Not sure yet, but we need to cross. Trust me, we want what's in there."

"And what is there, exactly?"

I told him what I had seen.

He whistled softly. "They sound like celestial weapons."

I'd never heard of celestial weapons. "What do you know about them?"

"Not much, only that they were forged and used by gods."

"Why would any god leave weapons here?"

"We're in the underworld, remember? They're not meant to be found by anyone from our realm."

They'd been stored here by a god, perhaps with the idea that the owner would one day return for them.

"Maybe we can use them to drive out the dragons," he added.

I had a feeling celestial weapons were only designed for one purpose. "No killing, remember? Besides, that's what the stone is for." I patted the slight bulge in my pocket.

"Did you see any way for you to reach the bridge?" he asked.

I told him about the indentations in the wall. "Still too risky for me, though."

"I can get us across," Max said. He glanced at the gaping hole beside us. "Just promise me you won't let go."

"I promise."

Max stretched his neck, preparing to shift. "I thought we'd be naked the next time you rode me, but it is what it is."

"You're a real charmer, you know that?"

Grinning, he transformed. Bones cracked, joints popped, and fur sprouted until a white wolf stood before me. The beast was even larger and more formidable than Max in his human form, and that was saying something. Four massive paws rested on the ground. Their claws looked sharp enough to shred granite.

I climbed on his back and held on tight. He bolted forward, and I clung to his hide like my life depended on it—because it did.

He jumped, using the indentations in the stone wall to gain momentum for the final leap to the bridge. He pushed off with his paws, and we soared toward the bridge. Two front paws landed with a hard thud and the bridge swayed as the wolf bounded toward the other side. My foot swung out to the side and slammed against the side of the bridge. Pain shot up my leg, and I swallowed a cry. As long as it wasn't broken, I'd manage. I'd need my foot intact if I had any hope of making it back in one piece.

We reached the narrow passage, and the wolf slowed to

a stop. There was no way he could fit through the gap in his beast form. I climbed off his back and turned away to let him shift without an audience. It was a contrary move, really. If anybody liked an audience, it was Max Kane.

When I finally dared to look, he'd transformed into a different outfit from the one he'd been wearing.

"How did you do that?" My crew didn't have that ability.

"I'm the White Wolf. I can do a lot of amazing things." He wiggled his eyebrows suggestively.

We turned sideways and squeezed through the gap, continuing to the next cavern.

"Is there anything else I need to know before we get there? Any obstacles?" he asked.

"Nothing obvious, but I was incorporeal so I might not have triggered any traps."

"Let's hope we're right about this being some kind of godly storage unit." If the owner didn't expect them to be discoverable, that decreased the likelihood of an ambush.

We crept toward the weapons attached to the far wall.

"Interesting design," Max remarked.

Carved into the stone behind the weapons was the head of a bird. I'd been so intent on the weapons, I'd missed it the first time around.

"Is that a phoenix?" Max asked.

My heart skipped a beat. "I think it's a falcon. Is there a falcon god?"

He shrugged. "Not sure. Maybe they're just a fan."

We edged forward until we were within reach of the weapons.

"Your arms are longer," I said.

He nodded. "Be ready to run."

My heartbeat thrummed in my ears. "One, two…"

He tried to swipe the staff from its hook, but it remained intact.

"I didn't say three!"

Ignoring me, he stared at the staff still attached to the wall. "It's stuck."

We had to hurry. I muscled my way ahead of him and reached for it.

Laughter bubbled from his throat. "If I couldn't budge it with these muscles, what makes you think you can?"

I plucked the staff from the wall like it was affixed with sticky tape. "I guess it needed a woman's touch."

He grinned. "I mean, we all need that." He gazed at the staff now clenched in my hand. "Feel anything weird? No poison infiltrating your bloodstream?"

I shook my head. "Nothing yet."

He nodded at the wall. "Next one."

"Do you think it's wise to take them all? Maybe we should only take one each and leave the rest."

He chuckled. "You think a god is going to let it go because only two of his precious weapons are missing? Go big or go home, Aster."

He was right. If we were going to court the ire of a god, we might as well take the lot.

I held my breath as Max attempted to liberate the axe. Same result.

He folded his arms. "Do you think this is a King Arthur and Excalibur situation?"

"I doubt it. I'm a thief, remember?"

"And I'm worse."

I glanced at him. "This isn't a competition."

"It kind of is."

I removed the axe from the wall with the same ease as the staff. It was so light that it didn't feel like a solid object.

Max wiggled his fingers, and I passed it to him. He gave it a practice swing. "What a beauty. I don't rely on weapons, but I might be tempted to learn."

I frowned. "What if it's not very effective?"

"Don't let the weight fool you. That's the sharpest blade you'll ever hold." He returned his attention to the remaining weapons. "I'll carry the next two, and then we'll bolt."

"What about the bridge? You'll need to be in wolf form." Despite the light weight of the weapons, my hands were only human sized, and they'd be busy clinging to Max.

"I wish we'd brought a sack," he said.

"It isn't like we expected to find a cache of celestial weapons. We came for a single crystal."

He removed his new shirt. "We can use this. You can wear it like a backpack." He created a sling, and I placed the two weapons inside. Together we knotted the ends and slid it over my shoulders. The only real weight I felt was from the shirt itself.

"I'll take it off to get through the narrow passageway," I said.

"Let me grab two more, and we're all set."

I turned away from the wall so he could more easily pop the items inside the makeshift backpack. It was then that I noticed a crack forming in the entryway. Dust and debris fell from the fissure as a line traveled along the wall toward the place where the weapons had been affixed.

"I think we have a problem."

He followed my gaze. "Yeah, I see that."

I snatched the final two weapons from their respective spots and shoved them into the improvised pack. The fissure reached the empty hooks just as we turned to run.

The wall exploded.

A powerful force propelled us toward the entrance.

Rocks smacked the back of my head and legs. I pitched forward and skidded along the cave floor, scraping the skin from my knees and palms in the process.

I scrambled to my feet and continued running. The shrieking of birds jolted me. I spared a glance over my shoulder to see a murder of black crows with their wings aflame.

Max blew past me and squeezed through the narrow gap. By the time I made it through, a white wolf stood ready for me. I jumped on his back and gripped his fur as he shot forward.

The crows spilled through the gap behind us. No bridge required for the birds. They poured across the chasm and pecked us. Their beaks weren't sharp enough to pierce the wolf's thick hide, but their fiery wings were a problem. The wolf's white fur smoked as the crows set Max alight, and I immediately used one hand at a time to douse the flames. The stench of singed fur burned my nostrils, and I hoped Max healed as quickly as I did.

The bag pulled away from my back as the crows tugged the fabric in an attempt to reclaim the weapons. I balanced myself and twisted my body to swat them away. Clenching my thighs as tightly as I could, I slipped the bag off one shoulder and switched it to my front, sticking my head between the handles. It was awkward, but not as awkward as dying at the beaks and wings of crows.

Max didn't bother to use the indentations at this end. He simply sailed through the air. I pulled the axe from the bag and started swinging. Feathers floated around us as I dispatched dozens at a time. At the other end of the bridge, the crows had formed a blockade. They crushed their bird bodies together, creating a wall of fire.

The White Wolf didn't slow his pace. He plowed

straight through them. As we sailed through the air, heat scorched my chest, and I realized the bag was on fire.

Max landed on the rocky slope and fought to gain purchase. We slid backward toward the murky abyss, and he clawed at the hard surface to stop our descent. The crows crowded around us in an effort to push us to our doom.

I continued wielding the axe, slashing their feathers at each opportunity. There were too many of them.

I stuffed the axe in the shirt, and part of the weapon poked through the other end. Great. The burns had formed a hole.

Max struggled to keep us from falling. Although we'd stopped sliding backward, he seemed stuck and unable to defend himself against the onslaught of crows.

I had to do something.

I relaxed my legs and leaned my hands on the wolf's back to vault over his giant head. I landed on the ground and pivoted to face the crows. I raised my hands and let light burst from my palms. The crows shrieked in protest and scattered.

I watched as Max crawled to safety. He was wise to remain in his animal form. His thick hide would protect him.

Light beamed across the chasm. The crows flew toward the weapons cave as though being chased by an unseen predator. They squeezed through the gap in a frenzied manner, cawing and scratching at each other in their desperation to escape the light.

I closed my hands and plunged us into darkness once more.

Max returned to human form. His skin was covered in

angry red marks. He gazed at me with an inscrutable expression.

"We need to get out of here," I said. The crows were quite the display, and there could be more where they came from.

"If that was a falcon carved in stone, then why were crows defending the territory?"

I waited a beat for a 'birds of a feather' joke that didn't come.

"Is there a god of all birds?" he asked, sounding slightly dazed.

A deep groan emanated from deep within the chasm.

"Time to go." I ushered him to his feet, and we raced down the rocky steps, winding around and around until we arrived back where we had started.

"We'll have to risk the water," I said.

"We should have time left on the tonic."

I gazed at the dark water. "Not if we get lost." Or attacked. I kept that possibility to myself.

Max waded in and started swimming. His strokes were smooth and careful, and I realized he was trying to avoid splashing. Smart. If we could avoid attracting attention, we increased our chances of getting out of here alive.

We swam side by side, neither of us willing to veer too far from the other. It was too murky to see more than a few inches in front of us. I didn't realize the bag had grown loose until I noticed the staff floating between us. Max and I snatched the staff at the same time before it could float away. It would be awkward to swim with the stick in my hand. All I wanted was for us to be back in the Beast and on our way home.

My body snapped, and I stared at the steering wheel in

my hands. Holy hellfire. I turned to Max, who looked as stunned as I felt.

"What just happened?" he asked.

I glanced at the bulk of the improvised bag. "I think I activated one of the weapons."

"The staff is a teleportation device? In that case, you should've had it take us the rest of the way home."

"You're a spoiled brat, you know that?" I put the pedal to the metal and hit the road.

Max held onto the door as we flew over a bump. "We should do this again sometime. We make a great team."

I leveled him with a look. "Which part do you think we should do again?"

A flash of teeth nearly blinded me. "All of it, but I especially like the part when you're on top."

I groaned. "You almost had me."

"I know. That's why we should do it again. So we can finish what we started."

I returned my attention to the path ahead. "We agreed not to talk about it."

"Okay, then let's talk about something else. How would you feel about joining forces permanently? Your crew joins mine."

"I'm not a werewolf."

"You'd be welcomed by the pack, especially if you agreed to be my mate."

I looked at him askance. "Seriously? That's where your head is right now?"

I remembered Poco's remark about my romantic interest. She'd described him as dangerous and deadly. At one point, I thought her vision might've meant Lord Doran. Now I wasn't so sure.

"Fine. We'll deal with the dragons first, then we can talk about us," he said with a casual air.

"There is no us."

"Not yet."

I kept my eyes fixed on the path ahead, choosing my next words carefully. I didn't want to insult him; I still needed his help. "We got what we came for. Let's be satisfied with that."

"I'm never satisfied."

"Sounds like a 'you' problem."

He chuckled and settled against the seat. Crisis averted. All I had to do now was get the crystal to the canyon and figure out how to use it.

No biggie.

Chapter Eleven

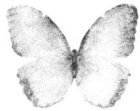

I sensed trouble brewing the moment the wind whipped past me, blowing down a weakened tree in the process. I parked the Beast in a small clearing, and we traveled the rest of the distance on foot.

"What's going on?" Max had to shout to be heard over the noise.

"Nothing good."

Each step grew harder as the wind pushed against me, forcing my eyes closed. Peering through two slits, I saw the funnel in the distance. It tore through the forest with abandon. I'd heard of tornadoes happening before the Great Eruption, but I'd never experienced one. The sun's disappearance had resulted in changes in weather patterns, and even locations like Tornado Alley no longer suffered from unexpected twisters.

The presence of a tornado in the middle of The Wild was unprecedented and suggested supernatural forces at work. I wasn't aware of any elemental witches powerful enough to conjure a tornado of this caliber.

I dodged a falling branch and remained huddled with Max against the base of a large oak tree as the air blew a torrent of leaves and sticks to the ground. The forest was already in poor condition; this unnatural event would devastate what remained. Even worse, the massive oak that served as our shield was now directly in the path of the twister.

"We need to move." I bolted from behind the tree, although my speed was slowed considerably by the strong wind. Max fared better against the natural nemesis. I could tell he was holding back for my sake.

Lightning flashed in the sky. The sharp angles of light contrasted beautifully with the black canvas. If I weren't in danger of dying, I'd sit here and watch for another strike.

The ground trembled as we raced away from the tornado's path.

"A tornado and an earthquake?" Max queried.

It *was* strange. There could be an air witch and an earth witch working together, but the odds were low that there'd be coordinated magical activity that didn't involve me.

This was something else.

We sought refuge behind a huge boulder, and I was thankful for the respite.

"Maybe we angered the god by taking his weapons and now he's coming after us," Max said. "Who's the god of natural disasters?"

My body stiffened at the mention of natural disasters. If this was the work of the calamity demon, heads were going to roll.

Max gave me a speculative look. "You know the god?"

"No, but I know the demon." And, more importantly, I knew how to defeat it.

"Stay here," I ordered. I didn't wait to see whether he

complied. I scrambled from shelter and headed for the canyon, ducking under flying debris and leaping over branches along the way. Anger boiled the blood in my veins. I couldn't let my emotions get the better of me, though. I needed to stay sharp if I expected to stuff the calamitous genie back in the bottle. First I had to find the guilty party because that was where I'd find the amulet.

As the tornado continued along its path, I spotted the cause of all this chaos. The enormous demon lumbered toward the dragon-filled canyon. It wouldn't be difficult for the demon to cause an avalanche that crushed the dragons where they stood.

I couldn't let that happen.

I rushed toward the cliff where I'd first encountered the dragons and found members of my crew strapped in bungee cords attached to a giant boulder. They'd clearly come prepared.

Tyson was the first to notice me. "I can explain."

"Not now." A gust of wind rushed past me, and I struggled to remain upright. Scarlet grabbed me as I skidded toward the edge of the cliff.

"There's no river this time," Tyson said. "I thought it would be less dangerous."

"It's a calamity demon, not Poseidon," I snapped. "The demon will use any tools at its disposal."

As if on cue, the ground shook again. That got the dragons' attention. Multiple heads lifted, searching for the source of the unrest. A few took to the air.

Tyson observed the dragons in flight. "What if the demon and dragons join forces and unite against us?"

"Maybe you should've thought of that sooner," I told him.

There was no chance of that happening, though. The

dragons wouldn't respond well to a demon in their territory, especially one that felt threatening to them.

Two dragons must've identified the demon as the cause of the commotion because they flew in tandem toward the creature. Fire streaked from their gaping jaws.

Moments later, fat drops of icy rain fell from the sky.

"I guess that's how the demon plans to defend itself against firepower," Bear surmised.

"It'll work, too," I said.

Raindrops plummeted to the earth like winter soldiers parachuting into battle. Cold water spilled down my face to the point where I could no longer see. I wiped my eyes continuously until I regained my vision.

The dragons attempted to approach the demon, but between the heavy rain and sliding debris, they were unable to gain traction. I watched one open its wings and attempt to hover, but the wings were too drenched to function. Its fire slowly diminished to darkened dust.

"If the dragons can't move, they can't leave," Scarlet said.

"What did you think would happen?" I asked.

Tyson cringed. "That if they think this is the demon's territory, they'll leave at the first opportunity."

"Or they'll burn the demon to a crisp when they all breathe fire at once," Bear said.

I shook my head, disappointed. "Your plan was to let the demon do as much damage to them as possible and then stick it back in the amulet? You know I'm the only one who can do that."

Tyson patted my shoulder. "Which is why you're here."

I brushed off his hand. "You didn't expect me. You deliberately waited until I was gone so I wouldn't interfere."

"That was the preferred outcome," Bear admitted.

I couldn't believe how careless they'd been.

The demon raised its huge arms toward the sky, and the rain stopped. The dragons seemed more riled than subdued by the display of power. They rose to their feet and flapped their wings. More dragons flew to join the initial two.

"That demon is toast," Bear whispered in awe.

"They can't kill it, remember? They can try, but the calamity demon can't be killed."

"Can't be killed at all?" Tyson asked. "Or can't be killed by traditional methods? Maybe dragon fire is the demon's one weakness."

"And you thought you'd experiment? You all could've been killed along with the dragons." I held out my hand. "Who has the amulet?"

Bear reached beneath his shirt and pulled a chain over his head. "Can you at least wait to see what happens next?"

"A tornado is tearing apart The Wild, destroying trees that were barely standing as it was. I don't need to see what else it can do." I snatched the amulet from his grasp.

"What does the amulet do?" Max asked.

Tyson clapped him on the shoulder. "Watch and learn."

Max stared at the hand on his shoulder, and Tyson quickly withdrew it.

The earth shook again, and we clung to the bungee cords to keep from falling into the canyon. As I reached for the cord, the amulet slipped from my fingertips. I watched the necklace slide down the rough terrain and catch on a jutting rock.

I let go of the cord and started toward the amulet.

"Aster, no!" Scarlet's voice pierced the air.

Thanks to the icy rain that had fallen, I slid on the slick

rocks. Elbows and knees cracked against the cliffside as I tumbled toward the necklace. It didn't matter how many bruises I got. Nothing would matter if I didn't retrieve the amulet; it was the only way to stop the demon.

Gravity worked against me, and I slid toward the rock faster than I anticipated, unable to stop myself. I skimmed over the rocks and crags until I reached a wayward branch that stuck out of the cliffside. I curled my body around the branch like a sloth to stop my descent. Another tremor rocked the canyon, and I gripped the branch in fear as I heard a cracking sound.

My weight was too much for it. As the branch broke, I reached for a rock—anything to keep me from plummeting to the bottom of the canyon—but grabbed empty air instead. My back slammed against an outcrop, causing pain to radiate down my spine. I used the heels of my boots to try to slow my fall. Sweat coated my palms as I reached for another limb. My hand slid down the bark; my pulse raced. Below me was a straight shot to the bottom.

I flipped to face the wall and gripped the limb with both hands. Cheering voices from above spurred me on. I pulled myself from the limb to an outcrop, taking as much time as I needed to make the transition. My heart jumped each time another tremor occurred, but I kept going. The necklace dangled a few feet above my head.

As I raised my hand to take it, icy drops began to fall again. They pelted the necklace, knocking it from its perch. The amulet sailed past me, and I stuck out my foot to catch it. The chain looped around the base of my boot, and I had to keep my leg at an awkward angle to prevent the chain from slipping off. I maintained my composure and practiced steady breaths as I bent my knee. Keeping one hand and one foot on the cliffside, I brought my knee as close to my body as possible. I held my breath as I attempted to transfer the chain from my boot to my hand.

More cheers erupted above, including a shrill whistle from Max, and my heartbeat accelerated. I was close now.

Slowly, I placed the chain around my neck. Only when the amulet rested against my chest did I dare to breathe again. I curled my fingers around the stone to reassure myself that it was there. The earth trembled again, but I hugged the face of the cliff and kept my balance. Picturing the demon inside the amulet, I uttered my grandmother's incantation for the containment spell, "i dici te."

The rain ceased, along with the mighty roars of the dragons. A surge of energy jolted me, and I knew the calamity demon had returned to its prison.

Out of the corner of my eye, I observed the dragons as they flew to the basin, the threat extinguished. The different species had joined forces to defeat a common foe. Whatever these dragons were doing here, they were in it together.

I took my time climbing to the top. My body was sore, and bruises were visible on my arms and legs by the time I reached the cliff where my friends' outstretched hands pulled me to safety. Max hovered in the background, clearly prepared to let my friends make amends by coming to my aid.

They unhooked themselves from the boulder, and I noticed their matching guilty expressions. They knew this wasn't over, that my safety and the containment of the demon wouldn't be enough to quell my dismay. Hugo's actions were bad enough, but the wizard had always challenged my authority. I expected better from the crew members standing before me.

I marched past them to the Beast. Between the fallen trees and the scattered debris, the tornado's path was apparent. I was relieved to find the Beast upright and unharmed. Thank the gods.

I climbed behind the wheel without a backward glance.

Max appeared by the driver's side. "I'll make my own way back from here."

I nodded stiffly. "I'll touch base with you when I figure out the best way to use the crystal."

His gaze drifted to the bag full of weapons in the back seat. "I suppose you want to keep hold of the weapons."

"I think that would be best." Although I had no intention of sharing the bounty with my crew, not after the stunt they'd just pulled.

I drove away, leaving skid marks in the dirt. They'd made their way to the cliff; they could make their way back. It wasn't much of a hardship considering they could cover the terrain on four legs.

Bonnie was alone when I arrived at the campfire. She'd gone to the trouble of preparing kebabs, for which I was both surprised and grateful. Bonnie was rarely proactive when it came to serving others.

She looked me up and down when I entered the clearing. "What happened to you?"

I ignored the question. "I need water."

She pointed behind me. Wordlessly, I retrieved the jug and guzzled water until my thirst was quenched. Survival was thirsty work.

The rest of the crew appeared in the clearing with their heads hanging. I ripped the chain off my neck and thrust my hand in the air.

"Whose bright idea was this?" I demanded. I couldn't believe after what had happened the last time that anyone in the crew would dare use the amulet again, not when they knew the dangers involved.

Nobody reacted.

I shook the amulet. "When you raised the idea before, I shot it down for a reason. You knew what this demon could do. You knew you couldn't control it, yet you went behind my back, which is so much worse. What if I'd been gone for days? The demon could've destroyed far more than the dragons by then."

"If it's any consolation, I didn't know until the experiment was underway," Scarlet said in a quiet voice. "At that point the only option seemed to be to pitch in."

"Honestly, I wish you had known so you could've talked them out of it," I replied. I turned to address the rest of the group. "We've already dealt with one betrayal in this group. We can't tolerate another one. We agreed not to use the calamity demon, so whoever did this acted in direct contravention to the group's decision."

I couldn't help but look at Bonnie. She was the most likely member to have acted in defiance. The pregnant werewolf seemed to think she knew best on a regular day, so it wouldn't surprise me to learn she thought she knew best during a crisis, too.

Bonnie flinched under my incriminating gaze. "Don't look at me like that. It wasn't me."

She wouldn't lie; I knew that much. I hated the alternative even more. If it wasn't Bonnie, that meant it was someone I trusted more.

"It was me," a voice said.

I twisted to see Hattie standing at the entrance to the clearing. "I told them to use the amulet. I'm sorry. I thought I had a solid plan."

I was at a loss for words. Of all the possible scenarios, this wasn't one I envisioned. "Hattie, what are you even doing here?"

Bonnie passed a charred kebab to Bear. "Did I not mention she was here? Oops."

Her quiet presence didn't surprise me. Hattie had always been stealthy. She was lighter on her feet than any werewolf I'd ever known.

"You and I discussed the calamity demon. Why would you think you knew better?" I asked.

Hattie lowered her gaze. "I thought you might not make it back alive. I didn't want the end result to be that none of us survived."

I exhaled. As much as I wanted to yell and express more outrage, I understood.

"You're lucky nobody was killed," I told her.

"Let me make it up to you."

I folded my arms. "How do you expect to do that?"

"There's a place I found that might be helpful to you. Olive gave me permission to tell you about it."

My ears perked up. "I'm listening."

"Meet me at Olive Branch tomorrow, and I'll show you."

Tomorrow sounded good to me. I wasn't in the mood for any more surprises today.

"I'll escort you back to Oglethorpe," Bear offered.

"Tyson will do it," Bonnie said quickly.

"I don't care who does it," I said, "as long as it isn't me." I'd need to find a new storage space for the amulet, as well as the stash of celestial weapons. My crew had shown they could no longer be trusted. Even if it had been Hattie's idea, they could've refused.

But they didn't.

"I'm going to shower," I announced.

Bonnie held out a kebab. "Eat first?"

I felt too nauseated by betrayal to eat. "Someone else can have it."

"I'll give it to the bean," she said, and bit into the hunk of meat.

I exited the clearing and headed toward the waterfall that doubled as a shower. After the day I'd had, I only wanted to be alone. I didn't even want to think. I simply wanted to close my eyes and wash away the stink of disappointment.

I arrived at the watering hole and sat on a log to take off my boots. A purple and black butterfly settled beside me, as though waiting for me to finish. The blood in my veins chilled.

Although it was possible this was an actual butterfly, the odds were extremely low. Butterflies hadn't been seen in The Wild in my lifetime. Then again, most vampires in this region didn't have the ability to shift either. It was one of those genes that simply didn't get passed down to the local generations.

The wings stretched and went perfectly still. Slowly, I peeled off my left glove. No sudden movements. If this was a vampire, I had to act oblivious and lull it into a false sense of security.

The swift transformation threw me. I expected popping and cracking sounds, but maybe that was only werewolves. I stared at the vampire now standing in front of me and was in no doubt as to her identity.

"Isobel Markham, I presume."

She tilted her head, a curtain of raven hair shifting with it. "You'll put that glove back where it belongs if you know what's good for you. I have no intention of suffering the same fate as my John." She flashed a set of sharp fangs.

"Although you should know he'll be back to his old self soon enough."

That got my attention. "How?"

"I found him the best wizard that money can buy, and he's working on a pair of magical glasses that will allow him to see again."

She found Birney the best wizard that money can buy—and she bought my location with a jar of honey.

"Great," I said. "All's well that ends well."

Her eyes narrowed. "Do you seriously believe I'd allow your transgression to go unpunished?"

"I didn't realize you were in charge of dishing out justice. I thought Lord Doran was judge, jury, and executioner in The Wild."

She flipped her dark hair over her shoulder. "You might be able to run rings around Doran and his Keystone rangers, but I'm another story."

I opened my arms. "Then why am I not dead yet?"

Her gaze raked over me. "Because I wanted to see you first. I've heard so much about you over the years, you see. It's hard not to be the tiniest bit interested in such a worthy foe."

I let my glove drop to the ground. Her eyes tracked its descent.

"You're welcome to keep your weapons, although fair warning, Birney is very eager to cut off both your hands and mount them on his wall."

"That'll make for charming decor."

"Thankfully, I have places of my own and won't need to look at them." She began to walk in a slow circle around me. "Tell me about this magic of yours. I've never heard of a witch with your abilities."

"Do you want to interview me or kill me?"

She laughed. "I do appreciate a woman with a strong personality."

"I inherited it from my grandmother."

"Ah, yes. The indomitable Maya Goodfellow. Another name I'm familiar with."

"You knew her?"

"Only by reputation. If it weren't for her, your coven might still be intact. I imagine that fact disrupts your sleep on occasion."

I turned as she walked, tracking her movements. "I believe you'll find it was the vampire retaliation that destroyed my coven."

Isobel clucked her tongue. "Lord Doran can be quite vicious when the situation demands it. Just like when his poor family was killed." She shook her head. "I would've hated to be those responsible. They had no idea what kind of monster they'd unleashed."

"According to you, my grandmother was the real monster."

"Her massive ego was the real monster. It endangered your entire coven."

I laughed. "I don't think it was her ego who wanted freedom from vampire rule."

Isobel came to a halt. "Maybe not, but her ego spurred her to make rash decisions at the expense of others. Half your coven might have lived had she not decided to attack Klondike."

I thought of Hugo and how foolish his efforts had been. Had my grandmother's action been comparable? I'd been too young at the time to be included in any planning, and they'd made certain to exclude me when the crucial moment arrived. They'd gathered their blades and bows and marched off to their collective doom. Of course, the 'doom' part was delayed. The coven members who managed to return afterward were singled out and killed during the purge. My grandmother could've used me as a weapon in that fight, yet she'd chosen to keep me safe, stashed me away so I could live to fight another day.

Her reasons for launching a rebellion would haunt me. I'd always viewed them through a simple lens. She wanted freedom from oppression, but I began to wonder whether there'd been more at stake and that her reasons had been far more complicated than I could ever know.

"Are we finished yet? Because I really need a shower after the day I've had." I started to undress.

Isobel seemed taken aback my attitude. "Aren't you at all concerned?"

"That you'll talk me to death? Not really."

Isobel glanced warily at my hands. "You're not going to defend yourself?"

I stripped off my pants. "No, like I said, I'm going to shower." I tilted my head. "Unless you'd care to join me? There's plenty of room under the waterfall."

Isobel recoiled slightly. "Just stay away from John, and we won't have any problems."

"Lord Birney is the least of my concerns at the moment. In case you haven't heard, there's a dragon horde that's decided The Wild is a nice place to settle down and raise a family."

Isobel turned away as I removed my top. "John told me. He said he had no doubt you and your friends would take care of them."

"See? I may be an outlaw, but I have my uses. Kill me now and the dragons become your problem to solve." I turned toward the waterfall and hoped she couldn't sense the rapid beating of my heart. When I finally dared to look over my shoulder, she was gone.

I stood under the waterfall long enough to prune my skin. The hideout was quiet when I returned. It was Bear's turn to patrol, and he sat at the edge of the clearing, using a small knife to sharpen the end of a stick. He acknowledged me with a grunt, but we didn't speak. I was still angry. Nothing that a good night's sleep couldn't cure.

I climbed to my treehouse and settled on the mattress with my mother's journal. After the day I'd had, I felt the need to be close to her. I allowed a small bit of magic to shine from my index finger, enough to illuminate my mother's neat handwriting. I started at the beginning this time, smiling at the parts about my father, which usually involved him doting on her. He'd been a good husband and father. Despite his early death, I'd been lucky to have him in my life as long as I did.

I turned the page and immediately spotted my name at the top.

Aster continues to impress the coven. I wish I'd known as a young girl that I'd be the one to produce such a valuable witch. Maybe I wouldn't have felt so useless and unnecessary.

My chest tightened. It was hard to read about my mother's insecurities and not be able to comfort her. I skimmed through the next few pages and stopped again when I saw the mention of my grandmother.

Maya has told me about a prophecy that involves Aster. I think she might be reading too much into it in typical Maya fashion. She's always had a flair for the dramatic—like mother, like son. I asked her not to share the finding with anyone else in the coven until we learn more. I don't want them to treat her differently. Well, any more than they already do. I love that her magic is special, but I hate it too. I know it doesn't make sense to feel so conflicted. Her gift is monumental. Still, I fear for her safety. If the Fallen ever discover what she can do, they'll come for her, and I will be powerless to stop them.

I reread the passage. If my grandmother believed in this prophecy, then why did she attack Klondike instead of waiting for nature to take its course? Did she somehow think her actions were necessary to put me on the right path?

There was no one left to ask.

I continued to read, mesmerized by my mother's thought process, as well as the depth of her feelings when it came to me. She hadn't been overly demonstrative as a mother. Whenever I'd needed a hug, I ran to my grandmother. It must've cut my mother deeply to watch her beloved only child seek comfort from someone else. Guilt gnawed at me. There was nothing I could do now. The damage had been done, and my mother was long gone.

I feel caught between the power of Aster and the determination of Maya and worried that the two might someday meld together to form a weapon that all vampires fear. I do not want my child to bear this burden. She's only one witch and deserves to live a life that is hers alone. Maya seems to think Aster belongs to the coven, to the greater good, and treats her like an object to covet rather than a girl with her own destiny.

Had she treated me like an object? I hadn't noticed. She was my beloved grandmother, and I'd felt nothing but love and affection for her.

I read until my eyes betrayed me. Finally, I tore myself away and tucked the journal under the mattress. There was so much information to process. It was strange reading my mother's thoughts. I wondered whether she'd intended to destroy it at some point to avoid anyone else reading it. I can't imagine she ever intended for me to read it. It was cathartic to learn how conflicted she was about my magic, though. I'd somehow mistaken her fears for jealousy. There was comfort in knowing how much she cared and what she'd been willing to do to protect me.

For once, I slept well.

Chapter Twelve

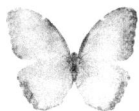

Knowing there was a secret to be revealed, Bonnie insisted on tagging along to Oglethorpe, which was fine, except for the constant complaints and demands for bathroom breaks along the way.

"Just you wait until you're pregnant," she huffed, climbing into the passenger's seat of the Beast after her third pitstop. Good thing there were plenty of trees between the hideout and Olive Branch because it seemed like she christened each and every one of them.

"I didn't say anything."

Her eyes turned to slits. "Your face did."

I shifted my focus to the road. "My face apologizes for whatever it said to you."

Behind me, Scarlet snickered. I was glad to have her as a buffer, even from the back seat. Bear and Tyson had agreed to do some maintenance around the hideout while the three of us ventured into the village to find out whether Hattie would make good on her promise to show me something helpful to atone for her role in the calamity demon debacle.

Olive Branch was still closed to customers when we

arrived, but the interior lights were on, illuminating Olive and Hattie inside. I knocked on the glass and waved.

"You have a restroom in here, right?" Bonnie asked, the moment Olive opened the door for us.

"I believe you've used it a few times before," Olive said.

"No need for sarcasm." Bonnie pushed past her and waddled in the direction of the restroom.

"Can I interest anyone in tea or baked goods?" Olive offered.

Scarlet raised a hand. "I'll take anything."

"Bonnie will, too," I said.

Olive smirked. "That's a given."

"Show them first," Hattie said cryptically. "They'll want to get started."

Get started on what?

Bonnie emerged from the restroom and joined us by the counter. "What's the big secret? I hope I didn't endure an uncomfortable ride for nothing."

Olive nodded to Hattie, who proceeded to roll up the rug behind the counter.

"Ta-da!" Hattie said.

I stared at the trapdoor. "Please don't tell me you're holding vampires in a dungeon."

"Nothing like that. Come on." Hattie tugged open the door.

I cut a glance at Bonnie. "You might want to stay up here."

Bonnie shuffled toward me with a stubborn look in her eye. "Hell no. I'm not getting left out. I want to see what's down there." She cast a hopeful look at Olive. "Is it a torture chamber?"

"Maybe some would consider it one. Depends on your interests." Olive handed me a flashlight. "There's no electricity down there, but I don't allow candles for reasons which we will become clear."

I passed the flashlight to Bonnie and descended the rudimentary staircase, careful to keep the light from my finger shining ahead of me. It would be far too easy to trip and break my neck on the narrow steps. There was no handrail, and I had to twist my feet slightly sideways so as not to lose my balance.

"Please be careful, Bonnie," I called over my shoulder. Her equilibrium was already off, thanks to her growing belly, and she'd been complaining about swollen feet recently. She was the poster child for abstinence in my opinion.

I arrived at a wall at the bottom and held up my hand to direct the light to the right. "You can't be serious," I said to no one in particular.

Books. Lots of them. There were shelves and tables overflowing with stacks that seemed to extend into eternity. I moved forward to make room for my companions. Each arrival held a flashlight, except for Olive who carried two large lanterns.

"It's a secret library," Hattie said, bubbling with enthusiasm.

"Gee, and here I thought it was a sandwich shop," Bonnie replied.

Olive placed one lantern on a table close to the bottom of the staircase and continued to hold the other one. "I've been storing these books for decades. I do my best to keep the damp from ruining the pages."

"If vampires knew about this place, they'd take a torch to it," Scarlet said.

Bonnie shushed her. "You can't say anything negative about our overlords, or Doran's girlfriend might get upset."

I glared at the pregnant werewolf.

Satisfied that she'd gotten under my skin, Bonnie turned her attention to other matters. "How is this going to help us?"

Only Bonnie would ask how books might help us in our quest for information.

"You're in need of research," Hattie explained. "We have information and lots of it."

She wasn't kidding. There had to be thousands of books down here.

Bonnie looked at me. "What are we looking for?"

"Start with dragons, and we'll go from there."

Olive laughed. "Dragons is a pretty broad category. Anything in particular?"

"How we can use the Ulunsuti stone to relocate the dragons without killing them is a good start," I replied. "Focus on Ustrina and Corniger dragons. Find out their preferred habitats." It would be best to send them somewhere they liked in order to discourage them from ever returning.

"I'll work on the crystal," Hattie offered. "I still have books with references that I haven't read yet."

"I'll focus on dragons then," Scarlet said.

"Information is power," Hattie said, "which is why the vampires don't want us to have access to it."

Scarlet opened a book in front of her. "In that case, Olive is the most powerful woman in The Wild."

A blush creeped into Olive's cheeks. "I wouldn't say that."

Bonnie held up a book with a torn dust jacket. "This one is good for when the bean is older."

"We're not shopping for the baby," I reminded her.

"All about you again," she huffed. "I should've known."

Hattie patted a pile of books. "I was so excited when Olive finally showed me this place. It was like every holiday rolled into one."

"I'll never get through organizing them on my own," Olive chimed in. "And I needed help from someone I could trust."

Hattie looked ready to burst with pride. "You can definitely trust me. I'd never tell anyone if it meant the books might be destroyed."

"There's also the small matter of Olive being executed," Scarlet said with an amused smile.

"Well, obviously I wouldn't want that either," Hattie said, "but look at all these books. Can you imagine losing so much information in one fell swoop?"

I stifled a laugh. Hattie's priorities were clear.

"If Lord Doran allows you to operate a used bookstore, why do you think he'd object to this?" Bonnie asked with a sweeping gesture.

"Because the bookstore is small and nonthreatening," Olive replied. "This, on the other hand, contains a wealth of knowledge."

"And the more we learn, the more likely we are to one day overthrow them," I added. One of these days, there'd be a rebellion the vampires couldn't quash.

We each claimed a space and started rifling through the books.

Bonnie stretched her back. "My feet hurt. I think I would've been happier on latrine duty."

I motioned to the steps. "You're welcome to leave."

"You said all hands on deck."

"I should've specified all *helpful* hands."

"Forget it. I'll keep looking." Bonnie cocked her head to read the titles on the spines.

We continued gathering our potential resources in silence. Eventually, Nike joined us and trotted daintily over the books like they were stones and the table was lava. The black cat didn't seem bothered by the presence of three werewolves.

I noticed Olive and Scarlet occasionally sneaking glances at each other and wondered whether there was interest brewing between them. I liked Olive, and she clearly had no issues mixing with supernaturals. She was smart, kind, and fiercely independent. She'd be a good match for Scarlet.

Hattie tapped the top of the first pile of books. "I flagged all the relevant pages in this stack. Want to see?"

"Not yet." I wanted to pull as many books as I could from the shelves before I settled at a table to review them.

"I think you're being overly ambitious," Bonnie said. "We'll never make it through all these in one day."

I flipped to an index and scanned the terms. "You're probably right, but..."

Bonnie groaned. "I know. Time is of the essence. You know, I pray for the day when time doesn't matter."

"You're about to give birth," I said. "I don't think you'll be experiencing that anytime soon."

Bonnie cradled her belly. "I don't know. Maybe time will stand still when I'm nursing my pup."

Hattie's gaze flicked to Bonnie's stomach, and I noticed the sadness in her eyes. She desperately wanted what Bonnie had. She was still young, and there was a good chance she'd meet someone every bit as worthy as Bear and build the life she craved.

"Find anything yet, Hattie?" I asked, hoping to redirect her focus.

"Nothing specific that would help us. The crystal can

do a lot of things but transporting an entire horde of dragons doesn't seem to be one of them."

"Then why go to all the trouble of getting it?" Bonnie grumbled.

"Yes, because you went to so much trouble, Bonnie," Scarlet shot back.

Olive leaned over Hattie's shoulder. "I think there's another way of looking at this passage. It says the crystal is a window into the past and future."

"Right, but we don't need a seer," I said.

Olive straightened. "A window doesn't just offer a view."

Scarlet's whole face brightened. "You can open it and climb through it."

Bonnie blew a stray hair from her eye. "Then why not call it a doorway?"

"These are often translated works," Olive explained. "The words won't be exactly right, which can alter the meaning slightly."

Hattie gaped at her employer. "You're telling us we can use the crystal to time travel?"

"I'm not sure. It might mean teleportation," Olive said. "The past and future might be poor interpretations of the text. The simplest explanations are often the right ones."

"In science, maybe, but magic seems way more complicated," Bonnie told her.

I was stuck on Olive's interpretation. "Does it say how to trigger its power?"

Hattie paused. "Nothing I can see."

What if I'd been wrong about the staff? What if the Ulunsuti stone had been responsible for teleporting us?

Another thought occurred to me. "If the crystal allows

the Uktena to teleport or time travel, then why didn't it use the stone to escape from us?"

"Could be there are limitations," Olive said. "I'll keep reading."

"Me, too," Hattie chimed in.

"Try to find out if only the one who possesses the crystal can use it, or if the possessor can teleport someone else." I'd managed to teleport Max along with me, so that fact seemed to suggest it was possible.

Hattie nodded. "Or a whole group of someone elses."

Scarlet tapped a page. "I've hit the mother lode. This book gives a list of known dragon species and their natural habitats."

"Is it post-Great Eruption, though?" Hattie asked. "Their habitats will have changed along with the environment."

Scarlet flipped to the copyright page. "It's a few years after the Great Eruption."

Which would've been when people were excited to discover the existence of dragons. It didn't surprise me that they would've gathered all the available information to disseminate it. Technology was unreliable at that point, and people had reverted to books again as their primary source of information. I wondered whether vampires in other regions were as antibook as the ones in The Wild. Maybe it was only House Nilsson.

"Hey, this one is blank." Bonnie sounded disgruntled by the absence of words.

"It's probably an unused journal," I said.

She frowned. "I don't think so. Seems too fancy. The cover is engraved and everything."

I abandoned my book and joined her at the other table. The black book was larger than most, and there were five circles embossed in gold on the cover. I picked it up and was immediately struck by its weight. Definitely heavier than a blank journal had any right to be. I flipped to the first page. The paper felt thicker and was creamier in color than the other books.

"This has to be something," I murmured. But what?

"Why make it so beautiful and then not write anything in it?" Bonnie asked.

The longer I held the book in my hands, the more I felt the low hum that seemed to build by the second.

"I don't think it's blank. I sense magic."

At the mention of magic, Olive wandered over to see the book. "It does seem too extraordinary to be useless, doesn't it?"

I concentrated on the book. I felt a push to unlock its secrets, as though it *wanted* to tell me everything it held between its covers.

"What kind of magic?" Scarlet asked from across the room. "Like a ward?"

I kept both hands on the book. "No, it doesn't want to keep me out. I think it wants to let me in." I just didn't know to access the information.

"Any idea where this book came from?" Scarlet asked.

Olive shook her head. "At the start of the Eternal Night when vampires started banning books and closing libraries here, villagers deposited their books in places designated as safe harbors. I know a lot of those books ended up here, but there's no telling where they came from originally unless it's written inside."

"Well, there's nothing written inside this one," Bonnie complained. "It would be nice if we could get it to work."

Hattie giggled. "It's a book. It doesn't 'work.'"

"Have you tried turning it off and turning it on again?"

Olive joked. Her cheeks colored. "Sorry, that's an old saying from before the Great Eruption."

But not necessarily a bad idea. I closed the book and pondered the beautiful cover. "Won't you be a good book and reveal your secrets?"

The book shimmered, and words took shape. "Codex of the Five Suns." So the gold circles on the cover were meant to be suns. Interesting.

The others crowded around me. "Open it," Hattie urged.

I opened the book to the first page. This time there was writing, although it was only the title page. I turned to the next page. It went straight to the text without a Table of Contents.

"Check for an index," Hattie insisted.

I flipped to the end. Sure enough, there was a detailed index. My gaze landed on the 'sun gods' entry, and my heart skipped a beat. Unfortunately, the list of page numbers indicated there were dozens of references throughout the book.

"If only it could show me the sun gods relevant to prophecies during the Eternal Night."

Hattie cast a speculative look at me. "Why would you want to know that?"

Suddenly, the pages began turning without my help. I watched them flip until they stopped in the middle of the book.

"Nice," Bonnie said. "What else can it do?" She leaned over and said, "Show us teleportation crystals."

The pages remained still.

"It's the Codex of the Five Suns," Hattie admonished her. "It won't know anything about crystals."

Bonnie shrugged. "Don't know unless you ask."

I smiled. It was nice to see Bonnie embracing a thirst for knowledge.

"I'm going to read this for a bit," I told everyone. "You can go back to your stacks, and I'll let you know if I find anything worth sharing."

I found a comfortable corner and nestled there with the book in my lap. I read about gods and goddesses I'd never heard of, as well as lands that no longer existed. Prophecies, however, were in abundance, and I wondered whether mine was among them.

"A lot of these prophecies involve the number three," I said to the others. "I thought the power of three was a witch thing."

"I think three is a special number in a lot of cultures," Olive said.

I rubbed my thumb along the edge of the page. "What about a triangle?"

"Three pointy ends. Equal sides if it's an equilateral triangle," Hattie interrupted. Olive and I turned to look at her, and she offered a sheepish grin. "What? I like geometry."

"Is there a prophecy that references a triangle with three women?" Poco had said that she saw important women in my life—women I hadn't met yet—as well as a triangle, and she specified that it wasn't a love triangle. Maybe it was the same prophecy my mother had referenced in her journal.

Hattie's eyebrows drew together. "That's a very specific question."

"I'm just curious." I didn't want to offer too much information, mainly because I had no idea how to interpret it. What if it was information I didn't want anybody to know, like I was part of a prophecy that would destroy the earth?

My grandmother destroyed a coven. Why not raise the bar? I wouldn't be a Goodfellow if I didn't excel.

"I thought we were supposed to be working on the dragon issue," Bonnie complained.

I peered at her over the top of the book. "And you are."

Grumbling, she returned her attention to the book in her hands. I waited until the others were engrossed in their own research tasks and whispered to the book. "Show me a prophecy with three women at its center."

The pages skimmed past me and landed on the blank page at the back.

"I'll take that as a no."

Hattie appeared beside me and interrupted my concentration. "Can we trade? That book seems far more interesting than the one I have."

"You should really work on your manipulation skills." I'd read enough of the codex for now. I passed the tome to her, and she handed me the book called *Monsters of the Underworld*.

Hattie skipped back to the table with the codex, and I dove into a chapter about the Uktena. The more I read, the more I agreed with Olive about her interpretation of the crystal's abilities.

Hattie's voice cut through the silence. "Ooh, this guy sounds cool."

"Does he sound cool in that he can help us, or cool as in he drives a fancy car and has plenty of fuel at his disposal?" Bonnie asked.

Hattie didn't seem to hear the question. She continued to read straight from the book. "He's a divine cobra named Uraeus."

"Interesting choice," I said. "Personally I would've gone with Snaky McSnakerson."

Hattie ignored me. "He protects Ra, the sun god, by destroying his foes."

"We could use a divine cobra," I remarked.

"Forget the cobra," Olive said. "We could use a sun god."

"Fair enough." I vacated my seat and joined Hattie at the table. "Is this part of the codex about sun gods?" The beginning seemed to include more general information.

"Sort of," Hattie said. "It's about the different phases the world will go through during its lifetime."

"Five suns?" Scarlet asked.

"How many have we gone through so far?" Bonnie interrupted. "Maybe this means we're due for another one."

Hattie shrugged. "I haven't gotten that far. I was too interested in the cobra."

I leaned over Hattie's shoulder and skimmed the passage. "Do we think this Uraeus is real?"

Hattie craned her neck to regard me. "Why not? Look at all the other creatures that sprang into existence. Why not a divine cobra?"

"If all these monsters are roaming the globe," Olive said, "then why aren't the deities? Shouldn't there be a host of gods and goddesses joining forces to bring back their beloved sun?"

"I've heard about minor gods and goddesses popping up in places," Scarlet said.

"Then where is Ra?" Olive asked. "Where are any of them?"

"Maybe if we found his cobra, we'd get an answer," Hattie said.

"I'd rather hunt for another creature," I said. "Isn't there a god with a protective raccoon or maybe a cute red panda?"

Hattie turned the page. "I can check the index." She let out a breath. "I swear the index is the best part of a book."

"Really?" Bonnie said. "I prefer The End."

"That's only because you didn't learn to read properly," Hattie said without glancing up from the book.

The color of Bonnie's cheeks deepened to a dark crimson. For a fleeting moment, I worried she'd resort to violence, but the mother-to-be simply waited a breath and said, "Maybe you could teach me. I'd like to be able to read to the bean when they're older."

You could've knocked me over with a hair from Bonnie's chin. I resisted the urge to sneak a peek at Hattie because I had no doubt she was equally stunned.

"I think that's a great idea," Olive interjected. "I have plenty of books you can borrow that would be ideal for learning. And they wouldn't bore you either."

Bonnie leaned an elbow on the table. "Good, because I lose interest pretty quickly if there aren't enough severed limbs."

"I hope you're not planning to pass that interest on to the kid," Scarlet said. "Maybe stick to nursery rhymes or whatever."

Bonnie grunted. "Are you kidding? Children's books are some of the most violent stories you can read. Have you ever read an old fairy tale?"

I nodded in agreement. "My grandmother used to read them to me and give me nightmares. Way more death and violence than you'd expect in a story featuring children. They were particularly unkind to witches. I remember asking her when I would start eating people."

Bonnie pounded a fist on the table in excitement. "Ooh, did you ever hear the story about the wolf that ate the little girl and her grandma? That could've been me eating you and your grandmother."

"And we blew down a bunch of houses when those poor pigs were trying to live in peace," Scarlet reminded us.

I laughed. "Okay, I guess your species didn't fare too well either."

"You were always portrayed as hideous," Olive said. "Unless you were trying to draw someone in for nefarious purposes, and then you'd make yourself attractive."

"I used to check for warts on my nose," I admitted. "I was obsessed with becoming ugly. I think I was seven when my grandmother finally told me to stop or she'd take the switch to my bottom."

Bonnie cast me a sly look. "I can think of two gentlemen who don't think you're remotely hideous, although there's no accounting for taste."

"I'd hardly call either one of them a gentleman," Hattie said. "One is the ruggedly handsome and powerful leader of the legendary Ghost Pack and the other one is a vampire."

I laughed. "I can see which one you favor."

"You have to admit," Scarlet said, "Max is objectively perfect."

"If only he had a perfect personality to match," I replied. "He acts like he's the god of The Wild."

"Because he basically is," Bonnie said. "He runs the show outside of vampire circles."

"He doesn't run *our* circle," I shot back.

"I don't know that we have a circle anymore," Bonnie said. "We're more of a pentagram."

"I guess we are." I didn't want to contemplate the demise of our crew. I knew between Hugo's death, Hattie's departure, and Bonnie's pregnancy, things would have to change, but I still wasn't ready.

Bonnie nudged me aside so she could view the codex. "What kind of bird is that supposed to be? Looks like a deranged chicken."

"I think it's a falcon," Hattie said.

My antennae shot up. "Show me."

Hattie pointed. The image did look more like a deranged chicken, but the one next to it made my pulse quicken. It looked very much like the image carved into the wall in the underworld.

"We're still in the section about Ra?" I asked.

"Yes, this chapter goes into more depth about his travels."

I edged Bonnie out of the way for a better view. "He had a flying chariot?"

"It was called a barque, but sure, chariot works."

I looked at her. "Are you mocking me, Hattie?"

She allowed herself a tiny smile. "Come on. It isn't every day I get to be smarter than you."

I clapped her on the shoulder. "Hattie, you're smarter than I am every day of the week and twice on Tuesdays."

Still smiling, she returned her attention to the book.

"I'd like to hear more about Ra," Bonnie interrupted. "He sounds like a badass."

"He was a sun god," Hattie continued.

Bonnie blew a raspberry. "No wonder he's gone. He's got nothing left to do in this world except watch the results of his failure. The guy had one job." She held up a finger. "One."

Hattie shot her a silencing look. "Ra would hop in his barque and travel from the underworld."

That made sense given where I found the weapons. I didn't see a chariot or a barque or any kind of godly transportation, though. If I had, I would've ridden that out of there instead of Max's bumpy back. Then again, if we'd realized the crystal doubled as a teleportation device, we could've used it sooner. Maybe the god had traded his chariot for a staff to move between realms. Or maybe Ra had nothing to do with the storage unit we found, although the evidence in favor of it was mounting.

"Does it mention his preferred weapons?" I asked.

Hattie heaved a sigh. "If you want to learn about him, you need to stop interrupting and let me finish."

Bonnie and I exchanged surprised glances and then burst into laughter.

"Our little girl is growing up," Bonnie remarked.

Hattie's scowl evaporated, and she continued her review. "During the day he rode the Mandjet, or the Boat of Millions of Years, and at night he rode the Mesektet."

"Wait, it's a boat?" Scarlet asked. "I thought it was a chariot."

Bonnie bristled with impatience. "Whatever. It's a vessel that glides through the sky. We get it. Continue, Hattie."

"When Ra traveled across the sky in the Boat of a Million Years, he brought light to the world."

"And then he'd swap vessels and travel through the underworld during nighttime?" Scarlet asked.

Hattie nodded. "He had to fight off monsters every night in order to return light to the world at daybreak."

Bonnie whistled. "What a thankless job."

"The divine cobra Uraeus protected Ra by destroying his opponents," Hattie continued.

"The opponents meaning the monsters in the underworld?" I asked.

Hattie shrugged. "I guess so."

"Now we know more about the cobra," Scarlet said.

Hattie followed a line with her finger. "His progress was viewed by some as his daily growth, death, and resurrection."

Bonnie squeezed next to her. "Does it say anything about weapons? How did he kill people? Dismemberment or more like Little Miss Sunshine over here?"

Hattie inched away from her. "Ra has also been associated with three parts of the day: Ra-Horakhty, the morning sun; the noonday sun where he's known as Amun; and the evening sun where he's called Atum. Each one is linked to primal life-giving energy. According to ancient Egyptians, Ra controlled the sky, earth, and underworld."

"The power of three," I murmured. Even ancient Egyptians put stock in the magical number.

"Unlike others, Ra is strictly a celestial god," Hattie continued. She flipped through the remainder of the chapter. "I don't see anything about weapons. Sorry."

"It isn't a definitive text," Olive interrupted. "There will be more information out there. We just might not have it in our makeshift library."

Hattie kept her gaze on the book. "What about Doran?"

The vampire's name grabbed my attention. "What about him?"

Her expression turned hopeful. "Do you think he might have access to more information about Ra?"

It wasn't a bad idea. He had agreed that we should help each other. Of course, he meant in terms of the dragons, not my personal quest.

"I think it's worth exploring," Hattie replied.

"I agree," Olive said, then just as quickly, "not that anybody asked. I know I'm not part of the crew."

Scarlet squeezed the woman's arm. "Of course you are,

Olive. Sometimes I feel like the entire human population of The Wild is part of our crew."

I didn't disagree. We wouldn't have endured as long as we had without their cooperation.

"He might," I said slowly. "I don't know."

If the celestial weapons belonged to Ra, then why was Max unable to take them? What did the Egyptian god have against werewolves?

"What is it, Aster?" Scarlet asked.

"Nothing. Just thinking." I didn't want to share too much about the weapons. I still felt uneasy about trusting them in light of the calamity demon debacle. I'd hidden the weapons under the mattress in my treehouse. Not the most creative hiding spot, but no one would have a reason to snoop, which was the reason I felt comfortable hiding my mother's journal there as well.

I ran my finger along the page, thinking. Max had been able to hold the weapons. I handed him the axe, and it didn't burn him or anything, but did he wield them? No, he turned furry and we escaped. I was the only one to wield the weapons. Maybe Max's joke about Excalibur wasn't that far off, although the measure couldn't be worthiness, or I wouldn't have been able to take them either. Still, there had to be a reason.

Scarlet sat across the table from me. "You look stumped."

I offered a weak smile. "I'm feeling ill-equipped to deal with life's big mysteries."

"I think we all feel that way on occasion," Olive piped up.

I chose to focus on what I could control—the research. "The falcon is an interesting choice. A phoenix would make more sense. At least that's associated with the sun and rebirth, like Ra."

"I can help with that one," Olive said. "Falcons were known for their strength, speed, and flying abilities. What better species to represent a sun god?"

Hattie bent over the text and read. "Ancient Egyptians even offered mummified falcons as gifts."

Bonnie cringed. "Don't even think about buying a mummified falcon for little Bonnie Bear. Hard pass."

Everybody laughed.

"What about crows?" I asked. "Are they related to Ra?"

"Probably just the underworld," Scarlet said.

So maybe the crows were protecting the underworld in general and not simply the celestial weapons. Made sense.

Olive held up a finger. "Actually, Hathor is associated with the crow."

"Who's that?" Bonnie asked.

"The Egyptian goddess of love, among other things," Olive replied. "She was also the protector of the dead."

That made even more sense.

By the time we left the secret library, my head was swimming with too much information. We now knew where the dragons belonged and what the crystal could do, although not exactly how to do it. More importantly, I learned I was a witch with no link to ancient Egypt, yet I seemed to have a connection to the weapons of their sun god.

Now I had to know why.

Chapter Thirteen

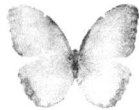

I used my three hours on watch duty to sift through the evidence Tyson and I had recovered from Tiffany's grave. I'd been so focused on the larger dragon issue that it was easy to forget about the rogue zombie. My instincts told me not to ignore our undead friend, though, so I decided now was a good time to listen.

We'd collected enough yew and mullein from the grave site to cast a locator spell, I just needed someone with the expertise to do it. Who better than a witch already in hiding? I was fairly certain I could retrace my steps to Patricia's invisible house, mainly because I'd made a point of noting a few landmarks when I left. In my experience, a powerful witch was ignored at your peril.

When Scarlet arrived to take over watch duty, I told her my plan.

"Are you sure you want to go by yourself? Maybe take Bear."

I slipped on my fingerless gloves. "I promised I wouldn't reveal her location to anyone." I wouldn't go so far as to say the witch and I had bonded, but I thought at the very least we'd reached an understanding. If I showed up with a burly werewolf by my side, she might misinterpret it as a threat.

"If she's that powerful, bring backup."

I held up my hands. "Don't worry. If things go sideways, the gloves will come off."

Scarlet smirked. "No pun intended."

I put on my golden cloak and chose an offering from our supplies that I thought would appeal to her. Then I loaded the quiver with arrows. I never knew who or what I might encounter in the forest.

It was fortunate that I knew The Wild as well as I did. That was the upside of spending the latter part of my youth hiding from rangers and exacting vigilante justice. I was able to retrace my steps to Patricia's hidden home without too much effort. This time, however, I gave the invisible door a polite knock instead of opening it.

"I know it's you," Patricia's voice called through the closed door. "What are you doing back here?"

"I need a favor."

"I thought we were already even."

"I brought an offering." It wasn't honey, but it would have to do.

The door opened, and Patricia ushered me inside. She wore a white smock and held a purple marker in her hand. "Quickly, before anyone sees you."

I snorted. "How much traffic do you think this part of the forest gets?"

"You're a wanted witch. Perhaps someone followed you." She ambled back to the kitchen counter, which was covered in sheets of paper. She appeared to be in the midst of a spell.

"No cookies today?"

"Unfortunately not." She placed the cap back on the

marker. "The cloaking spell is due for a touchup. It starts to weaken unless you give it a boost every now and again."

I noticed the same runes drawn on the sheets of paper. "I would think you'd know them by heart."

"I always practice them before I draw them on the house. You don't want to get one wrong and screw up the spell."

I lifted one of the sheets and studied the runes. "Do you think I could have this as bonus material?"

She looked me over. "What's the offering?"

I removed the three small pumpkins I'd shoved into my cloak pocket and set them on the counter.

Patricia nodded her approval. "What else do you need?"

I removed a small pouch from my other pocket and opened it for her.

She bent over and sniffed the contents. "Yew?"

"And mullein. Maybe something else too. I need to find the practitioner."

She took the pouch. "Easy peasy."

"How long will it take?"

"With all this content, it should only be a few minutes. Then you simply follow the bouncing ball." She compressed her lips. "Okay, it's more like a will o' the wisp, but there's no punchy saying for that."

I folded the sheet of paper and tucked it into my pocket. "Should I wait here?"

"Not necessary. If you start walking, it'll eventually make an appearance." I must've looked at her askance because she cackled. "No need to look so suspicious, my dear. I'm not playing you. After all, you know where I live."

True.

She handed me the purple marker, along with a blue-colored stone. "You'll need the marker for your runes. I assume art supplies aren't the kind of thing you have lying around in your treehouse."

"And the stone is to see the hidden object?"

"Good memory."

I slid the items into my pocket. "Thank you."

She shooed me away. "Off you get. This place isn't going to hide itself."

"Enjoy the pumpkins."

I left the house and started walking in the direction of the hideout, keeping an eye out for any signs of little glowing lights. After a few more steps, I realized I wasn't alone. I notched an arrow and aimed it at the darkness.

"You should know I rarely miss," I announced.

A familiar figure emerged from the trees, and I lowered my bow in a huff.

"Sorry," Bear said. "Scarlet told me to follow your trail but keep my distance."

"I could've shot you."

Grinning, he pointed a finger at me. "But the important thing is that you didn't."

In the distance, a faint light began to glow. "There it is!"

Bear turned to follow my gaze. "What is?"

"I need to follow that glowing fuzzball." I darted through the trees to catch up to it. Patricia wasn't exaggerating. The little burst of magic was reminiscent of a will o' the wisp.

Bear lumbered behind me. "Can I come?"

"You're here now. You might as well."

I kept my gaze firmly locked on the wisp for fear of losing sight of it. The blanket of darkness helped, but there were plenty of trees to block my view.

"Where is it taking us?" Bear asked, now keeping pace with me.

"Don't know yet. I'm tracking whoever released Tiffany from her grave."

Bear nodded. "Cool. I'm game."

The will o' the wisp picked up speed, prompting Bear and I to follow suit. My heart raced as I hurried after it.

The spell guided us to a comfortable house on the outskirts of Berthold. It shared the same charming Bavarian design as many of the buildings in the village, but this home was slightly larger than most. The will o' the wisp dissolved at the front door.

"This must be the place," Bear announced.

"Thanks, I kind of figured that out."

Before I could knock, Bear tapped my shoulder and pointed to the yard where a man was on his hands and knees, facing the opposite direction. He seemed to be gardening, judging from the way his backside would tip up and then back down again. Either that or yoga.

As we crept up behind him, I observed the patch of plants and vegetables. It didn't surprise me to learn that our necromancer was a wizard with earth magic.

I latched onto his shoulder and spun him toward us.

"I have permission," he practically shouted. "I can show you my license." He fumbled for his pockets.

"We're not vampires," I said.

He looked up at me with cold, dead eyes. Fish eyes, my grandmother would've called them.

"You're her," he said in a reverential voice.

"What's your name?"

He swallowed hard. "Burlington."

"Is that your first name or your last name?" Bear asked.

His gaze flicked nervously to the werewolf. "My first name is Gasper. Middle name is Beck."

"Gasper Beck Burlington." Bear grimaced. "Who saddled you with that one?"

Gasper's thin lips tightened. "They're all three family names."

No doubt. I wasn't familiar with any of them, though, so they hadn't been members of my coven.

"I found something that belongs to you," I said. "She was roaming around the forest, looking a little lost."

"Probably because she was in the wrong century," Bear added.

Gasper's eyes widened. "Where is she?"

"Gone," I told him.

He climbed to his feet. "Was she sentient?"

"Very much so." The tiny smile that followed my response unnerved me. "Gasper, you can't wake the dead."

"I believe I've already demonstrated that I can."

"Okay, you physically can, but you shouldn't. You need to stop and never do it again."

"Or what?"

I stared at him. "Are you fifteen? What do you mean or what?"

"What will you do if I refuse? Kill me? Somehow, I doubt that."

I tossed a glance at Bear that basically said *can you believe the stones on this guy?*

"You do know who this is, right?" Bear asked.

"The Hooded One." He grunted dismissively. "I expected her to be taller."

At least he didn't say he expected me to be a man. That would've stung.

"My name is Aster Goodfellow," I said, "and I've saved your ass more times than I care to count."

"Saved me from what?"

"Usually vampires," Bear interrupted. "This time, she's saving you from dragons."

He looked at me with renewed interest. "Is that what happened in Clayton? I heard the rumors, but I assumed they were false. What kind of dragons are they?"

"Does it matter?" Bear asked.

"I like dragons. I used to study them when I was a boy. I drew thousands of pictures of different types. Drove my mother to distraction with my endless questions about them."

I got the distinct impression this guy drove his mother batty even without the dragon obsession.

"Tell me something," I said. "How did you manage to get Tiffany's corpse to appear the way she looked when she died? Or was it some pre-Eternal Night chemical process?"

Another smile passed his lips. He was proud of this accomplishment, no doubt about it.

"I developed a spell that restores the corpse to its appearance at the time of death. The clothing she wore was the outfit she was buried in. Her hair was styled the same, too."

"Are you sure about that?" Bear asked. "Her hair was a couple inches above her head and solid as a rock."

"I believe that was due to a product called hairspray," the wizard replied.

Poor Tiffany. What a time to be alive.

"Why mess with the dead?" Bear demanded. "You have a license to perform earth magic and you risked it for a zombie?"

His eyes glinted in a way I disliked. "You didn't risk anything, did you? You knew you wouldn't get in trouble."

The wizard flinched. "I don't know what you're talking about. I took a calculated risk. Why do you think I traveled to the outer Wild to find my practice material?"

"Because it's remote, and that's the only place you could find a corpse that was intact," Bear shot back.

"Practice material?" I repeated, stunned by his clinical response. "Tiffany was a person."

"Hardly. She'd been dead since 1985." His eyes narrowed. "You're the reason I couldn't get back inside the cemetery, aren't you? I knew it wasn't anything I'd done!"

"You had permission," I said, continuing to unspool the thread I'd started, "but not from Lord Doran. That's why you went all the way to the outskirts of Poole. You were ordered to be discreet."

Gasper's fish eyes darted to the left. Gotcha.

"I went to Poole because that's where the cemetery is."

Uh-huh. "And you were pretty brazen, returning multiple times for your test subjects. You must have felt very confident you wouldn't be persecuted for your crimes."

The wizard folded his arms. "Nobody noticed until you went there, and that's only because Tiffany rose earlier than I expected."

"The average person doesn't scout The Wild," Tyson interjected, "but rangers do."

I didn't bother with the bow. I simply snatched an arrow from my quiver and jammed the tip in the side of his neck. Blood spurted from the wound.

"Is it poison?" he moaned.

"No, but while we're on the subject, I could use more sleeping potion for these babies." Hugo had left me high and dry in more ways than one.

"Let's play a game," Bear said. "You tell us who asked you to rouse the dead, and we'll tell you whether you're about to die a painful death."

Tears spilled from his eyes. "Can you at least pull it out so I can talk? It hurts."

I kept my grip on the arrow. "Who hired you?"

"No one, I swear," he whimpered. "It's my own form of pleasure. Some people read. I raise the dead."

Ever so slightly, I pushed the arrow deeper. An image flashed in my mind of Vincent Dufresne. The Master Inquisitor had tortured me in the White Fortress in an effort to learn more about my magic.

My body tensed. I didn't want to be anything like the ruthless vampire. I unstuck the arrow, and Gasper's hand clamped over the wound.

"Was it Lord Birney?" I asked. "Blink once for yes and two for no."

Gasper kept his eyes closed for a moment. Then he opened them and blinked once. "If you knew, why did you ask me?"

"Because I needed confirmation."

"You mean you can't go to Lord Doran with a hunch," Gasper said. "Is that your plan?"

"Never mind my plan." Digging a cloth from my pocket, I wiped the arrow clean and returned it the quiver. "It wasn't poisoned by the way. It's only a flesh wound."

Gasper exhaled with such force that I could smell onion and garlic on his breath. Delightful.

"Did Birney tell you why he wants you to reanimate corpses?" I asked, although I was more interested in why he'd hidden the information from Lord Doran.

"Of course not. He compensated me for my work, that's all. There was no discussion of future plans."

"Did he say anything indirectly that might reveal his intentions?" I pressed.

Gasper snatched the cloth from my hand and held it over his wound. "I was more interested in the necromancy itself. I find the whole thing fascinating."

I figured if I appealed to his curious nature, I might get more information. "What did you learn from your experiments that surprised you?"

His eyes sparked with inner light. "I'm so glad you asked. The dead can be imbued with qualities they didn't formerly possess."

"Like juggling?" Bear asked.

Gasper's brow furrowed. "I suppose." He shifted his gaze back to me. "If you're interested in speaking to someone special, I can arrange it for you. Surely someone in your position has burning questions to ask a loved one."

An image of my grandmother blazed in my mind. "You know that's not possible. We burn bodies now."

"If you know where their ashes are, I might be able to help you—in exchange for your silence, of course."

I stared at him. "You're telling me you can lord power over ashes?" I'd never heard of a necromancer with that kind of prowess.

"It's neither easy nor reliable, but I have a method."

I wasn't sure I wanted the details. "It doesn't matter anyway. Her ashes are gone." We'd sprinkled them in the river and watched them float away. "How about this? I'll take a bottle of sleeping potion in exchange for my silence." If he could wake the dead, no doubt he could put the living to sleep.

Gasper's eyes rounded. "You won't reveal what I've done?"

"I won't mention your name, as long as you promise not to do it again."

He nodded exuberantly. "I'll say my experiment was a failure, and I'll give you a sleeping potion. Just don't tell Lord Doran about me."

Bear answered before I had a chance. "We don't owe Lord Doran anything. We have a deal."

I decided to test Patricia's runes by drawing them all over my black cloak. I figured if the spell failed, the purple marker would barely be visible against the dark material anyway, so I wouldn't ruin a perfectly good cloak for nothing. There was, of course, the small matter of using the runes to sneak into Lord Doran's private home. If I failed, I'd have a lot more to worry about than a ruined cloak.

Thanks to Bear, I'd promised Gasper Beck Burlington that I wouldn't reveal his name. What I didn't promise, however, was not to tell Doran about Birney's secret scheme. I figured his lordship would be more willing to share his books with me if I could offer something worthwhile in return. Birney's employment of a necromancer seemed like a worthy trade to me.

With my hood drawn, I ventured closer to the house. There were a few rangers within view, but they were engaged in a game of croquet on the grounds at the side of the house. Once again, I envied the life of a breezy, carefree vampire.

I slipped through the front door and considered my options. A member of staff walked toward me, and my whole body tensed. The vampire passed by me without a glance. Even then, it took another minute to relax. I stalked through the house, peering in rooms for any sign of Lord

Doran. I found him in his study at the back of the house and took a moment to observe him. The vampire sat behind a desk, looking fairly miserable as he reviewed a stack of paperwork. So it wasn't all fun and games in a vampire's life. Good to know.

Slowly, I closed the door and locked it behind me. The vampire was too absorbed in his documents to notice. I climbed on top of the desk and notched an arrow, taking aim at his crotch. "Call for help and I promise to put you in excruciating pain."

"Hello to you, too, Miss Goodfellow," he said, maintaining a neutral expression. "I know some vampires have the power of invisibility, but why can't I see you?"

"Consider it an extra layer of security."

"I feel deprived. I like looking at you."

"Suffering is universal."

His mouth quirked, but he said nothing.

"What have you done for Clayton since our last meeting?"

He cocked his head. "Is that the reason you're here? To discuss restoration on behalf of Clayton?"

"I'd like to know the people won't be homeless for much longer."

"I'm sure you can offer them a few tips." His eyebrows knitted together. "Apologies. That was cruel."

Lord Doran was apologizing for an insult? I couldn't decide whether to be pleased by his sensitivity or insulted that he thought I couldn't handle it.

"I've acquired information that might interest you," I continued.

He leaned back against his chair and placed his hands behind his head. Lord Casual. "I'm listening."

"Birney is up to something."

"Birney is always up to something." He waved a dismissive hand. "You can lower your bow and arrow, assuming you even have them. We both know the real weapon is attached to you."

Obliging, I climbed down from the desk and perched on the edge of it. "And we both know I don't want to resort to using magic."

"Why not show yourself?"

"To keep your rangers from spotting me when you summon them."

He raised his hands. "I have no interest in summoning rangers or anyone else. Truth be told, I enjoy our private meetings. Makes me feel special."

"You're the thegn. Of course you're special."

"Is that the only reason?"

I ignored the question. "Whatever Birney's up to involves necromancy."

Laughter rumbled from his chest. "Necromancy? What the devil is he doing that would require walking corpses?"

"No idea, but I met one of them in the woods. Couldn't get rid of her until we beheaded her."

"Perhaps he's in the market for a corpse bride."

"Knowing Birney, I doubt it. He went to a lot of trouble. He specifically hired a wizard to raise the dead."

Doran frowned. "Where is he digging up bodies?"

"There was a cemetery outside Poole, but that one is no longer accessible to him."

"I see." He seemed to ponder the information. "You didn't happen to visit any other cemeteries, did you?"

"No, I figured I'd leave that up to you and your rangers."

"You mean rangers that should've noticed activity in a forgotten cemetery?" His expression darkened. "Any idea how far he's gotten with his plan?"

I shook my head. "A quick tour of the other cemeteries should give you a sense of it, although you should know that many of the empty graves near Poole were failed experiments."

"And the wizard?"

"Swears he won't do it again."

"And you believe him?"

"We may have struck a bargain."

He tilted his head. "Does that bargain involve your current invisibility?"

"Different bargain."

He smiled. "You're a very busy witch."

"Always."

"Perhaps you should consider a vacation."

"That's a luxury I can't afford."

Despite my invisibility, he looked directly at me. "Where would you go if you could?"

The question caught me off guard. "Anywhere?"

"Anywhere. Any time or place. Tell me something you've always longed to do for the sake of it."

There was something about being physically hidden from him, yet speaking so personally, that created a strange sense of intimacy between us.

"If time and space were no issue?"

"Whatever you like. I've always wanted to see the aurora borealis. Did you know The Wild was one of the best places to view them before the Great Eruption?"

I cocked an eyebrow. "Pretty lights in the sky don't really sound up your alley."

"You think you know my alley? That's presumptuous." Despite his words, he didn't actually seem bothered. "It started as a dream of my son's. When he died, I made it my own."

His honesty and vulnerability stunned me into silence.

"I've seen pictures in books, but it's hard to imagine what it would look like in person. Painted fire in the sky." He glanced upward as though envisioning it. "My wife was the artist in the family, and our son was picking up a few of her talents. He drew countless pictures of the northern lights." Doran shook his head in amazement. "You would think he'd witnessed them firsthand. So much detail."

"People thought they were magic."

He wore a vague smile. "For all we know, they were."

"What happened to your family?" Part of me didn't want to know the details. Doran didn't deserve my sympathy, yet the pain I sometimes saw reflected in his eyes suggested someone who still mourned. And that I understood.

"There was an altercation with wolves a few days prior to the incident. I intervened. Two of them were executed. I thought the matter had been resolved." He shook his head. "I was wrong."

"Why target your family and not you?"

"They thought they were targeting me. I was called away at the last minute and left them until the next day. When I returned, they'd been..." His voice broke. "Torn to pieces, along with the guards in the house. If I'd been there like I was meant to be..." He trailed off, giving his head a small shake.

"You can't blame yourself. Even if you'd been there, they still might have killed all of you. In fact, I have no doubt they would have."

"But at least I could've been there at the end. We would've been together."

"Is that why you have an interest in the arts? Because of your wife and son?" According to reports, he'd spent money to restore museums and other venues, although it was mainly for the benefit of vampires. The average person couldn't afford them.

A pained look crossed his rugged features. "It is. I continue to support the arts in their memories."

Maybe Lord Doran wasn't the monster we all believed him to be. "And what is it that interests you?"

His head lifted slightly as though my question had dragged him back to the present. He didn't look unhappy to be here.

My gaze locked on his fangs, and I wondered how they'd feel against my bare skin. I shook off the thought as quickly as it entered my mind.

"I would like to experience Fairbanks as it was before the Eternal Night. To venture out during the day in winter and enjoy the Celebration of Lights. There would be a lighted tree and fireworks. I've considered reviving events like that."

"What's stopping you?"

He lowered his gaze. "I thought my son would enjoy them the way I once did. After he died, I suppose my enthusiasm waned."

"That's completely understandable." I paused. "It isn't too late, you know. You could always test the waters with a summer solstice festival or a Celebration of Lights festival."

The vampire drummed his fingers on the desk. "I suppose I could." He angled his head, as though able to see me, and for a moment, I'd forgotten that he couldn't. "You haven't answered my question."

"I'd like to be with my family. I don't care where we are as long as we're together. My parents and my father's parents."

"Not your mother's?"

"I never knew them, but I was very close to my father's mother."

"Maya."

"Yes," I said quietly. I cleared my throat in an effort to change the direction of the conversation. "I was hoping for something in return for my Birney intel."

"And what's that?"

"Books."

He chuckled.

"I'm glad you find it amusing."

"I expected weapons, or maybe food for the poor."

"We're all poor except vampires."

His eyes sharpened. "Why books?"

"I'd like information on the Egyptian sun god called Ra."

"That's very specific."

"I'm a history buff," I lied. "That's an area where I'm deficient."

"I'll have the books sent to you. Just tell me where."

I laughed. "You're very funny."

His expression changed. "Show yourself, Aster. I want to see you."

Despite my better judgment, I lowered my hood to reveal my face. "What will you do about Birney? Report him to King Stefan?"

"Birney has always held the king's ear, whereas I've been nothing but a distant hum. For all I know, he's been telling the king I'm to blame for his recent injuries and the king has given permission to remove me from office."

"If that were the case, I doubt he'd be going about it in such a roundabout way. Maybe he did ask and the king denied his request, so he's going rogue. He can always tell the king you died at the hands of the Hooded One." I held up my hands and wiggled my fingers.

With preternatural speed, Doran reached for my hand and tugged me forward. He gazed at me with a mixture of desire and tenderness.

"I can't," I said, almost too quiet to hear with my own ears.

"Can't what?"

"You know what."

"Why can't you say it?"

"Because that would make it real." And there was no reality where Doran and I made sense together.

"Trust me, Aster. You are real to me either way, and so is the way I feel about you."

My throat thickened. "Stop."

"Why?"

"Don't make me say it." I didn't even want to think about it, let alone say the word out loud.

He rose to his feet, towering over me so that his tall body dwarfed my own. "Is it the purge?"

I looked up at him. "I can never get past what you did."

"What I did," he repeated.

"Yes." Despite my growing suspicion that my grandmother wasn't the saint I believed her to be, I still couldn't let Doran off the hook for her death and the destruction of my coven. It was a bridge too far.

"The world isn't black and white, Aster."

"No, it's pretty much black."

His mouth curved slightly. "I don't suppose you could be persuaded to look on the bright side of life either."

"I don't know why people still use that expression. There is no bright side."

"That's not true. There's you," he said. "You're the bright side."

"I'm surprised that would appeal to you."

He edged closer. "You appeal to me for other reasons. I didn't expect to feel anything for someone again." The muscle in his cheek twitched. "For you."

I flattened a hand against his broad chest to keep him at bay. "This is exactly what I'm talking about. When I look at you, I see the vampire responsible for the murder of my grandmother and countless others. I see the reason I lost my family and my home."

He flinched. "I know what it's like to lose a family."

"Then how could you do that to someone else?"

"I would've stopped it if I could."

"You're the thegn, Doran. You could've stopped it, but more importantly, you never should've started it."

I felt the powerful muscle twitch and yanked my hand away from his chest.

"I understand how you feel. Believe me."

I did believe him, and that's what made this moment so much harder than it should've been.

He took a step backward. "I'll see what I can do about the books. I have access to resources that you don't; it seems only fair I should offer them to you given all you do for The Wild."

I jostled the hood of my cloak. "I'm the Hooded One, remember? Not your associate."

"I know exactly who you are." He stared at me with such intensity—it seemed as though he was capable of devouring not only my flesh and blood, but my very soul. "Thank you for telling me about the necromancy. I know your group must've debated whether to share that information with me."

"I didn't tell them I was coming," I admitted. "They'd never forgive me."

His lips curved in a sad smile. "Do you think you could ever forgive me?"

I drew backward and lifted my hood. "Even if I could, today is not that day."

Chapter Fourteen

I spent the next day drawing runes on our treehouses and carving a reveal rune into five stones, one for each of us. Just because we'd never been discovered before didn't mean there wouldn't be a first time. If Birney was up to something, it was best to take precautions now that we had the means to do so.

After lunch, I retreated to my treehouse for some alone time. Today was supposed to be a day of deep reflection that I tended to ignore. Reflection usually meant dredging up bad memories. My mother's journal, however, had made me think differently about today. Her words chipped away at my armor, and I found my resistance weakening.

I closed the journal and slid it back under my mattress. Once again, I had to force myself to stop reading. As much as I enjoyed the glimpse inside my mother's head, it was also hard to process all those thoughts and emotions. So far, there were no more details about the prophecy. What I did read, however, reminded me how important it was to trust your family, even when they disappointed you. If I was handing out second chances, I might as well start with my crew.

I retrieved the bag from beneath the mattress and slung it over my shoulder. I found the crew gathered by the campfire and tossed the bag on the ground next to them.

"What's that?" Bonnie asked.

Bear bent over and picked up the axe that poked out from the bag. "These are some fancy weapons. Who'd you steal them from?"

"Ra, the sun god, apparently."

Four heads turned to stare at me.

"I think I might need details," Bear said.

"Max and I discovered them in the underworld after we'd taken the crystal from the Uktena. I thought the staff teleported us back to the Beast from underwater, but now I'm not sure."

Scarlet frowned. "You think it might have been the crystal?"

I nodded.

Bonnie struggled to her feet. "I want to see."

Bear rooted through the weapons and retrieved the staff for her.

"Why didn't you tell us?" Tyson asked.

"Because when I got back, you'd unleashed the calamity demon. I wasn't feeling generous with information."

Bear passed the axe to Tyson. "Then why tell us now?"

"It's Samhain."

Tyson's nose wrinkled. "What's that?"

"Samhain. It was an important time for my coven, and I decided to honor it by honoring you."

Tyson nodded, as though expecting my answer. "I mean, as long as you're honoring me, I wouldn't object to a steak."

"Isn't it also when the veil between the world of the living and the dead was believed to be at its thinnest?" Bear asked.

"It is."

"Before the purge, what did you do to celebrate?" Bear asked. "Was this the kind of thing where you danced naked under the full moon?" He shot a quick look at Bonnie. "Not that I'm imagining it or anything."

To my relief, Bonnie took the remark in stride and laughed. "I'd like to know, too. Maybe it's something we can celebrate with the bean next year."

Scarlet leaned over and whispered, "I like this Bonnie. Can we keep her?"

I clasped my hands in my lap. "The coven would spend the time in self-reflection, and we would acknowledge our flaws. Look for ways to improve in the year ahead. We'd write down an element of our life we wanted to change, like a habit we wanted to break."

Bonnie's head bobbed enthusiastically. "Sounds good. Let's do it."

I nearly choked on my own saliva. "Excuse me?"

"Vampires have ruined enough good things. No reason to let them have self-reflection on top of everything else."

Bear grinned at her. "Go on then, Bon. Tell us your flaws."

To my complete and utter shock, she seemed to consider the directive. "Well," she said after a lengthy pause. "I could stand to be more patient when dealing with others less capable than I am."

"Okay," Tyson said, drawing out the word. "Anything else?"

"I tend to leap before I look and make assumptions that turn out to be untrue." Her gaze met mine, and I knew she was referring to her jealousy over my friendship with Bear. She'd always been possessive of him, but her insecurities ramped up to a solid ten when I was involved. To be fair, even that personality quirk seemed to have calmed in recent weeks.

We continued around the campfire naming our flaws that we wanted to improve upon. It was a bonding moment I didn't realized I needed until it happened. The recent acts of disloyalty melted away against this backdrop of friendship and solidarity.

"Now we should honor the dead," I announced, once we'd finished.

"How do we that?" Scarlet asked.

I contemplated my meager possessions. There were no photos to place on an altar. We'd have to wing it.

"They don't show up, do they?" Tyson asked. "I don't think we need ghosts on top of a zombie."

"You don't actually summon your ancestors. You remember them as a show of respect," I explained.

Gazing at the circle of my friends, I felt a sense of peace. I may not have a coven anymore, or a family related by blood, but I had a family I'd created, and that was worth celebrating. I remembered Poco and her 'found family.' At the time I'd been uncertain of my crew, but all those fears had washed away in the days that followed. It was as though Hugo's betrayal and subsequent death had altered the dynamics between us. The unfortunate events showed us what we truly meant to each other.

"Thanks for sharing this with me," I said. "It means a lot."

Scarlet smiled. "It's nice. I agree with Bonnie. I think we should do it every year."

Bonnie patted her burgeoning belly. "Next year we'll

have a walking, babbling pup joining us. It'll be a good opportunity to teach this kid the names of our ancestors."

Bear lifted the staff from the pile of weapons. "I feel like this one would make an excellent spit over the fire."

Bonnie reached over and snatched the staff from him. "This is a celestial weapon, you giant nutball. You don't want it anywhere near a fire. Who knows what might happen?" She turned the staff over, appearing to examine every inch. "Aster, are you sure this thing belonged to a god? It looks so basic. Other than the glow you saw, there's literally nothing special about it."

Bear nudged her shoulder. "I agree. Any god worth his salt would've decorated it with glitter and pretty gemstones."

"I don't see what purpose it serves," Tyson added. "Would a god really need a walking aid?"

"I don't know. He rode everywhere in a chariot, so maybe he did need help," I said.

Bonnie studied the top end of the staff. "There's a notch here."

"And what? You'd like to see how a ruby looks there?" Bear teased.

Bonnie's eyes grew wide. "Not a ruby." She swiveled toward me. "But what about the crystal?"

"We need the crystal for more important things than sprucing up an old stick," Tyson admonished her.

Bonnie shook the staff at him. "I'm not trying to beautify it anymore. I'm solving our dragon problem."

Tyson eyed her closely. "How?"

Bonnie turned back to me. "Aster, can I please have the crystal? I'd like to check something."

Having just gone through a ritual that strengthened our bond, it seemed disingenuous to refuse her. I reached into my pocket and produced the crystal from the buckskin pouch. "Please be careful. We need it for the dragons."

"No kidding. Why do you think I want it?" Bonnie made thoughtful noises as she lodged the crystal inside the notch. The staff began to glow with a pale yellow light that reflected the crystal, causing Bonnie to nearly drop the staff.

"By the gods," Tyson said under his breath.

"Did the staff glow like that when you used it?" Bear asked me.

"No, but it was underwater, and I wasn't expecting it to do anything. It did glow a bit when I found it, but not yellow. I think it was white."

"The yellow is the same shade as the crystal," Scarlet said. "It seems to be taking on the crystal's power."

"You said Ra was a sun god, right?" Bonnie asked.

I nodded. "Egyptian."

"By itself, the crystal might only be able to teleport a couple dragons, but I bet we can harness the god's power to amplify the magic, or whatever you'd call it, so that it encompasses all the dragons," Bonnie said.

Scarlet contemplated the stick. "You think the staff acts as an amplifier?"

"You saw the way its color reflected the crystal's," Bonnie pointed out.

I gazed at the staff. "Bonnie, you're a genius."

Bonnie attempted to bow, but stopped halfway, wincing. "Too inflexible now."

"But don't we want to send the dragons to their respective homes?" Scarlet asked. "It won't be a single destination."

I remembered how I'd inadvertently activated the teleportation power the first time. "No, but I think I can control that part." As long as I focus on sending the right dragons to the right locations when I hold the staff, it should work.

Scarlet bolted upright. "Someone's coming."

Tyson scented the air. "I'll check it out." The werewolf disappeared from the circle and returned a few minutes later with a young man on a bicycle.

I straightened. "Marcus, what's wrong?"

"Something's happening," he said between heavy breaths.

Bonnie polished a potato on her chest and bit into it. "That's vague and unhelpful," she said, crunching.

"There's a horde..."

I tensed. "Dragons?"

"No." His brow rippled with confusion. "I think they might be zombies."

Tyson swore. "That lying son of a bitch," he tacked on at the end.

The necromancer had told us just enough to send us away. Clever.

"It's Samhain," I said, feeling like a grade A moron. "His power will be at its peak now."

This was meant to be a night for remembrance, a time to honor the loved ones we'd lost as well as our ancestors. It didn't surprise me that Birney intended to twist such a solemn occasion to suit his own purposes.

"I don't get it. He's not summoning spirits," Tyson said. "He only wants the bodies."

"It'll maximize his power over the bodies, though," I explained. "Where are they headed?"

"Hard to tell," Marcus replied. "I thought it was one of the villages, but they bypassed Whitehead, which means the next stop is Klondike." He tugged his ear. "But that doesn't make sense, does it?"

"It does, actually." I sprang to my feet. I had to warn Doran. "How fast are they moving?"

"Well, they're walking corpses, so not very fast. You can pick up their trail easily enough. They reek like hell, and a few of them have lost limbs along the way."

Scarlet grimaced. "Lovely."

"We'll take the Beast," I said.

"How much damage can they do?" Bonnie asked. "They're dead."

"They're freakishly strong," Bear said.

"And they'll keep coming unless you behead them," Tyson said. "Trust me, they can do a lot of damage if you don't figure it out fast enough."

The zombies would reach Doran unless we got to them first. That must've been Birney's plan all along. I had to stop them.

"If they're headed to Klondike, who cares?" Bonnie asked, her mouth full of potato. "Let the vampires deal with them. It isn't like they'd be racing to our rescue."

"It's called being the bigger person," Bear told her. He leaned down and kissed her cheek.

"We're not people. We're wolves."

"You can stay here," I said. "I'm going to stop the zombies." Not a sentence I ever thought I'd utter.

"Can I take the axe?" Tyson asked, eyeing the celestial weapon still on the ground.

Bear gave me a pointed look. "Axes are great for beheading. Just saying."

"Take anything we can use for beheading," I agreed.

Scarlet nodded at the staff. "Maybe you can teleport them back to their graves."

"They'd just climb back out again," Tyson said. "We need to kill them all."

Bonnie perked up at the mention of killing. "I'll come." She tossed the remainder of her potato into the fire. Nobody tried to dissuade her.

"Thank you, Marcus," I said.

"I can come, too," he said. "I have my bike."

"Your parents would never speak to me again if I put you in harm's way. Go home and stay safe."

He didn't argue. Instead, he told me the exact location where he'd seen them, so we could intercept them before they reached Klondike.

I left my longbow behind this time. My arrows would be useless against the undead. I withdrew the celestial sword and brandished it in the air.

"To the zombie apocalypse!"

Scarlet stayed behind, much to her disappointment. The four of us piled into the Beast and took off. Marcus's instructions were spot on. We parked the 4x4 and ran to block the path that led to Klondike.

The zombies were dressed in a range of styles, although I spotted at least one undead that also looked to have died in the 1980s. I would've died, too, if I had to wear my hair in a side ponytail.

At the back of the horde, I spotted a man in a black mask with red stripes. Even in the darkness, I could see the gently curved horns that emanated from the top of the mask.

Gasper.

"Hold them off," I ordered.

"Wait, where are you going?" Tyson called.

But I was already running.

Gasper may have been truthful about the spell, but he'd withheld the part about a mask. I'd bet all the silver in The

Wild that the mask was the source of his power, which was the reason he failed to mention it. I should've known the wizard wasn't skilled enough to master a spell of this magnitude without primordial help. I had no doubt Birney had procured the mask for him, and Isobel might even have acquired it during her travels.

The source of the mask wasn't important right now, though. Its destruction was the priority.

I knew the precise moment Gasper spotted me in the crowd. His shoulders stiffened, and he shuffled backward, although I suspected he had to stay within a certain range of the zombies or risk losing his power over them.

I pushed my way through the throng of undead bodies, pausing momentarily for a closer look at one corpse in a blue suit made of crushed velvet.

Gasper decided to try his luck with a bit of acting and started to drag his feet like the zombies. He seemed to think I'd be fooled into believing he was part of the horde rather than its master.

I shoved two more zombies aside and reached the wizard. I didn't bother to greet him. I simply grabbed the mask and yanked it off his face.

"No!" He tried to reclaim it, but I threw it to the ground and crushed it with the heel of my boot.

The corpses crumbled to dust.

"No fair!" Bonnie yelled.

Gasper fell to his knees in tears. "Why would you do that? Do you know how valuable that mask is?"

"I don't care what it's worth. I care what it's being used for."

The wizard gazed at me in wonder. "Why would you want to protect him? He's a vampire."

"And why would you want to do the bidding of a vampire?"

"I was paid handsomely. What do you get out of it?"

"Integrity."

Gasper offered a weak laugh. "In a world like this one, who cares about integrity?"

"That's the problem. It's in short supply, yet greatly needed."

Gasper started to collect the broken pieces of the mask. "Maybe there's a spell that can repair it."

"I'm not getting through to you, am I?" I stepped on his hand as he reached for another piece. "The mask is no longer in your possession."

Gasper made a whimpering sound. "Do you have any idea what they'll do to me when they learn that I've failed?"

"That's what happens when you make a deal with the devil, Gasper." I used my boot to drag the pieces toward me.

"Do we just leave their remains?" Tyson asked, jogging over to us.

"The dust blends in."

Tyson contemplated the ground. "How are you going to convince Doran that this was intended for him? Maybe we should've let them get closer to Klondike before we stopped them."

"I don't need a giant display to persuade him." He'd listen to me—at least I thought he would.

I hoped he would.

Gasper remained on his knees, staring at the remnants of his failed project. "You have to protect me. If they find me, they'll drain me alive. Birney said so."

"Maybe you should've considered that before you opted to do their dirty work," Tyson told the wizard.

Gasper clasped my hand. "Please. Isn't there anything you can do? You spoke of integrity. Shouldn't that extend to those of us who've made mistakes?"

"Your mistakes are littering the ground in front of us," Tyson snapped.

I quieted Tyson with a look. "We don't have a protection program, but we do need magic users."

Tyson's face reddened. "You can't be serious."

"Gasper's proven he's more than capable."

"I'm very capable." His grip on my hand tightened. "I beg you to get me out of here before they find me."

I looked him in the eye. "We'll hide you if we have your word that you'll help us with a few potions."

"We have what we need, and it isn't him," Tyson insisted.

"Hugo left a hole in our magical supplies. Gasper can help."

Bear rushed toward us. "Never mind that. We need to go. Rangers are on their way."

Gasper's eyes widened. "I'll do anything! Take me with you."

Bear frowned at the wizard. "Why would we do that?"

I hauled Gasper to his feet. "We're not taking him to the hideout, but I have another idea in mind."

We stuffed him between us in the vehicle and drove like mad to the outskirts of the village.

"What is this place?" Gasper asked. His nose scrunched. "Is this *a barn*?"

"It's the former workshop of two cobblers," I said. "It's a quiet space where you can contemplate your poor life choices until we give you information for your next assignment."

The wizard tried to poke his head outside, but I clawed his face and pushed his head back inside. "You'll have everything you need in here. If you value your life, you'll stay put until we tell you otherwise."

"What about food?"

"We'll have it delivered. The only thing you need to worry about is staying alive."

Gasper turned to assess the interior. "I suppose it does have a homely feel to it. What about tracking, though?"

"Between the stench of the zombies and the wolves, they won't be able to pick your scent out of the crowd," Tyson assured him. "Vampires aren't as skilled in that department as we are."

"But if the vampires start knocking on doors, they'll find me. They're very thorough."

I held up a purple marker. "I have a fail-safe."

Gasper frowned. "You're going to draw?"

"On the outside of the barn. The runes will hide the building from anyone who doesn't possess a particular stone."

"Shouldn't I get a stone so I can find my way back here?" Gasper asked.

"No, because you're not allowed to leave, remember? If I give you a stone, you'll be tempted to go walkabout."

Gasper nodded slowly, as though still trying to process his current situation. "Will I get access to my materials?"

"When the time is right, you'll have what you need," I said. "In the meantime, lay low and don't let anyone see you."

Tyson gestured to the equipment. "Might be a good opportunity to learn a new skill. I understand the village is in need of a new cobbler."

"What happened to the previous one?"

"Two," Tyson corrected him. "They got sick, but the Green Death is over. If you die, it'll be…"

I cut him off. No need to frighten the wizard any more than he already was. "Just stay put, Gasper. We'll be in touch."

Chapter Fifteen

Donning my rune-covered cloak, I returned to Lord Doran's house early the next day to tell him about the thwarted zombie apocalypse, as well as our plan to relocate the dragons without bloodshed. I also wanted the books he'd promised.

Instead of his study, I found the imposing vampire in the living room. He sat on a worn leather chair with his boot-clad feet propped up on a footrest and an open book spread across his lap. He looked surprisingly domestic.

I removed the hood and unhooked my cloak to reveal my presence.

Doran simply glanced up from his book and smiled. "I have the materials you requested. As a matter of fact, I was enjoying one of them myself." He tapped the book on his lap. "Thought I'd learn a little about your friend, Ra." Carrying the book under his arm, he crossed the room to retrieve a bag on the coffee table. "The rest are in here."

"Thank you. We have a plan to deal with the dragons, if you're interested."

"Without killing them?"

I nodded. "What will you tell the king when he decides it's time to wrangle them for his own purposes?"

"Leave that part to me. It's the least I can do."

"You're welcome to do more. The Ghost Pack will be helping us execute the plan. There's always room for one more." In reality, the wolves would act as backup in case our plan backfired and we had to run for the hills.

Doran slipped the book he'd been reading into the bag. "It sounds like my presence won't be necessary." As he passed the bag to me, our fingers brushed. The unexpected contact jolted me, and I jerked the bag toward me, prompting a vague smile from him. "And the zombie situation?"

"No longer an issue, but you should know there was a giant swarm of them headed here yesterday."

"Yes, I'm aware. My rangers spotted you fighting them and left you to it."

"How heroic of them."

"They assumed if they joined the fray that you'd end up fighting each other, and I've expressly forbidden it."

That got my attention. "You have?"

"You're not to be harmed or touched in any way. That's a direct order from me."

My natural defiance kicked in, inching up my chin. "I don't need your protection."

His expression darkened. "And I didn't ask for your opinion on the subject. I've simply decided it's in The Wild's best interest to keep you alive. Nothing more."

"I think it's you that needs protection. In case you haven't figured it out yet, those zombies were intended for you. Birney assumed you wouldn't know how to kill them.

In light of Hugo's recent actions, it would be easy enough for him to pin the blame on a wayward wizard if things went south and you survived."

Footsteps drew our attention to the entryway where Lord John Birney himself entered the room. He wore a floor-length fur coat and sported the magical glasses that Isobel had mentioned.

Doran instinctively positioned himself between us. I would've laughed if I weren't so thrown by Birney's sudden appearance.

"John," Doran said carefully. "I wasn't expecting you."

"Clearly. Otherwise, I doubt you'd be consorting with my mortal enemy." He wiggled the frames. "Yes, I can see you, my dear."

"For what it's worth, I didn't mean to blind you."

Doran shot me a quizzical look. "He tried to murder you, yet you're apologizing to him for defending yourself?"

Birney spoke before I had a chance to respond. "Oh, little witch, I should thank you for the gift you bestowed upon me." He removed his glasses. "A vampire's other senses are heightened when his vision is taken from him. I wouldn't have learned that without your contribution."

"Then why bother with the glasses?" I asked.

He bared his fangs. "Because I like to see my food before I taste it. A pity you didn't kill me when you had the chance."

"And stoop to your level? No thanks. I want to affect change without causing death and destruction."

"The two most useful weapons in your arsenal when you're extinguishing the flames of rebellion." Returning his glasses to the bridge of his nose, he turned his smirk to Doran. "Ask me how I know."

Birney wanted to provoke me. Nice try.

"Residents keep rebelling to express their dissatisfaction with your leadership. Maybe if you took time to listen to the complaints, they wouldn't feel the need to resort to violence."

"Name a complaint," Birney demanded.

Doran pivoted to face me. "Yes, I'd like to hear more."

"No fair trials for nonvampires. You can execute us on the spot without repercussions. I can present you with a whole list of items if you're genuinely interested." At least sixty of them, in fact.

"You're kissing the wrong ass, my dear," Birney cut in. "Today I intend to declare myself Protector of The Wild and take over this one's duties." He inclined his head toward Doran. "Under my care, the Forgotten Land will thrive and flourish as it should."

Doran barked a laugh. "And how do you expect to do that?"

"Kill you and declare a state of emergency. The king will approve it, of course. He'd have no reason to suspect foul play."

"You've basically had your sight restored," I said. "Don't you want to travel again? Why tether yourself to a place you loathe?"

Birney spread his fur-covered arms. "What makes you think I loathe it here? Women, booze, gambling. Plenty of distractions from the reality of our situation."

"And what situation is that?" I asked.

"That we've been relegated to the worst prison in the world, and most of you don't even realize you're inmates." He shrugged off the coat and tossed it over the back of a chair. "It's warm in here. Must be the delicious company getting my blood pumping."

Doran observed Birney with a blank expression.

Despite The Wild's history with Doran, my gut told me we'd be worse off without him. Birney was the kind of vampire capable of turning neighbor against neighbor, playing on their fears and using them as weapons. Out of the frying pan and into the blazing hot fire.

"I should kill you both where you stand and be done with it," I declared. "Neither one of you deserves control of The Wild. You've proven yourselves equally poor caretakers."

Birney's mocking laughter filled the room. "And here I thought you two had become close friends."

I recoiled. "I could never be friends with the vampire who murdered my grandmother and half my coven. I tolerate him out of necessity."

Birney made a noise of delighted surprise. "Ouch, Doran. How does it feel to hear such vitriol from a woman you so clearly desire? Did you think you'd finally found love again after your dearly departed wife?"

A low growl emanated from Doran. "Mind your tongue, Birney, or you'll find it shoved in a very uncomfortable place."

"Go ahead and kill him," I told Birney. "I'd rather have you in charge than the vampire that destroyed my life."

Birney performed a mock belly laugh. "Do you truly believe Doran was capable of such carnage? My darling bloodsicle, Doran doesn't have the stomach for the hard work. That's why he's been a thegn as long as he has. He doesn't have what it takes to rise up the ranks. Why do you think the king is so fond of me? I take care of the difficult messes in the Outer Territories, and he can look the other way. He considers anyone west of Minneapolis to be savages anyway."

My head felt dizzy. Doran wasn't responsible for the

purge? Why didn't he tell me the truth when he had the chance?

Doran uncuffed his sleeves and rolled them to his elbows, revealing a set of powerful forearms. "The king appointed me to The Wild because he trusts my judgment in all matters. He keeps you visiting one spot after another because he knows you're incapable of an honest day's work."

The vampires glowered at each other.

Birney let loose a shrill whistle, and rangers flooded the room. A quick glance at Doran showed his shock.

"Michaels? Fullerton?"

The rangers ignored him and joined Birney across the room.

"While you've been busy befriending outlaws, I've been gaining the loyalty of your men." Birney clucked his tongue. "It seems they enjoy a good time in a gambling house as much as I do."

He'd won the rangers over with poker and booze? It figured. Good riddance to them as far as I was concerned, although I could see why Doran might feel differently about the situation.

"And what do you plan to do? Have my own rangers kill me?" Doran asked.

A sickening realization wound its way through my system. I looked at Doran. "The day your family was killed, you said you were called away at the last minute and that's why you weren't there during the attack. Who was it that called you away?"

Doran blinked. "It was Birney." He turned to the earl. "You were drunk at a poker game and out of money. You needed me to bail you out."

Birney clucked his tongue. "Such a tragedy."

"Why?" Doran's voice cracked.

"Your wife was in my way. She had too much influence over you. The king's budget for The Wild is so very limited, yet she had you spending money on the arts." Birney grimaced. "Such a waste."

Rage painted Doran's face. "And now you've decided I'm an obstacle, too?"

"Times change. Needs change. I think the good people of The Wild will enjoy the spectacle. The public execution of their former oppressor, and his mistress who traded their safety for love."

Birney had already prepared a narrative to present to the people. Unbelievable.

"I'd hoped to accomplish it with zombies so that I could present an alibi to the king, but desperate times call for desperate measures."

"You seem to be forgetting about the dragon problem," I said. "Kill me now, and you'll be dead when the dragons burn this place to the ground."

His upper lip stretched and curled, streaking his face with an eerie malevolence. "Why do you think I chose now to strike? You've all been so preoccupied by the dragons that you failed to see the real threat right in front of you."

Doran exposed his fangs. "You don't care about The Wild. You only care about power."

Birney threw his head back and laughed with unbridled glee. "What else is there, my boy? Power grants you access to all the good things in our immortal lives. Why not be a god among men?"

I was struck by their different outlooks. All this time I believed Doran only cared about himself. Even knowing what happened to his family, I thought his grief had caused him to turn his gaze inward and remain there.

But I was wrong.

Doran cared about The Wild and its inhabitants. The presence of dragons concerned him because he recognized the danger they presented to everyone. None of it mattered to Birney. If all the villages in The Wild were brought to ruin, he'd simply enslave people to rebuild them.

"I can kill you and your rangers right here and now." One quick movement—the simple raise of a hand—and I could obliterate them all.

"But you won't," Birney said with smug satisfaction. "You already said as much. You want to be better than me, but instead you'll be dead."

"Your zombie army failed, and now you think a few rangers will be able to accomplish a task they've failed to do for years?" I shook my head. "You're either very optimistic or very stupid."

"The necromancer was a poor choice, I agree. He lacked the skills, as well as the discretion." Birney smiled. "Which is why he'll be buried along with his failed experiments."

"Good luck finding him," I shot back, although my insides twisted at the thought of Gasper in peril because of me.

My concern must've shown on my face because Birney said, "Doesn't feel good, does it? To be responsible for ending the life of another."

"If that's your attitude, then why do it?"

He dusted off his sleeves. "Oh, it isn't *my* attitude. That's a weakness I simply don't possess."

"It isn't a weakness to have compassion."

He eyed me with amusement. "Are you sure about that, pet? After all, I'm the one in charge, and you're the one about to die."

Doran jumped on the nearest ranger, and I sprang into action. My movements were a blur as I notched arrow after arrow tipped in Gasper's sleeping potion. I hit the rangers in quick succession, and they fell to the floor. I avoided the rangers currently in Doran's double headlock. I didn't want to risk putting the thegn to sleep. The arrow meant for Birney only skimmed his shoulder as he ducked. Before I could reload, he pounced. I used the arrow to knock off his glasses, and his fangs sank into my arm. They sliced through the fabric of my cloak and pierced the skin. Blood trickled from the wound.

Birney inhaled, his chest expanding. "I don't need to see you when I can smell you, pet. One of the most glorious scents in the world. Fresh, metallic, and full of delicious magic."

I opened my hand and aimed it at Birney's heart. "Let there be light," I said. Maybe I was capable of revenge after all.

Doran appeared between us like a mountain between two rocks. He grabbed Birney by the neck and squeezed. At first I thought he was trying to asphyxiate the earl. Then his fingers curled tighter, prompting Birney's tongue to slide between his lips, and I understood.

"You might not want to watch this," Doran said through clenched teeth.

No, I didn't. As much as I wanted Birney to die, this was more brutal than anything I was capable of.

I turned to face the wall. I heard the sound of bone crunching, followed by a pop. I remained rooted to the floor until I felt Doran's hand clasp mine.

"Let's go," he said.

He slung the strap for the bag of books over his shoulder and guided me from the room. Neither of us spoke.

"What will you tell the king?" I asked, once we were alone. "If you blame another group, the king will seek revenge."

"I won't allow that. I'll take his body to the river where it will never be found. I'll tell the king Birney was attacked by dragons."

"Your rangers won't tell?"

"No," he said darkly.

I didn't want to know the details. My heartbeat finally slowed its frantic pace. I was glad the earl was dead. I only wished I'd been the one to kill him. "I'm sorry it was you."

"I'm not. You didn't want to lower yourself to his level." He shrugged. "I'm already there."

Except he wasn't. Not really.

I lifted my face to his. "Why didn't you tell me you weren't responsible for the purge?"

His eyes fixed on me, and heat flared in those gold flecks. "Would you have believed me?"

I didn't know how to answer him. Maybe? But probably not.

"Birney ordered the execution of the entire coven. He did it without my knowledge or consent. By the time I learned what was happening, the damage was underway."

"Even Isobel told me it was you."

"The only reason you and the other members of your coven survived was because I put a stop to the slaughter. When I asked the king for money to rebuild your coven, he refused. Agreed with Birney that you deserved your fate."

My mouth opened, but I couldn't seem to form words. All this time, I thought Doran was a hypocrite. The type of vampire who grieved his murdered family for decades yet ordered the same treatment of his enemies. The truth, I now knew, was very different.

"For what it's worth, I'm sorry about what happened to your grandmother and your coven. It wasn't right."

A lump formed in my throat. "She would've killed you, you know."

"Still, the retaliation was brutal and inhumane. It never should've happened."

"Thank you," I whispered. His apology meant more than I could express. Vampires didn't apologize. They did what they wanted and expected you to accept the consequences of their actions without complaint. But Doran wasn't like other vampires, at least any others I'd met. His leadership role had been constantly undermined by Birney.

That wouldn't be a problem anymore.

When we arrived at the barn, blood had been splashed across the runes, and the doors were wide open. There was no need for the reveal stone. It seemed that Patricia had sold us out to Birney before his death.

I sprinted through the open doorway to find Gasper seated at the table. As the wizard had anticipated, his attackers had drained his body of blood. On the table in front of him, a shoe without a sole was turned on its side.

"Looks like he decided to learn a new skill after all," Tyson said.

I felt a pang of guilt. I believed Birney's death would prevent him from murdering Gasper, but it seemed the earl had been one step ahead of me.

"I promised to protect him."

What good was talk of integrity when I failed to demonstrate it? The wizard might have been better off finding his own hiding place. Instead, I'd forced him to remain here.

"This isn't your fault, Aster. The wizard chose his path, and he paid the price for it. That's not on you."

"How long ago?" I asked.

Tyson leaned forward and sniffed the body. "Very recent. Bonnie was here a few hours ago, and he was perfectly fine. Even asked for one of Rita's pies from the pub."

I continued to stare at the wizard's lifeless body. "Did she get it for him?"

"She did."

I nodded. "Good. Will you help me build a pyre?"

Tyson looked around the barn. "I see a few pieces of wood we can use. I'll get it started."

"Thanks."

He picked up a spare wooden beam that rested on the floor at the base of the wall. "What about the witch?"

"I don't think we'll see Patricia again."

"A new hideout?"

I shook my head. "A new land." She was too smart to stay in The Wild after her betrayal. I wondered what she'd received in return for her treachery, not that it mattered. Deep down I knew I couldn't trust her; I just really wanted to. Patricia had sold her soul when she traded another's life for her own ill-gotten gain.

The werewolf gathered the materials and vacated the barn, leaving me alone with Gasper's body.

"I'm sorry I failed you, Gasper," I whispered. "That wasn't my intention."

The wizard knew, just as I did, that we all did what we felt was necessary for survival. Despite my revered status, I was no saint. I'd stolen more times than I could count. I'd wounded vampires. I'd blinded Birney, and I'd been willing to kill him out of anger. Under my leadership, my crew had killed vampires and werewolves alike, as well as a few horses—unsanctioned by me, the same way the death of my grandmother had been unsanctioned by Doran.

But that didn't change the fact that they were still dead, and no necromancer on earth could bring them back.

Chapter Sixteen

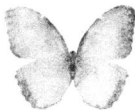

I sat in my treehouse with the celestial staff across my lap and focused on the Ulunsuti stone. With thoughts of my coven weighing heavily on my mind, I was curious to see whether the crystal could also act as a window to the past as the book suggested.

I conjured a memory of my grandmother to help the crystal along. She and I stood in the clearing where I liked to practice archery. Adjusting my shoulders, she critiqued my stance for what was likely the hundredth time. My deadly accuracy was all thanks to her incessant reminders. There were so many reasons I was grateful to her—I couldn't begin to count them all. I'd forgotten how youthful she was. Never a crone. 'A seasoned maiden,' she'd call herself and laugh.

Another image slid into place—this one unfamiliar. My grandmother entered a room filled with a dozen witches and wizards, and I felt as though I was right there with her. I recognized each one of them, as well as the location. It was the ritual room, where the coven stored objects used in our annual celebrations and events, including Samhain. It was a strange location for a meeting, though, as most coven rituals occurred in the great outdoors.

"We need Aster if we expect to win," Luther said, pounding his fist on the table.

"Absolutely not," my grandmother replied hotly. "I told you before she's off-limits."

"Then we should call off the attack," Luther said. "We're not powerful enough on our own."

"She's a child," Kendra interjected. "I don't care how powerful she might be, I agree with Maya—we don't use children as foot soldiers."

Sweet Kendra. Stern Luther. All gone. I could point the finger at Birney and let hatred burn in my heart, but they all knew what they were doing. They'd attacked Klondike with the full knowledge that the odds were stacked against them.

"Aster's fate lies elsewhere," my grandmother said cryptically.

"Aster's fate lies with her coven," Melanie insisted. "What's the point of possessing so much power if we don't use it to defend ourselves?"

"Except we won't be defending ourselves," Kendra countered. "This time we'll be on the attack."

"A rebellion has been brewing for years, you know this," my grandmother said. "Now is the time to strike."

Luther pivoted to face her. "You know something," he accused. "Why not tell us instead of leaving us in the dark?"

My grandmother hesitated. "I had Helen tug on a thread I uncovered. I'm not willing to divulge more than that."

"Aster is destined for greatness," Kendra said, "of that I have no doubt. The gods don't grant a gift like hers unless they intend for her to play a major role in events."

"She isn't Jason organizing her Argonauts," Garrison

sniffed. The wizard hadn't liked me. I recalled his sharp tone whenever he said my name. His permanent scowl had earned him the nickname 'Frowny Face' amongst the children in the coven. Needless to say, we weren't the most creative group.

My grandmother splayed her hands on the table. "Enough about Aster. We're here to discuss our plans, which I've made clear do not include her."

"And Helen agrees with your assessment?" Luther pressed.

My grandmother nodded. "She couldn't see as clearly as she would've liked, but she believes our actions right now, regardless of the outcome, are necessary to Aster's later success."

"Success at what?" Garrison demanded.

My grandmother regarded him coolly. "Bringing back the sun, of course."

I dropped the staff on the floor of the treehouse. My heart racing, I retrieved the staff and checked that the crystal was still lodged in place.

My grandmother's actions during the rebellion hadn't been the result of arrogance or anger. They'd been a calculated risk in connection with the prophecy about me. Death. Destruction. In her mind, they were necessary steps in order to put me on the path to literal enlightenment.

The question was—did it work?

I had no idea.

Still clutching the staff, I climbed down the ladder to join the rest of my crew. There was one crisis left on this week's agenda, and I was anxious to get it over with. We'd been fortunate there hadn't been another attack on a village so far, but we all knew it was only a matter of time before a few dragons decided to stray from the flock and leave destruction in their wake. Also, given the king's interest in them, there'd be royal soldiers showing up any day now to collect a couple specimens. We had to act before that happened.

We'd arranged to meet the Ghost Pack at the canyon. I carried the staff and monitored my words and thoughts carefully to avoid teleporting somewhere inconvenient. I had no clue how sensitive the stone and staff were, so I figured it was best not to recite proverbs such as 'the road to hell is paved with good intentions,' or else I might find myself on a more dangerous path than this one—and that was saying something.

Max was already at the top of the cliff when we arrived, flanked by Ina and Lavonne. He motioned to me, indicating he wanted a private audience with me before we began.

"Maybe he's going to ask you to join the pack," Tyson whispered.

I shot him a silencing look as I joined Max out of earshot of the group.

Max immediately zeroed in on the crystal. "You prettied up the staff."

"It's part of the plan."

"To distract the dragons with shiny objects?" He shrugged. "It works for cats. Why not dragons?"

I shook my head. "You're an ass."

He smacked his backside. "No, I have an ass. A very nice one, in fact. I'm sure you've noticed it."

"Speaking of asses, Birney's dead."

He lifted an eyebrow. "You?"

"Doran."

Max offered a grunt of approval. "Would've been more poetic to sacrifice him to the dragons, but I'll take what I can get."

"I invited the thegn to join us, but he respectfully declined."

"Because you'd be working with our pack?"

"He didn't specify."

"Well, it isn't like we need his help when we've got magic." Max cast a speculative look at the canyon. "What's the plan now, commander?"

"The White Wolf is asking me? I thought you were large and in charge."

His mouth opened, and I braced myself for an inappropriate retort.

"If it isn't the White Wolf himself," a voice interrupted.

I turned to see Doran standing behind me. "You changed your mind."

The vampire's gaze remained pinned on Max. "Upon reflection, I thought it best to be present. I can see the benefits of working collaboratively in light of recent regime changes."

"I'd hardly call Birney's removal a regime change," Max countered.

I stepped in front of Max to block the vampire's view of him. "I think that's a great idea. Thank you." I pivoted to face Max, whose face remained cool and impassive. "Right, Max?"

I might've stepped on his foot. Hard.

"Yes, I agree," Max said, albeit reluctantly. "Collaboration over annihilation. That's my motto."

Despite their words, the werewolf and the vampire continued to size each other up. I could tell this collaboration wouldn't be easy. It was, however, a step in the right direction. Today, dragons. Tomorrow, The Wild.

I adopted my sternest look. "Can we put a pin in any grievances? The dragons are waiting."

They abandoned the staring contest. Mission accomplished.

"Tell me more about the plan," Doran said.

"If the staff and crystal work together the way we envision, then the dragons will be relocated without the use of force," I explained.

He narrowed his eyes. "All of them?"

"Yes."

Doran scratched the back of his neck. "So they float into the air and we hope a stiff wind blows them to their next destination?"

"It's more of a mass transit situation," I told him.

Doran shook his head, appearing mildly amused. "Just be sure not to send the casual observers along with them."

I carried the staff to the edge of the canyon, checking on the Ulunsuti stone every so often to ensure it was still there. I was anxious about losing the crystal at the pivotal moment. No one would ever be able to forgive me because we'd all be dead.

"Tell me again about Plan B," Bonnie said as I threaded my way through the gathering of wolves. We'd encouraged Bonnie to stay at the hideout, as though that might actually happen. The werewolf had threatened us all with bodily harm if we mentioned her condition one more time. I didn't always like her, but it was hard not to respect her.

"Aster is our backup. She'll fight fire with fire," Tyson said.

I gave a weary sigh. He and I had been over this multiple times already. "First, it isn't fire; it's light. Second, the goal isn't to fight. We want a peaceful transition." The alternative was too dangerous.

"What we want is a dragon-free zone," Bear said.

I held up the staff as I pushed my way to the edge of the cliff. "Ask and you shall receive."

The view was the same as before—a dozen different species all mixing and mingling like one big, dysfunctional dragon family. Like us. They had their Hugo, and we had ours. Admittedly their Hugo caused far more death and damage, but that didn't mean the rest of them deserved to die.

I peered at their silhouettes in an effort to identify the leaders of the pack. They were the ones I intended to target. Of course, there was always the chance the leaders would fight back against the perceived threat before I had time to activate the stone.

I backed away slowly to update the team. "I'm ready. I don't think they noticed me."

"Even that one?" Bear pointed behind me.

I turned just as a massive red dragon emerged from the shadows on the other side of the canyon. Its serpentine body and ribbonlike scales distinguished it from the other dragons we'd identified.

"Well, that's unfortunate," I said.

Bear shrugged. "You know what they say about the best-laid plans."

"Is Jacob here?" I asked. I hadn't noticed him in the crowd, although his presence had been requested for precisely this reason.

"I'm here." The old man used his wooden cane to tap the wolves aside and let him pass.

"Please tell us it's a harmless species," Bear said. "Maybe draco maximus puppykus." He cut a quick glance at Doran. "That wasn't actual Latin, you know."

Jacob gazed at the serpentine dragon in wonder. "I can't

believe it. It's a viper. They're based in Asia. I'm not sure why it would've come all this way."

I observed the red dragon as it sailed down toward the horde. Its body rippled like a line of flags in a breeze. "I think it's a solo. I didn't notice any others like it." And they'd be hard to miss.

Max waltzed over. "Does this screw up the plan?"

"Not necessarily. It just means I need a minute to get up to speed." I turned back to Jacob. "Is there anything I need to know?"

His face scrunched as he tried to conjure more dragon facts. "They fly without wings."

"Sort of observed that one already," I said. "Where in Asia should I send him?"

Jacob tugged his ear, thinking. "Is China still there?"

I bit back a smile. "As far as I know."

"What? It's a fair question," Jacob said. "The world isn't what it used to be."

"Never is," Tyson agreed.

Jacob inclined his head toward the viper. "Anywhere in China should do the trick." As I turned to face the canyon, he added, "Oh, and that species is a little bit psychic."

Bonnie frowned. "Is that like being a little bit pregnant? Because I can assure, there's no such thing."

Doran stared intently at the old man. "Define psychic."

"It can influence other dragons without vocalizations." Jacob's brow wrinkled as he continued to concentrate. "It's like the cuckoo bird. It takes over the territory of other dragons through deceptive practices and ends up in charge of them."

"Maybe this dragon is the reason they all ended up here," Tyson suggested.

"Yes, but why here?" I asked. "If the viper isn't even

from this continent, why lead an entire horde to this particular place?"

Max joined me at the cliff's edge. "Maybe he's the last of his kind and he's been roaming the globe searching for others like him. The other dragons are his adopted pack."

There was a note of compassion in his voice I hadn't heard before.

"If that's the case, do we even want to separate them?" Scarlet asked.

"I don't know." The presence of the viper was definitely a wrinkle I hadn't anticipated.

Max snarled. "I vote they stay together."

I rubbed my temples. "Okay. If we keep them together as a group, where do I send them?" Where was enough space so the huge horde didn't end up encroaching on someone else's village?

"Mount Gongga," Jacob piped up. "Sichuan province, China."

"Are you sure?" I asked.

"Yes. It's the Daxue Shan mountain range, between two rivers, Dadu and Yalong. People evacuated during the Great Eruption, and no one ever returned." Jacob's eyes sparkled with satisfaction. "By the gods, I love when my brain actually works."

Tyson clapped him on the shoulder. "So do we, friend."

"I wonder if the fact that the viper is psychic means it'll be resistant to magic," Doran mused.

I heaved a sigh. Always something. "There's only one way to find out." I looked at Max. "Are you ready?"

He cracked his neck. "Back up, people. Give the White Wolf space to work."

I resisted the urge to roll my eyes. Max was putting his life on the line for this when he could've simply walked away. If he wanted to be an arrogant asshat in the process, then so be it.

He waited until he had sufficient room, and then the beast from within exploded. Bones bent, broke, and reformed. Fur spread across his body like a wave on the sand at high tide.

He wasn't kidding about needing space. Max was tall, but the White Wolf was massive. A howl tore from his throat. So much for our quiet entrance.

I peered down at the dragons to see whether the sound had registered. Only one dragon was looking in our direction. Unfortunately, it was the one whose attention we least wanted to attract.

From the depths of the canyon, the viper stared at us. Nobody moved. I was fairly certain nobody breathed.

The red dragon surged toward us, unleashing a blood-curdling shriek.

I climbed on the wolf's back and kicked my heels against his sides, spurring him into action. He ventured down the side of the cliff, and I clung to him, keeping my eyes pinned on the dragon. My fingers gripped the staff.

Any second now.

When the full expanse of the canyon came into view, I thrust the staff into the air, and activated the Ulunsuti stone. It took a moment for the dragon to spot the shiny object, and I held my breath again, awaiting a reaction.

The dragon's body undulated as it hovered in midair. It seemed temporarily mesmerized by the sight of the crystal. I couldn't tell if the response was good or bad.

Hundreds of dragons lifted their heads and turned to regard us.

Okay, it was bad. Very, very bad.

A collective sound erupted from the basin, piercing my

ears and shaking loose stones from the canyon walls. A chill ripped through my body when I realized that every dragon below now seemed to be focused on us. The red dragon's head swung away from us, and it seemed to be communicating telepathically with the rest of the horde.

I imagined the directive wouldn't take long to convey —*kill* was only one word, after all.

The dragons charged. They moved like a block of rock that had been carved from the same mountain.

Squeezing the staff, I raised it higher and focused on the location in China.

My hand began to glow. No, no, no. Not now.

The light from my hand filtered through the crystal and emanated yellow rays. In a matter of seconds, the entire canyon was bathed in simulated sunlight. The dragons slowed their ascent. Their heads turned left and right, signaling their confusion. The light seemed to be disrupting the red dragon's psychic connection.

The dragons grew quiet. Some hovered while others returned to the basin. The red dragon remained between us and the horde. It, too, appeared bewildered, except the confusion had angered it. When its gaze settled on me, an earsplitting shriek followed.

My heels squeezed against the wolf's body, spurring him onward. As I held the staff aloft with the crystal aimed at the dragons, I concentrated on Mount Gongga, Sichuan province, China.

The viper was only ten feet away now. Any closer and we'd be swallowed whole. Light poured from the staff, growing so bold and bright that I could no longer see. I closed my eyes to avoid the intensity of the light. Max must've suffered from the same issue because he lost his balance, and we started to skid. I clenched the staff as we toppled over. My shoulder smashed against a jagged rock, and I cried out.

When I opened my eyes, the canyon was dark and the viper was gone.

All the dragons were gone.

Max was on his side, still in wolf form. I crawled across the rocks to reach him. Blood stuck to his white fur, and I noticed a gash on his leg.

I stroked his soft fur. "Can you stand?" I hoped he could because there was no way I could carry him. I peered at the cliff's edge where our friends were gathered. The climb would be perilous, but I had to try.

A piece of thin material slid down the side of the canyon, and I realized it was a set of bungee cords tied together to form one long rope. My crew to the rescue.

I created a harness with the end of the cord and attached it to the White Wolf. The others began to pull from the top end. Slowly, the wolf was lifted up the canyon wall. I waited patiently for my turn and enjoyed the silence of the canyon. Much of The Wild was quiet, but this was on another level. I started to understand the dragons' attraction to this place. The canyon offered solitude and peace. I hoped China was even better for them.

It was an uncomfortable ride to the top, and I grit my teeth most of the way. By the time I reached the others, Max was already back in human form and wrapped in a blanket with Lavonne tending to his wounds. I passed the staff to Tyson as Scarlet checked me for injuries.

Doran stared at me with an inscrutable expression. "It's as though you harnessed the power of the sun itself."

I looked down at my hands. "It wasn't just me," I insisted. "The staff and the stone..."

Max ambled over to join us. "It was incredible. I've

never seen anything like it, and believe me, I've seen some shit."

Doran pivoted to face him. "I'm a vampire. I've seen far more than you could imagine."

I didn't have the strength to elbow them. "It isn't a contest."

"The crystal and staff are a dangerous combo," Max said. "If they fell into the wrong hands, the results would be catastrophic."

"Which is precisely why I'm holding on to them," I said.

"Aster's more dangerous than either one of those things," Doran argued.

"Well, the only thing I'm falling into now is my bed," I said, in an effort to reduce the tension. "Crisis averted."

Doran observed me. "As much as I appreciate what you did for The Wild, there's too much power concentrated in your hands."

Max barked a laugh. "I knew you'd turn on her."

The vampire sneered at him. "I'm not turning on her. I simply think it's too risky to leave so many powerful objects in one place."

"No need to resolve this now," Scarlet intervened. "For now, we should be happy with today's outcome. This easily could've gone another way."

"And we didn't kill each other. Bonus." Tyson held up his hand for a fist bump. He quickly lowered it again when he realized there were no takers.

"I think we all know where the real concentration of power is," Max countered. "Why don't you and your kind spread the wealth a little, then maybe Aster will consider doing the same?"

"Aster's been spreading my wealth for years," Doran said with a vague smile.

Max had the right idea. We finally possessed bargaining chips. It would be foolish not to use them to our advantage.

I faced Doran. "Promise you'll rebuild Clayton."

"The king..."

I shook my head. "Forget the king. I'll give you the crystal."

Bear and Tyson objected in unison. I held up a hand to silence them.

"Use the money from the sale of the crystal to fund the restoration," I continued.

"You want the crystal to be sold to the highest bidder, which means vampires," Tyson said heatedly. "We can't turn over a powerful stone like that."

"The crystal isn't that powerful on its own," I argued. "It's mainly a teleportation device." There was also a good chance someone with malicious intent would be unable to activate the crystal. I kept that part quiet; I was ruthless enough to want Doran to fetch a good price for it.

"Portal witches are expensive and not readily available here," Doran said. "Teleportation will be enough of a draw."

"We also have a list of demands. Those you can present to the king."

"Sixty-three of them," Scarlet interrupted.

"Sixty-three demands sound excessive," Doran said.

"They're not unreasonable," Scarlet told him. "One of them is to add more lights to villages like Poole."

"Quite a few of them involve lighting infrastructure," I added.

"I'd be happy to consider these demands, as well as any other requests you might have for me." The gold flecks in his eyes seemed to shine brighter when he looked at me, and I averted my gaze.

"How about we start with the first sixty-three on the list and go from there?"

Doran offered his hand. "I believe we have a deal, Miss Goodfellow."

"You can call me Aster." His hand felt smooth compared to my own calloused skin.

Smiling, he said, "And you can call me 'my lord.'"

Energy crackled in the air as we approached the center of Clayton, the location of The Wild Charter signing. Lord Doran had suggested Klondike or the White Fortress, but his ideas had been nixed. Clayton felt like the right choice.

A procession of vampires snaked their way to the makeshift dais where Lord Doran sat, appearing more regal than I'd ever seen him. The House Nilsson standard hung behind him. His posture was ramrod straight and his chin slightly lifted.

He was proud.

So was I.

Trumpets blared, signaling the start of the event. Groaning, Bonnie clamped her hands over her ears.

"I like the sound," Bear said. "It's exciting."

"The whole event is exciting," Hattie agreed. "I'll remember this day for the rest of my life."

Lord Doran rose to his feet to address the gathered crowd. "Residents of The Wild, thank you for joining me today for this momentous occasion. Today, on behalf of House Nilsson, I make sixty-three promises to you and everyone who lives within our borders."

Scarlet clapped her hands excitedly.

Bonnie cringed. "Great gods above. Is he going to read all sixty-three clauses?"

"It's a formality," I whispered.

"He's going to need a glass of water before he's finished," Tyson said.

On cue, a vampire delivered a full pitcher of water and an empty glass to Doran's side. Tyson gave me a pointed look.

Doran motioned for the crowd to settle. "Today is one for the history books," he began, "and you can tell your grandchildren you were here."

Bonnie cradled her bump. "We can tell our child they were here, too."

A cheer erupted from the crowd. Doran paused until they grew quiet again.

"I hereby release my role as treasurer and consent to the creation of a special committee to handle finances. I also agree to the creation of a justice committee, which will include at least one member of each resident species." He carried on with his speech, and every so often was forced to stop for applause. He appointed representatives in each village and agreed not to raise taxes without the consent of those representatives.

People jostled for a better view, and every so often I had to offer a sharp elbow to someone who passed too closely to Bonnie. Better my elbow than her claws.

"My back hurts," Bonnie complained, pressing her hands against her lower back and attempting to stretch.

"No wonder. Your stomach is the size of Mount Everest," Bear replied.

Bonnie's head swiveled toward him. "I'm sorry. I must've misheard you. I thought you compared my stomach to the tallest mountain in the world, but I know you would never be that insensitive to the mate who is nurturing your unborn pup."

Bear blinked but wisely said nothing.

"We will build a new public library in Klondike," Doran continued. "And it will be accessible to all residents."

Hattie bounced on the balls of her feet in response to that announcement. So many of us would benefit from an abundance of books.

"Is he also building a ladder to the sky in order to lasso the sun?" Bonnie whispered. "I mean, I'm all for change, but the list is going on forever."

"It's *our* list," Scarlet hissed.

Tyson snorted. "Only you would complain about this."

Bonnie scowled. "When you're carrying the weight of two werewolves, then you can let me know what I should and shouldn't complain about."

Tyson cast a quick glance at Bear and grimaced. It seemed nobody could say the right words in front of Bonnie today.

"Big day." Max squished in beside me.

"When did you get here?" Scarlet asked.

"Been here the whole time. I'm tall enough to see over everyone from the back. Besides, I didn't want to distract Aster from watching her boyfriend's big moment. I have to admit, he looks very sexy holding that pen."

I pressed my lips together. I wasn't playing this game with him right now. I only wanted to relish the moment.

"I thought you were her boyfriend," Tyson said.

Max sighed. "From your lips to her ears."

Tyson flicked my earlobe. "Her ears are right here."

I swatted the werewolf's hand away. "Can we not do this? I'm trying to commit this historical moment to memory."

"In that case, I should talk more," Max said. "That way I'm sure to be in it."

Doran held up his pen. "Once I sign this historic document, it will be sent via messenger to King Stefan for His Majesty's seal of approval."

That, of course, would be the true test. Would House Nilsson agree to these radical changes? If not, Doran could end up with his head on a spike.

The vampire made a big show of scrawling his signature.

Bear leaned over and whispered, "I bet he made loops. He seems like someone who'd have fancy handwriting."

"This is the start of something big," Hattie said. "I can feel it."

Bonnie rubbed her stomach. "Very big," she agreed.

Today heralded a new beginning—for all of us.

Chapter Seventeen

Scarlet took a step backward. "Your side needs to be higher."

I glanced at my handiwork. The streamer was, indeed, attached to a lower branch on the tree, creating a slant. "If I move it, the material will rip."

"Why do they make streamers so delicate?" Scarlet complained. "Now we have to leave it crooked."

"Bonnie won't care."

We looked at each other and laughed.

"Fine, I'll try to fix it without ripping it." I slid my finger underneath the thin material to reach the sticky ball I'd used as an adhesive.

"Too bad Hattie didn't want to come," Scarlet said. "I was sure she'd get over her crush, especially now that she's not living with us."

"Hattie's a teenager. Crushes are dramatic at her age."

"I wouldn't know."

"Oh, come on. You didn't have a crush at her age?"

"I was too busy trying not to die." Scarlet admired the adjusted streamer. "Perfect."

I took a bow. "Only slightly more challenging than hitting a target."

Scarlet glanced at the clearing. "We should've invited more guests. You know Bonnie. She'll count heads."

"And compare attendance with what? It's not like we've ever thrown a baby shower before."

"Good point." Scarlet rolled up the remaining bit of streamer. "Maybe we should've included Max and a few members of the Ghost Pack."

I gave her a sharp look. "That's too much encouragement."

Scarlet laughed. "I don't think Max needs encouragement."

That much was true.

"For what it's worth, I think he's a catch."

I snorted. "Easy for you to say."

"It isn't easy for me to say. That's my point. If he's getting my blessing, then he's worth consideration."

I groaned. "I hate when you're reasonable. It's so unfair."

Scarlet returned the unused decorations to the box of supplies. "Speaking of reasonable, I still can't believe Doran signed the charter. It feels like a new beginning for The Wild."

"We still need King Stefan to sign off." Until the ink was dry, I'd remain cautiously optimistic.

"I don't know that any of it would've happened without you," Scarlet said. "I think Doran only did it to win your approval."

My cheeks warmed. "I don't think that's true, although ultimately, I don't care why, as long as it's done."

She nudged me. "Come on, admit it. You like that he's made such a grand gesture to prove himself to you."

As far as I was concerned, he'd already proven himself, but I couldn't bring myself to say the words. Lord Doran was still a vampire. The thegn of The Wild. And I was still an outlaw with a price on her head. Doran and his rangers might be willing to look the other way, but there were plenty of vampires that wouldn't.

Footsteps trampled over the dead leaves, and Tyson arrived in the clearing, breathless. "They're coming."

"Relax," Scarlet said. "They're here for a baby shower, not a battle."

I observed our efforts. Lanterns surrounded the clearing, casting a soft glow around us. Presents were wrapped. Food was ready and waiting. Glenn and Rita had even donated a couple growlers of beer from the Dancing Dragon. It was more of a feast than we'd had in ages.

Bear appeared, gently guiding Bonnie by the elbow. "Why are we going here?" she asked as she stumbled into the clearing. Her equilibrium was only getting worse as her stomach grew larger and rounder.

Her gaze snagged on the streamers first and then moved to the wrapped gifts piled on the ground.

"Ta-da!" Tyson said, spreading his arms wide.

Bonnie's eyes narrowed. "What's all this?" Her nostrils flared. "I smell food."

"Because we have food, and lots of it," Scarlet told her. "This is a celebration."

"But we just did the whole Samhain thing," Bonnie said.

"Before the Great Eruption, people celebrated the birth of a child with an event called a baby shower." I gestured to the gifts. "That's what this is."

Bonnie looked blank. "Where's the water for the shower?"

"It's not that kind of shower. It's just what they called the event."

"That's stupid."

I smiled. "I agree. Can we focus on the food and presents?"

Bonnie's round face brightened. "Yes, absolutely." She wiggled her fingers. "Presents first."

She hurried to sit on the boulder that Scarlet had covered in purple material to indicate a throne. It wouldn't be the most comfortable seat for a pregnant werewolf, but it was the best we could do.

Bear gave her a small box from the top of the pile. It was wrapped in gold, red, and orange leaves that had been stuck together to create a sheet of paper.

Bonnie tore at the wrapping, scattering leaves at her feet. "I hope it's a raw steak."

Bear patted her shoulder. "I hate to disappoint you, but nobody's wrapping raw steak, Bon."

"Maybe we should start with the food if you're hungry," I offered.

"No, no. This is good." Bonnie opened the box and pulled out a small wooden stick with a pointy end. "Oh, wow. Baby's first stake."

Tyson puffed out his chest. "I whittled it myself."

Bonnie clutched it to her chest as tears formed in her eyes. "It's the perfect weapon. Our baby will love it."

"I hope they never need to use it," Scarlet commented.

"You'd better teach the kid to be careful, though," Tyson said, "or they might poke out an eye."

"Better someone else's than their own," Bear quipped.

Tyson grinned. "Unless that someone else is you."

Bonnie reached for another present. "This is great. If I have a baby every year, will I get more gifts?"

Bear threw his hand against a tree to steady himself. "Let's see how one goes before we launch our own pack."

Bonnie tipped back her head to beam at him. "Our own pack. That has a nice ring to it."

"What about joining the Ghost Pack?" Scarlet asked. "Have you given that any more thought?"

"Their pack is so big," Bonnie commented. "I worry we'd get lost in the shuffle."

"Strength in numbers, though," Tyson said. "And Max is a quality dude."

"He's definitely on the level," Scarlet agreed.

I started to feel as though there'd been a previous conversation I'd missed. "Is everyone thinking about joining the Ghost Pack?"

They exchanged uneasy glances.

"Max made us an official offer," Bonnie said. "Didn't he tell you?"

I blanched. No, he didn't tell me, probably because he knew I'd have mixed feelings. "We've been so busy with the whole saving The Wild thing. I guess he forgot."

Tyson clapped my shoulder. "It isn't like you'd be left on your own, Aster. He's made it pretty clear he wants you ... to join, too."

"I'm a witch," I objected.

Tyson shrugged. "Doesn't seem to be an issue for him."

"Maybe not, but it doesn't mean the rest of the pack will accept me." And I wasn't convinced it was the right move for me.

"We'd still be together," Scarlet said, watching me carefully. "Just as part of a larger group."

"We'd split our duties with hundreds of other wolves," Tyson said. "It would ease the burden on us, especially when little Bonnie Bear joins the crew."

Bonnie looked down at her stomach. "I think I ate too much."

"You haven't eaten yet," I pointed out.

Bear rubbed her shoulders. "She's talking about breakfast."

"Can you get me a cup of water, please?" she asked.

Bear dutifully crossed the clearing as Bonnie concentrated on unwrapping the next present.

"It's a rattle," Tyson said.

She paused, midtear, and glared at him. "Why would you do that? Do you know how rare it is that I'm surprised by anything? Let me have this."

Cringing, Tyson slunk behind Scarlet.

"You haven't opened mine yet," I said.

"It's an embarrassment of riches," Bear said, grinning as he carried the cup of water to her.

Bonnie's face paled. "Shit."

Bear rushed to her side, spilling half the water in the process. "What's wrong?"

"Pain," she said through gritted teeth.

"Contractions?" Bear asked.

She gripped his arm and squeezed hard. "I think I might be giving birth to a pain demon."

Bear turned toward me with crazy eyes. "Is that a thing?"

I bit back a smile. "I think she means the contractions hurt."

As Bonnie's breaths grew louder, her nails sank into Bear's skin. "This bean might be more lima than string."

"As long as it's fully baked." Bear squinted at us. "Has it been in there long enough?"

Scarlet shrugged. "How should I know?"

"You're a she-wolf," he practically yelled.

"I've never given birth!" Scarlet shot back.

Bonnie growled. "I need everybody to pay attention to me!"

Bear eased her off the boulder and onto the ground. "Okay, we can do this. Don't you worry about little Bonnie Bear."

"I'm worried about *me*," Bonnie ground out.

"Anybody else see that?" Tyson asked.

Scarlet frowned at him. "I think we all see it, Tyson."

"Not Bonnie. That."

I followed his gaze across the clearing where white light sparked in midair.

Bonnie drew up her knees and panted. "Somebody needs to take off my pants."

Tyson cut a glance at Bear. "Bro, that's your job."

Bear crouched in front of Bonnie and unfastened her pants. "I don't need to tell you this is how we got into this situation in the first place."

The light sparked brighter as it seemed to burn a hole through the fabric of reality.

"I think it's a portal forming," I said.

Bonnie moaned. "Not now!"

"Well, you wanted to be surprised," Bear said.

Scarlet looked from Bonnie to the circle of white light growing brighter by the second. "I don't have any weapons close by."

Tyson's body started to twitch. "The wolf in me wants out. Whatever this is, it isn't good."

"This wolf wants out, too," Bonnie said between desperate breaths.

My first thought was that someone was coming to reclaim the celestial weapons. I scooped my longbow off the ground and notched an arrow, taking aim at the widening portal.

Bonnie released a primal scream that set my teeth on edge. Bear's encouraging words faded to the background as a flash of color appeared in the circle of light.

Three royal soldiers stepped through the portal, followed by a familiar figure.

Vincent Dufresne. Master Inquisitor.

The inquisitor emerged from the portal in a dark blue pinstripe suit paired with a black collared shirt. His black shoes were so polished that they shone almost as bright as the portal itself. His hair was slightly longer now, tapering at the neck.

"Raise those hands of yours, Miss Goodfellow, and your friends die."

Each soldier raised a gun, no doubt filled with silver bullets.

A primal scream bubbled inside me as I recalled my last meeting with the renowned vampire. He'd tortured me in an effort to learn more about my magic. Even worse, he'd enjoyed it. Later, when I'd escaped and defended myself against Lord Birney, Dufresne had simply watched as I fled the White Fortress. Although I thought his reluctance was strange at the time, I'd been too concerned with survival to give it further thought. I'd found Max and rode away to safety. My only backward glance had been reserved for Lord Doran.

I didn't like my odds. *Maybe* I could take out the vampires in quick succession, depending on their skill level, but I had no idea whether there were more behind them. I also wasn't keen on attacking King Stefan's soldiers. I was hunted enough in The Wild. No need to add the king himself to my list of hunters.

Bonnie howled, prompting an echo of howls from the other werewolves.

"Aster," Scarlet said slowly, sinking her question into my name.

"We command your cooperation in the name of the king," one of the soldiers ordered.

"Are you out of your mind?" Bonnie shouted.

"We're kind of in the middle of something important," Bear told the intruders.

Beside me, Tyson's skin rippled, and I knew he was ready to unleash the hound. I couldn't let the situation escalate. If something happened to my friends—to the baby—I couldn't live with myself.

I stepped forward and positioned myself between my crew and the interlopers, keeping my eye trained on the Master Inquisitor. If anything happened to my friends, I'd fire an arrow straight through the place where his heart should be.

Dufresne pointed. "The redhead's the one you want," he said.

"My hair is auburn."

"If she's the light bringer, why does she use a longbow?" one of the soldiers asked.

Tyson cut a glance at me. "Light bringer? Cool nickname."

Four more soldiers poured through the portal. There was no way I could hurt them without putting the baby at risk, and with Bonnie about to give birth, we weren't able to flee if I temporarily blinded my friends.

One of the soldiers issued a warning shot that skimmed right over Bear's head. "Hey!" His face contorted with anger, and his skin started to ripple.

I tossed my bow and arrow to the ground and stuffed my hands in my cloak pockets.

"Good choice." Dufresne snapped his fingers at the soldiers. "It's only her we want. Leave the rest." He eyed me closely. "Unless she resists. Then kill them all."

"Aster, don't!" Scarlet shouted.

I couldn't see another option that didn't endanger my friends. Soldiers flanked me. One of them slapped anti-magic cuffs on my wrists and urged me toward the portal.

I couldn't bring myself to look back at the clearing. As the portal closed behind me, the last sound I heard was the wail of a newborn pup.

Don't miss the final book in Aster's trilogy, as well as the conclusion to the entire Midnight Empire saga, in **Midnight Burns**.

Also by Annabel Chase

Crossroads Queen

Pandora's Pride

Spellslingers Academy of Magic

Wings and Blades Academy

Magic Bullet

Federal Bureau of Magic

To learn more about my books and register for my VIP List to receive FREE bonus content, visit www.annabelchase.com.

Printed in Great Britain
by Amazon